E.M. Delafield

(1890-1943) was born Edmée Elizabeth Monica de la Pasture. She adopted her pseudonym "E.M. Delafield", a loose translation of her French ancestral name, because of the popularity of her mother's numerous novels, written under the name Mrs Henry de la Pasture. Her father was Count Henry de la Pasture of Llandogo, Monmouthshire (his family had come to England after the French Revolution), and after his death her mother married Sir Hugh Clifford, in 1910. E.M. Delafield served as a V.A.D. in Exeter from 1914–1917 and was then appointed to the Ministry of National Services in the South-Western Region at Bristol where she served until the end of the First World War. Her first novel, *Zella Sees Herself*, was published in 1917 and she was to write a further three before marrying Major Arthur Paul Dashwood O.B.E., the third son of Sir George Dashwood, sixth baronet, in 1919. They spent two years in the Malay States, afterwards settling in Devon where they had two children.

E.M. Delafield had written eighteen books when she was asked by Lady Rhondda to contribute a serial of some kind for the weekly *Time and Tide*. The result was *Diary of a Provincial Lady* (1930) which made E.M. Delafield one of Britain's best-loved writers of the 30s. *The Provincial Lady Goes Further* was published in 1932 and in 1933 E.M. Delafield's American lecture tour was serialised in *Punch* and formed *The Provincial Lady in America* (1934). *The Provincial Lady in Wartime*, appeared in 1940, and Virago published an omnibus of all four Diaries in 1984.

E.M. Delafield's writing provided her with a necessary life-line as well as additional income. Herself a provincial lady, her writing combined elegance and wit with a deep interest in the lives and conditions of her class, an interest reflected in her role as a Justice of the Peace and her involvement with Women's Institutes.

Her other work includes *The War Workers* (1918), *Humbug* (1922), *What is Love?* (1928), *Women Are Like That* (1929), *Thank Heaven Fasting* (1932, also published by Virago), *Nothing is Safe* (1937) and *No One Now Will Know* (1941). A regular contributor to *Punch* and *Time and Tide* she also wrote three plays, *To See Ourselves* (1930), *The Glass Wall* (1933) and *The Mulberry Bush* (1935). The first of these was a dramatisation of *The Way Things Are* (1927) and was staged in both London and New York. At the age of fifty-three, E.M. Delafield collapsed while lecturing in Oxford and died some weeks later at her home in Cullompton, Devon.

VIRAGO
MODERN
CLASSIC

NUMBER

290

E.M. DELAFIELD

THE WAY
THINGS ARE

WITH A NEW INTRODUCTION BY
NICOLA BEAUMAN

"I left the room with silent dignity,
but caught my foot in the mat."

GROSSMITH, *Diary of a Nobody.*

Virago

Published by VIRAGO PRESS Limited 1988
Centro House, 20–23 Mandela Street, London NW1 0HQ

First published in Great Britain by Hutchinson & Co. 1927
Copyright E.M. Delafield 1927

Introduction Copyright © Nicola Beauman 1988

British Library Cataloguing in Publication Data
Delafield, E.M.
    The way things are.—(Virago modern classics)
    Rn: Edmée Elizabeth Monica de la Pasture
    I. Title
    823'.912[F]   PR6007.E33
    ISBN 0-86068-435-0

Printed in Great Britain by Cox & Wyman Ltd.
of Reading, Berkshire

A good many of the characters in this novel have been drawn, as usual, from persons now living; but the author hopes very much that they will only recognise one another.

E. M. DELAFIELD.

Introduction

"It dawned upon her dimly that only by envisaging and accepting her own limitations, could she endure the limitations of her surroundings." The last sentence of *The Way Things Are* (1927) is, like the title, pure E.M. Delafield. It is weary, accepting, ironic, yet contains the undertone of tragedy that is the hallmark of all her books. It conveys the realism and detachment necessary to an impassioned feminist statement (albeit one that few feminists would recognise). And it is perfectly judged in the way it mixes the lightly amusing read demanded by the lending libraries with a statement about the female condition that is so crushing in its implications as to be almost unbearable.

E.M.D. (which is how she was known to her friends) was her typically unassuming self when, in 1933, she referred to

a colloquial expression of which I once made use as the title of a novel: *The Way Things Are*. It epitomises all that I have consciously striven for throughout the whole of my writing life: ability to observe impartially, unbiased either by sentiment or by cynicism, and courage to record faithfully and without dramatic emphasis.

These phrases are of course so all-embracing they could be applied to any writer who, in avoiding romance, fantasy and sentiment, opts for verisimilitude and "felt life": most novelists observe impartially and record faithfully. What *is* rare is to make the reader laugh throughout three hundred pages while doing so.

This is E.M.D.'s funniest novel, its first few chapters

i

bearing comparison with the work of Jerome, the Grossmiths, E.F. Benson, Evelyn Waugh, P.G. Wodehouse and Nancy Mitford. But because it has a darker side it has suffered the fate of any other novel that defies easy labelling: the reading public likes to be told if a novel is funny/problem/social comedy and so on, and tends to forget about those which lie outside an obvious category.

Hence the greater success of the book for which *The Way Things Are* was the inspiration, and which remains its author's best known: *The Diary of a Provincial Lady* (1930). Rachel Ferguson (a novelist contemporary with E.M.D.) once described *The Diary* as containing passages

of absolute genius, and that is not a word one flings about lightly, and this book was an unmistakable success because it was earmarked as a frolic. But the good things and subtleties in her "straight" novels are far worse submerged by this same general effect of flimsy treatment … She is, by those who seem to have missed the point of her, roughly rated as an agreeable rattle. These assessors would probably dismiss the works of Jane Austen as nice books for the beach, and do not perceive that *petit point*, though very small indeed, may be exquisite.

The other reasons for the popularity of *The Diary* are that it can, and indeed should be, read in snatches; its heroine, although harassed, is not unhappy; the absence of a lover and the introduction of other, funnier elements (the French governess, the Plymouth pawnbroker) keep the tone light-hearted; and the diary form, for stylistic reasons, can (in the hands of E.M.D.) be consistently funny. Consider the following passage:

Robert startles me at breakfast by asking if my cold—which he has hitherto ignored—is better. I reply that it has gone. Then why, he asks, do I look like that? Refrain from asking like what, as I know only too well. Feel that life is wholly unendurable, and decide madly to get a new hat.

If this was transposed into the third person with the narrator "reading" the provincial lady's thoughts, this would be a rather more ordinary, self-pitying married exchange.

Even written from the narrator's point of view, however, *The Way Things Are* is a very funny book, and many people prefer it to any of E.M.D's other works because of the variety of themes underlying the humour; it has always been my favourite out of the forty or so titles. "Unbrokenly hilarious" was the opinion of the witty and perceptive reviewer in *The Times Literary Supplement*, who added, "we may feel that to laugh at Laura all through three hundred pages of what is torment for her is cruel; but there is no keeping a straight face". Then comes the nub. Is laughter compatible with realism, asks the reviewer, i.e., does the novel fit into a category?

So rippled with enjoyment, in fact, is the surface of this sardonic narrative, that one cannot at times help feeling that despite the almost hallucinatory naturalism of the dialogue, this world is not— worse luck—the world we encounter.

But to thousands and thousands of middle-class married women with children this world is indeed the one we encounter. (Whether this novel is one that can be appreciated by readers outside this group is a question I cannot answer.) The details may have changed, but there are enough timeless qualities to make the insights quite as relevant as they were sixty years ago. Any woman who has found herself in a domestic situation from which, for reasons of love, loyalty, convention or finance, she cannot escape, will identify with the heroine; and most will sympathise with her acceptance of "the way things are".

The storyline is minimal. The *TLS* said:

There is no plot here that it is important to tell or to refrain from betraying. Laura Temple has a husband, Alfred, as stolid as a leg of mutton; she has a country house that is too large and an income that is too small; she has children she cannot discipline, servants she cannot keep and neighbours who are bored. Up the stagnant reaches of her existence there floats one day—incredibly!—a lover . . .

There is also a sub-plot concerning the local bright-young-thing's "pash" for a successful author, and Laura's sister's marriage to "the richest commoner in England". But most readers will find this infinitely less interesting than the story of Laura.

As with the title, her name is in itself significant. No one could accuse E.M.D. of having created merely a caricature—we sympathise far too much with Laura for this to be possible—yet it is at once apparent that she is *not* presented as a rounded character whom we can imagine "off the page". Instead, being an archetype, a symbol of Wife and Mother, she is given the Christian name so often used by interwar novelists to suggest the kind of staunch, quietly charming, sensible woman who is always the wife, never the mistress. (Nowadays the name Kate has much the same impact: it is redolent of good sense.) In addition, her surname makes it clear that she is custodian of the temple, the hearth and home, and as such is bound to its demands and strictures as firmly as she would be by any religion.

The other characters also have names with larger meanings, although they too have enough individuality to be far removed from stereotypes. Alfred is the loyal but dull family man (he would be Freddie if he were at all dashing); Edward is the conventional son and Johnnie (not John) the more flamboyant one; Lady Kingsley-Browne is the statutory neighbourhood title whose hyphenated names have the cachet the single would lack; Mrs Bakewell is the smugly competent (bake well) homemaker; the lover's name (Duke, short for Marmaduke) is exotic and his surname (Ayland) suggests distant lands romantically far away from the demands of household, neighbours and children; while Gladys and Nellie were cliché names for 1920s servants (indeed Virginia Woolf's cook, whom she lavishly immortalised in her letters and diaries, was called Nellie).

Among all these people moves Laura. Aged thirty-four, she married in 1919 and has produced two sons. She is not in love with her husband (when she renounces her lover she knows "that she [is] going back to an existence in which love-making played no part at all") but "had been rather anxious to be married, just when she first met Alfred".

Laura could scarcely believe that she had once lived with Aunt Isabel, during the war, and had endured her with equanimity.

"After all—a home of one's own—" thought Laura.

It was a wordless recognition of what Alfred had done for her in marrying her.

At the heart of the book lies E.M.D.'s belief that married women are trapped. They wish to be married for reasons of economics and prestige and they do indeed feel gratitude to the man who provides for them. They think they married for love:

In the course of seven years of child-bearing and rearing, housekeeping, writing stories to augment her income, and talking about the bulbs to her neighbours, Laura had almost forgotten that she once thought herself destined for a *grande passion*.

When the wives find that they are unhappy, either because they are bored or harassed or because they lack companionship ("she did, however, very frequently wish that Alfred would make love to her, or even, if that was too much to expect, that he would make personal remarks to her"), they realise that they are snared like animals in a trap. Lacking the financial resources to leave their husbands, and knowing that the divorce laws would deny them custody of their children, there is no way out. "How trivial, and yet how infuriating was life, with recalcitrant nurses and husbands and children, and nothing to look forward to ever, and at the back of everything an eternal sense of one's own inadequacy."

This was a theme to which E.M.D. would return: in *Thank Heaven Fasting* (1932), a novel that was written and sold as a lightly readable story about the difficulty of getting married and the heroine's rapture when she finally achieves it, which appeared, however, in a dust jacket that shows a girl looking out from between prison bars. And in *Three Marriages* (1939) in which E.M.D. was even more vehement, the heroine, Cathleen, receives a proposal.

She was being offered a home, and a life of her very own—instead of one spent in the houses of other people—and somebody to take care of her—and a fine, splendid position, and the status of a married woman.

It was really too good to be true ...

But when Cathleen falls in love with someone else her husband is unforgiving. Quite apart from never again having anything to look forward to (Laura Temple also feels this acutely), she knows that the

old, cheerful life, when the daffodil-painted walls of the nursery and the round nursery table with the blue-and-gold chain had seemed to Cathleen like a fairy-tale come true, was spoilt for ever.

She came to feel that it was she who had spoilt it, and the sense of guilt seeped into her days and nights so that she was never wholly without the consciousness of it.

This would be the Emma Bovary theme once more except that, this being middle-class and middle-brow England, the women are not obsessed with romance and the lovers are properly temperate. The most they hope for is sometimes to be able to "meet in freedom and happiness without fear of hurting anybody else, and without need of concealment" (*Three Marriages*). That they cannot, because of their children and through fear of hurting their husbands, of whom they are "very fond", was an oft-used subject, most famously by Noel Coward in his play *Still Life* (1935) and then in the film *Brief Encounter* (1945). And there are passages in *The Way Things Are* which appear to have lent inspiration to Coward, especially the final scene between Laura and Duke in the tearoom of the Army and Navy Stores (Coward's Laura and Alec meet in the station buffet) when their final moments are beset with trivia—"'Bleck or whyte' said the waitress abruptly, poising two vessels above the two cups on the table."

The tyranny of the marriage vows is, then, the subject of *The Way Things Are*. Women get married in order to have status, financial support and children. The men, placed through an accident of sex in the dominant role, exploit their superiority; worse, they contrive that their wives remain forever inferior. The law denied women freedom should they seek it; the god of respectability stopped them doing anything that might draw attention to themselves; lack of financial autonomy made them feel worthless; their husbands, because of inhibition, laziness, egoism and thoughtlessness, did not provide the companionship, let alone the sexual love, their wives craved; and woman's subordination, encouraged by her lack of self-esteem, was satisfactorily established.

Alfred in *The Way Things Are* was drawn in a far harsher light than the husband in *The Diary of a Provincial Lady* was to be two years later. In *The Diary*, Robert is a figure of fun, someone who is treated by his wife with that mixture of affection and exasperation which so often stands for married love. We do not expect him to do much more than grunt from behind *The Times* or once, boldly, tell his wife that he had missed her while she was away. But Alfred has cherished his wife so little that we learn at once that she has a "secret sense of her own futility and weakness". He criticises her weak handling of her sons but does not help her to be more effective, or to moderate her undisguised adoration of Johnnie. He refuses even out of kindness to go along with the domestic strategems that Laura thinks absurd but necessary, such as eating the last piece of toast so that the cook will not think she should prepare less in future. He insists on ringing the bell merely to ask whether there is enough hot water for his bath. He complains because his wife has (uninvited) guests for tea on the servant's afternoon off. And he often has to assert his dominance in the only way he understands:

Alfred was in that frame of mind in which nothing would serve him but to ring the bell—an act of despotism disliked at least as much by his wife as by the servants whom it was designed to summon.

"Dear, what do you want?"

"Haven't we any jam in the house?"

"Has she forgotten the jam?" said Laura coldly. "I suppose as none of us ever eat it, she didn't think it worth while."

"Ring for it."

"Please do ring, if you really want jam," Laura replied icily.

"How is she to learn, if we don't tell her?" was the indirect retort of her husband.

The short sentences, and the lack of interior monologue on the part of the characters, are intended to make this conversation, and so many like it, funny rather than sad, and of course we cannot help but laugh. But behind the most innocuous seeming exchanges lies a contempt for men which often verges on hatred. One of the remarkable aspects of this novel is that it can be read on so many levels: we can laugh at Alfred; we can smile wryly; or we can absolutely loathe him. As for example, in the sugar-beet conversation. Alfred is insistent on discoursing on sugar-beet at lunch-time: "'I'm glad they're taking it up round here. (Edward, not with your mouth full.) Did you say the Home Farm had (Never let me see you do that again!)—had decided to give it a trial?'" And so on. Then, a few days later, husband and wife are for once alone together. Laura reflects:

If only Alfred would talk about sugar-beet now, instead of at lunch-time, when she couldn't possibly attend!

There had been a time, however, when Laura would have regarded sugar-beet, viewed as a conversational topic between a man and a woman, as frankly impossible.

The great attraction of Duke is not primarily sexual: it is

that he is *interested in Laura*. She "yielded to the insidious rapture of talking about herself exactly as she wished herself to be talked about". He sees her as an individual, turns her from someone submissive and indecisive who "had ceased to exist" into a normally happy woman, is interested in her writing (which everyone else views as something secret and eccentric) and wants to be with her, whether or not she has planted the indoor bulbs in time or put the jam on the table or pretended to care about sugar-beet. Which is why, when it appears that they will not be able to meet again (the ending is inconclusive), Laura wakes to a sense of gloom that, surely, gives her affinity with the heroine of a tragedy. Granted, she has a roof over a head, her children are healthy, she has a few people of whom she is fond. But, in the context of respectable, middle-class England, there is a note of real desolation and despair. Will anything interesting ever happen? Will Laura ever again experience the sense of joy that comes from sharing her thoughts with someone who cares? Will life ever consist of anything except "the children, her marriage vows, the house, the ordering of the meals, the servants, the making of a laundry list every Monday?"

These last, the shackles of domesticity, provide the imagery for *The Way Things Are*. The book is not just a fascinating social document about the way a medium-sized home was run in interwar Britain; it also reveals how much more our grandmothers and mothers were bound by the fetters of housework than we are today, and in this respect we should read this book with a sense of empathy and a sense of compassion. For E.M.D. was not a radical feminist, she was a realistic one. She believed it better to try and accept things laughingly than to impose drastic changes. If, without cook and parlourmaid, "the days seemed to be entirely occupied in small dustings and cleanings, and the evenings in lighting the lamps, drawing the blinds and the curtains, and clearing away the things from the dining-room table", why does Laura not leave the things on the table or only clean once a week? The answer is that it was not until after the Second World War, when middle-class women could no longer employ servants to help them, that they even imagined they could subdue the tyrant housework.

The house was a tyrant, the husband was often a tyrant, and so, it appears, were the children (especially boys). Although Laura reads manuals about how to bring them up (she also has a copy of Marie Stopes in her drawer) their writers do not seem to give her very positive advice. "Never meet opposition with opposition" they say, without, apparently, stooping to explain what else should be done when Johnnie throws himself upon the floor and shrieks. They recommend "pleasant, gentle reasonableness" without explaining why Laura is "almost always mysteriously tired after quarter of an hour spent in the undisturbed company of her children". The explanation lies, in fact, with the author: E.M.D. was sharing the knowledge common to all mothers that there *is* no remedy when a child shrieks on the floor or when exhaustion sets in after fifteen minutes. Like so much else in life, it is "the way things are".

Throughout the book E.M.D. displays the resignation instilled into those of a Catholic background; if there is a tinge of masochism it must have originated at the same source. The humour and the delicate perception cannot be a product of a religious upbringing (and must indeed have been the factors that induced the twenty-one-year-old E.M.D. to

renounce her vows and, after a year as a novice, leave the
convent in which she imagined she would spend the rest of
her life). The wit, the inability to see anything but the funny
side of life, and an extraordinary warmth, are what make this
novel unique. Anyone who has ever laughed at the sentence
from the Grossmiths quoted on the frontispiece ("I left the
room with silent dignity, but caught my foot in the mat") will
laugh at this. And one can but echo Rachel Ferguson when
she refers to E.M.D.'s

completely perfect novel, *The Way Things Are*, about which I dare
not let myself go. I have read it at least fifty times and shall read it
fifty more; it satisfies on every count and yet it is precisely this book
which, to judge from the blank stares of my friends when I talk
about it, is her least known.

This, in future, will not be so.

Nicola Beauman, London, 1987

Chapter I

"DID I tell you what Johnnie said, after he'd had his reading-lesson to-day?"

"No."

Laura embarked upon her anecdote.

She had not intended, nor even wished, to tell it. She knew well that her husband did not want to hear it.

Nevertheless, she told it. And her secret sense of her own futility and weakness took all conviction from the manner of her telling, so that even a much more amusing story than that of a five-year-old's repartee would have been bereft of sense and all spirit.

When the recital of his son's witticism had petered out, Alfred Temple said, "H'm," compromising between a short, unamused laugh and a curt ejaculation, and then he and Laura were silent again.

They had been married seven years.

Every evening after dinner they sat in the drawing-room, or, on those rare summer evenings when it was hot, in the garden, and Alfred talked not at all, and Laura, in spite of almost frenzied resolutions to the contrary, found herself preparing to talk—and often, indeed, actually talking—about the children, the servants, or the question of expense.

Their elder son, Edward, was six years old, and Johnnie was five.

Between nine and ten o'clock, Alfred Temple, as usual, fell asleep behind *The Times*, and Laura, also as usual, told herself that it was only a question of concentration, and that an occasional snore could not annoy her unless she allowed it to do so. And at the seventh snore she cleared her throat loudly and suddenly, and Alfred woke with a start.

"I wish we could get the children in to the dancing-class at Quinnerton regularly," said Laura.

"They're a bit young, aren't they?"

"Edward is just the right age. And it would be good for Johnnie. Besides, I like them to see something of other children."

"They're always going out to tea."

"That's another thing, we ought to ask the Allington children here, but nurse, for some reason or other, has taken a dislike to their nurse."

"I shouldn't let nurse regulate your invitations, I must say."

Laura gave him a look, and compressed the corners of her mouth into an expression of controlled patience.

She was not really feeling impatient with Alfred, but it seemed necessary to let him know that she considered his opinion of no value whatever on the question of her relations with nurse.

Alfred had sometimes said, and frequently implied, that Laura was ruled by her servants.

Laura, in return, said and implied that Alfred did not

know anything at all about the domestic problem from the inside.

She often felt that Alfred did not understand her, and that he still less understood what a difficult and fatiguing affair life was for her, and it also vexed her to know that their ideas differed widely on the important subject of Edward's and Johnnie's upbringing, but nevertheless, Laura knew that she and Alfred were what is called "happily married."

Only, somehow, Laura was not happy, and she sometimes felt that perhaps Alfred was not happy, either, although he did not seem to think about it a great deal.

It might, perhaps, have something to do with the undoubted fact that their income was not quite adequate to their demands upon it. Laura, copybooks to the contrary notwithstanding, knew well that riches can do a great deal towards contentment, and that pleasure in life is not produced in an atmosphere of unpaid bills and economical dinners. Sometimes Laura visualised herself as the wife of a man much poorer than Alfred—obliged herself to cook a great part of every meal eaten in the house, and able to afford only one maid, to help her with the children, and to keep the house clean, and to do the sewing. Of course, they'd be living in a smaller house, two reception, five bedrooms, and one bath, h. and c., and usual offices, half an acre of garden, a job gardener, and rent and electric light bill to pay.

As it was, they lived at Applecourt, which had belonged to the Temples for three generations, and the house had nine bedrooms, two bath-rooms and three sitting-rooms, and two kitchens and a pantry, and a good deal of passage-way, and a staircase with two landings, and no lighting whatever.

And there were—or, very frequently, there were not—a cook-general, a house-parlourmaid, and a children's nurse. A gardener received thirty-five shillings a week and a cottage and helped Alfred with the cleaning of the car, and worked in the garden and in the kitchen-garden.

Laura had been brought up in a house that entirely resembled Applecourt, except that it had been more comfortable, because everything had been much less expensive and difficult, in the time before the war.

Throughout the war she had lived and worked in London, boarding very comfortably with an aunt who had a house in Wilton Crescent.

Laura could speak French fluently, and play the piano not very well, and she had qualified as a masseuse in 1915. Ten years earlier she had supposed herself to be a good dancer, but the dancing of ten years earlier was not the sort of dancing to produce in a present-day ballroom—and Laura had learnt no other. Her tennis had also become inadequate, in much the same way. There were depressing times when she felt that her prettiness had shared the same fate as her accomplishments.

At twenty, it had been a universally acclaimed prettiness, of a slim, Grecian-nymph type, a matter of outline and features rather than colouring. It seemed to her that she had altered wonderfully little, even in fourteen years. She was still slim, upright, and without any grey at all in her brown hair. There were faint lines round her mouth and round the corners of her eyes, but her forehead was smooth, except for two little vertical marks between her dark eyebrows.

Her colour had never been very bright—she was paler now, that was all. And her face and hands were thinner.

Nevertheless, Laura knew that, by some indefinable process, she had ceased to be very pretty. People no longer looked at her as though struck by her appearance.

She sometimes rather forlornly told herself that her particular type of beauty was no longer in vogue. Girls, nowadays, didn't look like Grecian nymphs.

They had no particular features, but they had beautiful teeth—Laura's teeth had always been too prominent—and good complexions, and they moved and held themselves well.

Shingled hair suited them.

It had not suited Laura, and she had compromised with a bob that always seemed to herself to be either just too long or just too short. She was still able to get most of her clothes ready-made—but she had to go to the better-class London shops for them. Never more could she hope to "carry off" a cheap, bright-coloured cotton frock, bought from the big draper's shop in Quinnerton.

These considerations formed a kind of vague, unsatisfactory background to Laura's life. In the foreground were Edward, Johnnie, Alfred, the servants, the management of their home, and the Nursing Association, the Women's Institute and the Girl Guides, of Quinnerton. The relative importance of these things, to Laura, was

measured in terms of her own emotional reactions to
them.

Johnnie came first.

Although Edward was her first-born, it was Johnnie
that she loved best. Edward was a good little boy, not
imaginative, mildly averse from any form of lessons, and
finding his chief amusement in kicking at a ball, or in
running rather aimlessly about the garden, making as
loud and incoherent a noise as possible.

Johnnie also made a noise—and a much louder noise
than Edward's—but it was never an incoherent noise.
He was articulate, sensitive, passionate and intelligent.

Alfred Temple said that Laura adored Johnnie, and in
a sense it was true. But the term was only a relative one.

Laura herself felt that Johnnie was her chief preoccupation, and the source both of her deepest discomfort and
her sharpest joys, but at the back of her consciousness
was a profound conviction that her own emotional capabilities had never really yet been fully roused.

At thirty-four she had just begun to wonder if they
were ever destined to be roused at all.

Perhaps if she had ever been in love. . . . Or had she
ever been in love?

It was ridiculous to ask oneself such a question. No
other woman in the world, Laura felt intimately convinced, could have experienced such a doubt. It was a
problem peculiar to her own unique psychology.

Certainly she had thought herself in love with Alfred.
But it had been an academic affair, rather than a passionate one. She had never lost her head, nor Alfred his.

They had been attracted by one another; they had found themselves to possess certain tastes in common. Alfred had admired Laura's looks, and Laura had admired Alfred's distinction.

Laura now admitted to herself—what she had not admitted to herself at the time—that she had been rather anxious to be married, just when she first met Alfred.

The war was over, and there had been a question of her returning home, which she did not want to do, and so many other people seemed to be getting married. . . . She wanted the experience of marriage, and she was just beginning to be rather afraid of missing it altogether, because so many of the men belonging to her own generation had gone.

It had been easy to fall in love with Alfred—in love, that is to say, as most people understand the words. If Laura had a lurking feeling, in those days, that a less deliberate process might better have suited her temperament, it had been stifled in the excitements of her engagement and marriage.

Alfred did not put his fondness into words—it was not his way. Laura, who was given to analysis, put it into words for him often enough—but only to herself, never to her husband. And although it reassured her to know that she did love her Alfred, and that he loved her, it failed to convince her that she had not missed romance altogether.

Laura, forlornly dissecting herself at thirty-four, was startled by the poignancy of her own regrets.

She studied a little psychology, obtained the loan of

a volume of Havelock Ellis, and felt so little exhilarated by the life-stories there set out that she had a brief reaction in favour of Thomas à Kempis. But his consolations were too cloying, his wisdom too trite, and his explanations explained nothing.

Laura was rather relieved, for she would not have liked to think of herself as a religious woman, although her careful agnosticism in reality belonged to her date just as surely as the habit of orthodox belief did to that of an earlier generation.

She sometimes thought—in her less candid moments—"A woman can live for her children."

Perhaps, indeed, some women could, but Laura, in reality, knew that she was not one of them. She could not possibly have lived for dear little Edward, with whom, in fact, she would probably have nothing whatever in common once his childhood's dependence was over—and Johnnie, of an individuality quite as strong as her own, would certainly neither expect nor wish her to subordinate her existence to his.

She wanted a life—an emotional life—of her own.

Laura, for the sake of her self-esteem, strenuously ignored the fact that in all probability she was sharing this desire with a large number of middle-class, middle-aged Englishwomen all over the country.

"Mum-mie-e-e!"

That was Johnnie.

"Was that one of the children?" said Laura, disingenuously.

"Won't nurse go?"

"She's down at supper."

"*Mum-mie-e-e-e!*"

"I'll just see," said Laura, halfway to the door.

"You'd much better leave him to nurse."

"Yes, but ——"

"Well, tell him that if he's simply playing the fool, I shall ——"

She went out of the room, closing the door with an effect of gentle deliberation, and then flying up the shallow staircase two steps at a time, and along the passage. . . .

"Coming, darling. *Don't* scream ——"

She opened the door of the night-nursery and slipped inside very quietly.

"Never let the child see that he has been the centre of unusual excitement," said the little book read by Laura during her children's infancy.

"What is it, Johnnie?"

"I heard you rush upstairs, and all along the passage," said Johnnie in tones of interest. He was sitting up in bed, in his blue striped pyjamas, with his curls all on end.

Those curls, to which Johnnie owed so much more in the way of leniency, and treats, and petting, and notice, than he would probably ever know!

Good little Edward's hair was quite straight, and cut rather short.

"Johnnie, what did you call me for?"

"Please can I have a drink?"

"Couldn't you have thought of that earlier?" said

Laura indulgently, pouring water into the glass on the wash-stand as she spoke.

"Yes," said Johnnie candidly. "But I just thought I'd like to see you. I feel rather lonely."

Edward was in the other little bed, but Edward was asleep. He always went to sleep early. Johnnie never did.

"Well, but don't call me for nothing, like that. It vexes daddy."

Laura bent to kiss him, and, as usual, Johnnie's curls and his smile, and the way in which his arms went round her neck, charmed her utterly.

"Darling!"

She kissed him half a dozen times, rejoicing in the warm, fragrant touch of his little soft face against hers.

"Now go to sleep, and let there be no more of you to-night."

"Yes, *some* more of me to-night," Johnnie answered, in the formula of his babyhood that had always made her laugh. She left him.

Outside the night-nursery door, she remembered remorsefully that she had forgotten to look at Edward, just as she always did forget to look at Edward when Johnnie was there.

The little lamp on the bracket against the passage wall was flaring, and Laura turned it down, noticing for perhaps the thousandth time that there was a black patch of grime on the ceiling above the bracket.

The house needed painting, and cleaning, and repapering. Some day they'd *have* to afford it.

Laura returned to the drawing-room, and to her arm-chair, and the half of *The Times* that Alfred had finished reading before dinner.

"Well?" said Alfred.

"Oh, it wasn't anything serious."

"I never imagined it was. He simply wanted to see if you'd come, I suppose?"

"He wanted a drink."

"Couldn't he fetch that for himself?"

"Of course not. For one thing, they're not allowed to get out of bed like that."

"Johnnie, of course, never does anything he's not allowed to do."

They both laughed.

"All the same, Laura, you're spoiling that child. Why not let nurse go to him, if he wants anybody?"

"She couldn't hear, from the kitchen."

"You could ring and tell her to go to the night-nursery, I suppose?"

"No, Alfred, I couldn't!" said Laura, speaking no less than the literal truth.

"I must have a go at the car to-morrow."

"Oh ——"

Alfred interpreted the sound of her ejaculation correctly, as he could hardly, indeed, have failed to do.

"You didn't want to go anywhere, did you?"

"I did rather want to go into Quinnerton, but of course I can manage ——"

"Wouldn't Wednesday do?"

"It's early closing. And Thursday is nurse's day out, and Friday the Stevensons are coming to tea."

"Well, all this taxi-work is playing the dickens with the car," said Alfred mildly.

"I don't see the sense of having a car if it isn't to be used," said Laura, also mildly.

"I wonder how many times in a month I drive to Quinnerton and back, or to the station, or half across the country," Alfred enquired into space.

"Mum-mie-ee-e!"

Laura tried to think that she had only imagined this familiar, distant sound.

It recurred, with increased volume.

"That naughty little boy," said Laura in an unconvincing way.

"Don't go. He doesn't really want anything."

Laura knew that this was true.

She hesitated.

The summons became an imperative shriek.

"Tell him that I shall come up and spank him if he isn't quiet."

Laura took advantage of the implied sanction and sped upstairs.

"Johnnie, be quiet. Daddy isn't at all pleased with you ——"

"I want a hanky, please."

"Aren't you *at all* sleepy to-night, darling?"

"No," said Johnnie pathetically.

She found him a handkerchief, tucked in the bedclothes, kissed him, told him to be a good little boy and go to sleep, and went out, forgetting to look at the placidly-sleeping Edward.

Outside the door of the night-nursery she remembered about Edward.

She turned down the little lamp on the bracket, that was flaring, and noticed the patch on the ceiling above it.

Then she went downstairs, and into the drawing-room again.

"Nothing, of course?" remarked, rather than enquired, her husband.

"Nurse will be up there directly," was Laura's evasive reply.

She looked at the clock.

It was nearly half-past nine.

No use pretending that it wasn't worth while to take up her sewing. There was plenty of time before one could think of going to bed. Laura, who disliked needle-work, took up her nightgown and began to mend the sleeve. She could not make things, and nurse did all the knitting and darning for the children, but there was no-body except Laura to keep Laura's clothes in order.

While she dealt inexpertly with the nightgown, Laura tried to think of a theme for a short story.

She had written short stories ever since her seventeenth birthday and could nearly always sell them to the more literary type of magazine.

Unfortunately, the higher the tone of the periodical, the lower was its rate of payment. But the guineas helped to augment the inadequate income of the Temples, and there had been times, in certain congenial surroundings, when Laura had been proud of her writings.

On the other hand, there had also been times when she had been ashamed of them. Times when elderly country neighbours had chaffed her about "writing stories with one hand, and pouring out your husband's tea with the other," or when mothers of young children had said that they supposed she didn't have much time for writing *now*, with two little boys to look after.

Laura, on these occasions, had felt that her behaviour was unlike that of other people, and, curiously enough, although she was perfectly ready to suppose herself utterly different to every other woman on earth in disposition, outlook, and mentality, she intensely disliked the thought of diverging from the normal in her conduct of life.

Conflict, in the language of psycho-analysis, was the almost incessant companion of Laura's psychological existence.

The hour between half-past nine and half-past ten passed exactly as usual.

"There's rather an amusing case in the paper," Alfred observed.

"What?"

"A husband who went off with his children's governess, and he's sixty-three, and she's twenty. The judge was rather funny about it."

"Let me see it when you've done," said Laura, not so much forgetting, as entirely eliminating from her consciousness, the fact that at a recent committee meeting she had emphatically seconded a resolution to the effect that the reporting of unseemly details in the Press should be protested against on an early and public occasion. . . .

"You can have it at once."

Laura put down her needlework, and for five minutes was pleasantly absorbed.

She exchanged a slightly ribald comment or two with Alfred, looked through the remaining Law Courts reports, and wished thoughtfully that there would be another case like the Crumbles murder.

"Is the water hot to-night?"

"As far as I know. It was hot just before dinner-time."

"Yes, but it's Nellie's evening out, and Gladys is hopeless about the boiler fire."

"I'd better go and see, then," said Alfred, unenthusiastically.

"No, don't! She'll only think that we think she isn't doing it properly."

Alfred leant back in his chair again.

Presently he said:

"I had to order some more oil to-day."

"Oh dear! The last lot isn't paid for yet."

There was a long silence.

The grandfather clock in the hall chimed ten.

"Oh dear," said Laura, five minutes later. She got up, opened the drawing-room door, stood for a moment listening, and then went back to the fire, leaving the door open.

"There's a most infernal draught coming in," Alfred presently observed, in an uncomplaining voice.

"I'm very sorry, darling, but I just want to hear if Nellie's come in. It's struck ten."

"Ring the bell and ask."

Neither Laura, nor, to do him justice, Alfred himself, treated this suggestion as being worthy of serious attention.

"I'll just go to the passage door ——"

The passage door divided the hall from the pitch-dark, stone-flagged passage that led to the kitchens and pantry.

Laura returned from her expedition worried.

"Not a sound. The lamp is still burning, though. Gladys may be sitting up to let her in, or she may have gone upstairs, and left the door undone."

"Nurse went up some time ago. I heard her."

"I know."

"You'd better speak to that girl before her next evening out. She's always late, isn't she?"

"Always. And next Sunday is her Sunday off."

"Well, tell her it's got to stop."

"If Nellie gave notice, I'm pretty sure Gladys would go too. They've always been friends."

"She won't give notice. She knows very well that she's supposed to be in by now."

"Hush!" cried Laura, darting to the passage door once more, and again returning disconsolate.

"I thought I heard her, but it was only Fauntleroy."

"It's time Fauntleroy was put out."

Laura opened the front door, and the Aberdeen terrier obediently disappeared into the night.

"Alfred, what had I better do?"

"Go upstairs before the water gets cold. I'll go round and see if the back door's fastened presently, and if it isn't I shall lock up, and Miss Nellie can ring the front-door bell."

"It's a quarter past. Even if her watch were slow it wouldn't be as wrong as all that without her knowing it."

"You'd much better go to bed."

Laura waited, drifted reluctantly upstairs, undressed with her bedroom door wide open, and in the bathroom gazed earnestly out of the window at the dark shrubs and bushes that surrounded the double doors of the yard through which Nellie should have returned on the stroke of ten o'clock.

On the way back to her own room, after a tepid and un-pleasant bath, she heard a footstep on the back stairs, and then the opening and shutting of a door.

"She's back," thought Laura.

It was a relief, but almost immediately she began to rehearse to herself the rebuke that it would be necessary to address to Nellie next day.

"Nellie, I really can't have this sort of thing going on."

"Have you any explanation, Nellie, of why you came in three-quarters of an hour late last night?"

"Nellie, what time was it when you got in last night?"

The variations of which this theme was capable seemed to be without number, as did the unsatisfactory replies with which Laura's imagination, quite against her will, continued to credit her house-parlourmaid.

She was still pursuing the distressing dialogue when Alfred came to bed, and it was the first thing that leapt to her mind when she woke.

Chapter II

LAURA woke at a quarter to seven, as she almost always did, and lay in bed and listened. If there was a distant sound of fire-irons it was all right. Gladys, at any rate, was downstairs. If there was the faint rattling of a chain, and the clank of drawn-back bolts, then Nellie was downstairs, opening up the house.

If voices, and the clatter of crockery, came from the direction of the nursery, then nurse was dressing Edward and Johnnie, and getting their breakfast ready. It was not necessary that these last sounds should be audible before half-past seven.

If, however, as was too often the case, perfect silence reigned, Laura knew that the maids had—probably with entire deliberation—overslept themselves. And her heart sank.

She ought to get up and go to the back stairs. She ought to knock on the door of the night-nursery.

She ought, at the very least, to Speak to Them, after breakfast.

Alfred lay sleeping on the far side of the double bed. They ought to have had modern twin beds, of course— much more hygienic, and, Laura could not help thinking, much more comfortable as well. They often talked about it. Or, rather, Laura often talked about it. Alfred, like so many husbands, was of a silent disposition.

Laura rehearsed the probabilities of the day that lay ahead of her.

Tuesday.

There wasn't enough of the beef left for anything except cottage pie. Her mind shuddered at being invaded so early by details from which she was at all times averse. She determined not to try and think of a pudding, although she could feel the thought pushing at the back of her mind.

Alfred was going to do something to the car. So she'd walk to the village for the Institute Committee Meeting at three o'clock. (What about pancakes—or were there no lemons? Rhubarb? The boys were sick of rhubarb. . . .)

The short story that had seemed rather good last night seemed idiotic this morning. Not worth working out.

Perhaps the post would bring an interesting letter.

(Jam-tarts—Johnnie would be pleased, but Alfred wouldn't eat jam-tarts—there might be a rice pudding for him. Laura made up her mind not to try and think of a pudding.)

Apples were over. There were such a lot of things to be made with apples—dumplings, fritters, apple-tart, apple-meringues, apple-charlotte, stewed apples and custard. . . .

At last. The sounds for which she was subconsciously waiting had begun. From the nursery, at the far end of the house, came distant yells. Either the boys were playing very happily together, or else it was one of Johnnie's

bad days, when he shrieked with temper at almost everything that happened.

Laura, who, although she would have denied it indignantly, lived in abject terror of these periodic attacks,
felt her latent uneasiness increase.

Chocolate pudding—they'd had it so very recently;
tinned fruit would be extravagant, and didn't really do
them any good, either; or —— No, she would not think
of a pudding. That would come quite soon enough, when
she had to go to the kitchen after breakfast. And after
she'd spoken to Nellie about coming in late.

Her anticipation sank to still lower depths. Perhaps
the post would bring letters. . . .

"Come in!"

Nellie entered, put down the little tray with the early
morning tea, and performed her usual functions, and
Alfred woke up. Although the separate items that made
up the morning were most of them rather disagreeable
than otherwise to Laura, she was eager to embark upon
them. It was better to do the things than to think about
them.

Just before the breakfast gong sounded she went to the
nursery and kissed the children. Johnnie seemed all
right. . . . Nurse said "Good morning" rather sulkily.
. . . She was an excellent nurse, but sometimes she had
injured feelings, for which no reason was ever forth-
coming.

"I shan't take any notice," reflected Laura, as usual.
"I daresay it'll have passed off by lunch time, or perhaps

it's simply my fancy." She went downstairs, racking her brains as to what could have offended nurse.

The post brought two bills, a circular, a postcard from Laura's younger sister, who was in Italy sketching, and a letter. The letter, in a large, square, expensive-looking mauve envelope, might be interesting. Laura opened it.

> *The Manor House,*
> *Quinnerton.*

Dear Laura,

We should be so pleased if you and your husband would come over to tea on Saturday next, the 17th. Mr. Onslow, the novelist, and his wife will be staying here, and I should so like you to meet them. He has read some of your stories!!

> *Yours ever,*
> *Gertrude Kingsley-Browne.*

Except for the two exclamation marks, Laura felt pleased.

"Lady Kingsley-Browne has asked us to meet the A. B. Onslows, Alfred."

"Good," said Alfred, without elation, as without rancour.

"You know who A. B. Onslow *is*, of course?"

"No."

"But, Alfred!"

"Does he write?" said Alfred.

"You know he does. You've read several of his books. You even liked them."

"What is he doing with the Kingsley-Brownes? Are they trying to foist the girl on to him?"

"I have no doubt they would, if he didn't happen to have a wife already," returned Laura uncharitably. "I think Bay-bay is supposed to have literary tastes, too."

Miss Kingsley-Browne, prettily called Bébée by her mother, was derisively referred to as Bay-bay by the Temples, in rather unkind mimicry of Lady Kingsley-Browne's pronunciation.

"What do they want us for—lunch or tea?"

"Tea, unfortunately," said Laura, in simple and sincere regret for the economy entailed by going out to lunch. "Saturday. I'll say Yes, shall I?"

"All right."

Laura began to think about her clothes, without much exhilaration.

"Hullo, mummie!" said Johnnie, at the open window.

"Hullo, darling."

"Mummie, have I got to put my boots on?"

"If the grass is wet ——"

"Of course it's wet," said Alfred.

"Yes, darling, put them on. And tell Edward to put his on, too."

"He has already."

"That's splendid. Run up and get yours, darling," said Laura, with entirely artificial brightness.

"Oh, bother," said Johnnie ferociously.

"Hasn't he got a nursery?" Alfred enquired coldly. He had but little patience with Johnnie at the best of times—and breakfast was the worst of times.

"Run upstairs, darling," Laura repeated.

"Need I put my boots on?"

"Nurse will help you," weakly said Laura, who had many times impressed upon nurse her wish that the children should learn to do things for themselves.

"I don't want my boots on."

"That'll do; go upstairs," said Alfred suddenly and severely.

Johnnie, muttering the nursery equivalent of curses, moved away from the window. Laura, out of the corner of her eye, saw him plunge morosely into the long, wet grass that fringed the tennis court. Her mind was divided impartially between the hope that he would not get a cold and the hope that Alfred would not notice. A great part of her life was spent in the endeavour to prevent Alfred from noticing what Johnnie was doing.

Had he gone?

Laura feigned absorption in Lady Kingsley-Browne's letter. Fortunately, Nellie had forgotten the marmalade.

"Ring for the marmalade, please, darling," said Laura.

"Not for me."

"She *must* learn to remember things."

"Mummie," said Johnnie, suddenly reappearing, "can I have a banana?"

"Go and put your boots on," Alfred shouted.

"Oh, don't!" said Laura involuntarily.

Shouting, with Johnnie, was always fatal. It was incomprehensible to her that his father had not learnt this.

Instantly Johnnie burst into roars of tearless anger, and flung himself flat upon the ground.

A short scene, upon familiar lines, followed. Laura profoundly disapproved of coercive measures, both upon general principles and from experience of Johnnie's peculiar reactions to a force of which he felt the tyranny, without being able to condemn it. At the same time, she had a thorough and genuine dislike of spoilt children, and a loyal determination to uphold Alfred's authority with his sons.

It sometimes seemed to her that every principle that she had ever had, she sooner or later sacrificed, either to Alfred, to Johnnie, or to the servants. And yet life continued to be a thing of conflict, of difficulty, and of ill-success.

"He's got to learn obedience," said Alfred, appearing to think that Johnnie had taken a step in this direction when, resisting to the utmost, he had been propelled upstairs by the superior physical force of his parent. "What's the matter with the child?"

"He gets like that, you know," said Laura unhappily.

The face of Edward inopportunely appeared at the other window.

"Hullo, mummie!"

"Go and play in the garden, darling," said Laura, with the utmost firmness, "or else up to the nursery."

Edward, thank heaven, always did as he was told; at least, as long as he was in sight. Therefore Laura commanded him, where she coaxed and even bribed Johnnie.

"Hop it," said Alfred, and Edward disappeared.

"There's no peace in this house," observed Laura's husband, not unpleasantly. "Aren't you going to eat that piece of toast?"

"I don't want it, thanks."

"Then I can ring."

"Oh, please eat it, Alfred. Or else I will. Otherwise she'll think she can send in less."

Laura saw no absurdity whatever in this domestic manœuvre, which she practised, in one form or another, almost every day of her life.

When she had eaten her undesired piece of toast, they left the dining-room.

The ten minutes most detested by Laura was close upon her. Instinctively she sought to postpone them by going up to the nursery, which she found empty, looking into the spare bedroom and opening the window there, and putting another log of wood on the drawing-room fire Then she had to go to the kitchen.

"Good morning, Gladys."

"Good morning, madam."

Gladys was twenty-six and Laura thirty-four. Gladys was the servant of Laura, paid to work for her. She had been at Applecourt only six months, and it was highly improbable that she would remain for another six. Nevertheless, it was Gladys who, in their daily interviews, was entirely at her ease, and Laura who was nervous.

"I'll just see what we've got in the larder."

The attenuated remainder of the Sunday joint was in the larder, with half of a cold rhubarb tart and a fragment of jelly.

"Better make the beef into cottage pie," said Laura.
"And what about a pudding for mid-day?"

As though these words possessed a magic, her mind, as
she uttered them, became impervious to any idea whatever. Just as though the word "pudding" had the power
to stultify intelligence.

Laura looked at the cook, and the cook looked out of
the little barred window of the larder, entirely detached.

"It's so difficult to think of a *new* pudding, isn't it?"
said Laura pleadingly.

Gladys smiled, as though at a small jest.

"We had chocolate-pudding just the other day, and besides, the weather's getting rather warm. The children
like jam-tarts."

"I'm right out of flour, madam."

"Oh. Well, the groceries will be here this afternoon,
won't they? But of course that'll be too late for the pudding. Yes. It's so difficult to ——" Laura checked herself just in time.

"What about ——" She searched her mind desperately. "What about ——? Have we any prunes?"

"I don't think we have, madam."

Laura didn't really think so either. It had been a forlorn hope.

With a supreme effort Laura said, "We'll have pancakes. There are plenty of lemons. Now what about
dinner to-night?"

With the least possible assistance from Gladys, dinner
to-night was outlined. A savoury instead of a sweet, as
usual. Mercifully, Alfred never wanted a sweet at night.

Feeling as though all food would be entirely distasteful to her for ever more, Laura left the larder and went to the kitchen. From the kitchen—where she saw Fauntleroy eating cold bacon on the floor, and indirectly rebuked Gladys by sending him outside—Laura proceeded to the store-cupboard, and after a distasteful five minutes there, compelled herself to say: "Please send Nellie to me in the drawing-room as soon as she's cleared the dining-room table."

"I was wishing to speak to you about Nellie, madam."

From an automaton, devoid of ideas, Gladys suddenly became a person of unsurpassed eloquence.

"I don't want to make unpleasantness, I'm sure, but I don't think Nellie and me can work together, not if she goes on the way she has done. It's the same every time she goes out ——"

"I know. Well, I'm going to speak to Nellie this morning, and I think you'll find ——"

"What I say is, it isn't fair. And nurse'll tell you the same, madam. If her and me can get in at ten o'clock, why can't Nellie? What I say is, it's not fair on nurse and I."

"It isn't fair on me, either," remarked Laura, but this was an aspect of the case that did not interest Gladys in the least.

"No'm, that's what I say; it isn't fair on me and nurse. I've never had to speak like this about any girl that I've worked with before, but Nellie's been queer-like ever since I came here."

"Yes, well, Gladys, you're quite right to tell me if

things aren't going well," said Laura unhappily. "Send Nellie to me in the drawing-room. I think you'll find things will be different."

Gladys committed herself to no fallacious expressions of optimism, and Laura left the kitchen, feeling as though her own stock of vitality for the day was already exhausted.

She supposed that she must, beyond a doubt, be the worst housekeeper in England.

The door of the drawing-room flew open, and the two little boys came in, leaving muddy tracks upon the carpet.

"Edward, your boots!"

"Mummie," said Edward earnestly, "do birds ever climb trees?"

Detachment of a high order is the reaction of the maternal mind to the inconsequence of childhood.

"Not exactly *climb* them," Laura said. "Go and wipe your boots, darling. Birds *alight* on trees when they're flying about, don't they?"

"What is alight?"

"Tell him, Johnnie. And wipe your boots on the mat, both of you."

"Alight is stopping to sit down," said Johnnie.

Laura experienced the faint thrill of pride that Johnnie's lucidity always brought to her.

"Is to-day Sunday, mummie?"

"No, darling, it's Tuesday. The day before yesterday was Sunday. Your boots, Johnnie."

Edward went outside and wiped his boots on the mat.

"Johnnie, darling, don't make me say it so often."

The house-parlourmaid Nellie appeared at the door of the drawing-room.

"Oh, Nellie —— Boys, go into the dining-room and wait for Miss Lamb. She'll be here directly. Come in, Nellie."

Laura seated herself before her writing-table.

"Mummie, why can't I stay in here?"

"Because it's lesson-time, darling."

"*Bother!*" said Johnnie.

"Bother," said Edward imitatively.

Laura's exasperated nerves would have welcomed the relief of slapping them both. The instinct of civilised generations behind her, no less than the knowledge that violence would only result in breeding more violence, restrained her.

"Go away, boys; I really mean it. Edward, hurry up." Her voice sharpened, because she knew that Edward could be easily intimidated.

He went out of the room.

"Johnnie, dear ——"

"Mummie, Nellie knows a whole poem called 'The Wreck of the Hesperus.' Isn't she clever?"

He smiled up at Nellie, who laid her hand on his curls, looking apologetically at Laura.

All servants adored Johnnie, who gave them a great deal of trouble and seldom obeyed them—but never spoke to them otherwise than politely. Edward, who was obedient, had no such instinct. He made personal remarks, and the maids merely tolerated him.

"Very clever, darling," said Laura. "Now run along."

"When will it be Sunday?"

"In four days. There's Miss Lamb. Run and open the door for her."

"It is open."

Laura knew that it was open, but had hoped that Johnnie didn't.

"Well, never mind—*go!*"

To her great relief Johnnie went, and Nellie promptly shut the door behind him.

When she turned round again the smile and the apologetic look alike had entirely disappeared from her face. The expression that had replaced them was one known to Laura, both on the face of Nellie herself and on the faces of several of her numerous predecessors. It was compounded of defiance, obtuseness, and a determination not to be "put upon."

"Nellie, you were very late again last night," began Laura. She knew that her cause was just, but the knowledge did not seem to lend her any self-assurance.

The interview ended, as she had all along felt that it would end, in an announcement from Nellie that she "wished to make a change."

"Very well, I will take a month's notice from you."

Now that the blow had fallen, Laura could be calm, and even firm. And anyhow, Nellie had always been unpunctual—a tiresome fault—and house-parlourmaids were easier to get than cooks-general.

She decided to write out an advertisement for the *Morning Post,* and to visit the Registry Office at Quinnerton.

"Very well. Thank you, Nellie."

"Thank you, madam."

Upon these empty courtesies Nellie left the drawing-room.

Laura got up and walked round the room, mechanically straightening the shabby mauve cretonne covers on the armchairs, straightening the piles of music on the top of the cottage piano, and shaking up the little striped purple bolster on the window-seat—all the time rehearsing her interview with Nellie, and thinking out excellent and dignified utterances for herself.

Then she saw that the vases needed refilling, and fetched a little water-can out of the hall. A cold northeast wind blew in through the open door, making her shudder, and adding to her general sense of unpleasing surroundings.

Johnnie's voice, in loud argument with his daily governess, reached her from behind the closed door of the dining-room.

Laura, physically and morally chilled, sat down before her writing-table.

> *Applecourt,*
> *Nr. Quinnerton.*
> *March 13th.*

Dear Lady Kingsley-Browne,

Thank you so much for your kind invitation. We shall be delighted to come to tea on the 17th, and should so much enjoy meeting Mr. and Mrs. Onslow. I have always admired his work.

> *Yours affectionately,*
> *Laura Temple.*

Lady Kingsley-Browne's note wasn't even dated. Laura felt faintly comforted by her own superiority.

All the same, she hadn't anything decent to wear on Saturday. It was a difficult time of the year for those who could afford only a winter wardrobe and a summer one, neither of which ever seemed to be wholly appropriate to the weather.

The kasha two-piece suit would be all right, but she had no really satisfactory hat to wear with it.

Laura drew a hat on the blotting-paper, frowned, and then wrote other letters.

At twelve o'clock she heard Miss Lamb go away and nurse call the boys for their walk. She felt impelled to go to the window and watch them start—sturdy little figures in their covert-coats, without caps or gaiters. Edward was bouncing a ball, and running to catch it. Johnnie was fitting a flower-pot on to Fauntleroy's head. Laura smiled indulgently, but was relieved when Fauntleroy broke loose and nurse caught Johnnie by the hand. They disappeared through the white gate that led into the lane.

Laura then perceived that she had allowed the drawing-room fire to go nearly out. She was obliged to work at it with the bellows for some time.

Her husband, whose occupation was that of farming his own land, did not come in until one o'clock, when he slightly annoyed Laura by going upstairs to wash his hands exactly five minutes after the gong had been rung.

Edward and Johnnie always had their dinner in the dining-room. No house-parlourmaid had ever consented

to the indignity of carrying up the nursery meals, and no
consideration would ever induce nurse to fetch her own
meals from the kitchen.

The Temples were not allowed by Laura to eat their
meals in silence. She had long ago informed Alfred that
such a course was uncivilised. Even the little boys were
encouraged to talk, provided that they did not interrupt.

To-day Laura wanted to tell her husband that Nellie
had given notice, but the presence of Edward and Johnnie
restrained her. She was obliged, instead, to give some of
her attention to the subject of sugar-beet. It might
have interested her more, but for her preoccupation about
Nellie and the necessity of addressing the boys in frequent
parentheses.

"I'm glad they're taking it up round here. (Edward,
not with your mouth full.) Did you say the Home Farm
had—(Never let me see you do that again!)—had decided to give it a trial?"

Alfred made a reply which unfortunately Laura did not
hear, owing to a mishap of Edward's with a spoonful of
cottage pie.

"*I* see," she replied interestedly, and looking almost unnaturally intelligent.

"It's a good idea, isn't it?"

"Very," said Laura emphatically.

"Mummie, do you know what Paris is the capital of?"

"Do tell me, darling."

"Did you read what the *Agricultural Journal* said about
sugar-beet last week?"

"I haven't read it yet, Alfred, but it's on my table."

"I know it is. I put it there a week ago. It wouldn't take you five minutes to read——"

"Daddy, do you know what Paris is the capital of?"

"Yes. Don't interrupt."

Edward looked rather hurt, and Laura said hastily: "I must read it after lunch. I want to very much indeed. Well, darling, do tell me about Paris."

"Look! There's a wasp!" said Edward, quite maddeningly.

"I want to send the *Agricultural Journal* on to the Men's Club this afternoon."

"Yes, I'll read it before post time, darling."

Alfred turned to his son.

"Now then, old man, what about Paris?" he said kindly. "You must learn not to interrupt when Daddy and Mummie are talking, you know."

Edward, who had obviously forgotten all about Paris, looked bored and made rambling and disconnected statements to which neither of his parents paid serious attention.

"How's the car getting on?" Laura asked, feeling that it was Alfred's turn.

"I haven't started on her yet. I shall do that this afternoon."

"I hope—(Don't fidget like that, darling)—I hope it won't—(and do keep your feet still; you're shaking the whole table)—be so very long before——"

"Pancakes," said Johnnie brightly.

Laura dispensed the pancakes.

Her hope concerning the car, never a very robust affair, died unuttered and unnoticed.

The conversation continued to be prosaic, lacking in grace, continuity, or purpose.

A vague recollection of a sentence, read somewhere, to the effect that it is always the wife and mother who is primarily responsible for the atmosphere of the home, depressed Laura's spirits.

Chapter III

AT THREE o'clock in the afternoon of the following Saturday Laura temporarily ceased to be a wife and a mother, and became a human being. She put on a biscuit-coloured kasha frock and the fur-bordered coat that matched it, and brown, low-heeled crocodile shoes over biscuit-coloured stockings.

When she had adjusted her small, soft velvet pull-on hat, Laura gazed earnestly at herself in the glass.

She thought: "I look nice—but there's no one to see it, really. Unless ——"

Unless was the unspoken tribute paid to romance, that lurking possibility to which Laura woke every morning of her life. She took out a tiny little rouge pad from under the handkerchiefs in the middle drawer of her dressing-table, used it very, very carefully, and then very, very carefully wiped the result off again.

Alfred disliked rouge, but very seldom noticed when she had it on.

From the nursery a loud wail came distinctly. Laura, catching up her gloves, hurried out of the room and along the passage.

It would have been impossible for her to go out of the house with that wail uninvestigated, although she knew that it had no serious significance, that it was in the nature of an isolated, casual wail—not the kind likely to be succeeded by a hurricane of wails—and that her presence, especially in outdoor attire, would hold nothing soothing.

She spent five minutes in the nursery, and found that Alfred, unusually, had brought the car round to the front door punctually, and was waiting for her.

"I'm so sorry," apologised Laura, energetically returning the frantic hand-waving of the children.

Alfred did not say, "You're not going to the North Pole. You'll be home again in about two hours from now," but it was Laura's misfortune to attribute such definite meanings to his silences, and to clothe them in pungent and unsympathetic language. She often held wordless and impassioned conversations with Alfred, replying to many things that he had not said.

To-day, as they drove, she tried not to think about the difficulty of finding a new house-parlourmaid, nor about Johnnie's temper, nor about Edward's loose front tooth, but when she had conscientiously banished these subjects, her mind seemed to become a blank.

If only Alfred would talk about sugar-beet now, instead of at lunch-time, when she couldn't possibly attend!

There had been a time, however, when Laura would have regarded sugar-beet, viewed as a conversational topic between a man and a woman, as frankly impossible.

"Who are these people we're going to meet?"

"The A. B. Onslows."

"Oh yes, of course. Did you say he wrote?"

"Alfred, you know he does. I told you the other day—and you liked that last book of his."

"I daresay," said Alfred indifferently.

"Well, don't talk about books, darling. That'll be safest, perhaps."

Alfred made an acquiescent sound.

They drove on in silence. Once Alfred said: "The oak'll be out before the ash this year, by the look of things." And once Laura, before she could stop herself, exclaimed: " I do hope Edward's second teeth won't be long coming through. Gaps are so dreadfully unbecoming."

Alfred made no reply, and she tried to hope that he hadn't heard.

The avenue of the Manor House was a long and winding drive, and the daffodils were in bloom under the trees.

"Much further out than ours," said Laura resentfully, and five minutes later she said the same thing to Lady Kingsley-Browne, this time in a tone of pleased admiration.

Their hostess was in the morning-room, to which the butler conducted them.

"My dear, how nice of you to come. How are you, Mr. Temple? Very busy, I suppose? The Onslows are so looking forward to meeting you both."

Laura murmured graceful disclaimers, and followed Lady Kingsley-Browne across the big square hall to the drawing-room.

Introductions were effected.

Mrs. Onslow, to Laura's slight relief, was older than herself, less good-looking, and with a figure no longer slim. Her clothes, on the other hand, were expensively beautiful.

A. B. Onslow was tall and attenuated, clean-shaven, and with a manner of rather elaborate geniality. His hair was brightly but unconvincingly dyed.

Lady Kingsley-Browne's only daughter was poised upon the window-seat, tall, slim, and rather strident, and with an air of almost phenomenal self-possession.

In the opinion of Laura Temple, Bébée Kingsley-Browne was neither pretty, clever, well-behaved, nor virtuous. Nevertheless it was impossible to deny that in some mysterious manner she attracted the admiration, and even the devotion, of a great number of men.

Even Alfred, loyal, unobservant, and non-susceptible, had admitted to Laura that there was *something* about Miss Kingsley-Browne.

"But *what?*" Laura had coldly enquired. And Alfred hadn't been able to say what—but there, he declared, it was.

It was there, too, in the opinion of A. B. Onslow. Laura saw that in exactly five minutes, while she exchanged intelligent observations about bulbs with Lady Kingsley-Browne and Mrs. Onslow.

"But, of course, living in London ——"

"Oh, but your lovely garden!" Lady Kingsley-Browne protested.

The Onslows owned a large house at Highgate.

"Mrs. Onslow has the most wonderful Dutch garden; and the rock-plant ——"

"One tries to pretend it's like a garden in the country
—but of course ——"

"I always think that Highgate—*or* Hampstead—give
one the advantages of both town and country," Lady
Kingsley-Browne declared earnestly. "We do feel rather
cut-off down here sometimes."

"One just can't get up to London and back in the
day," Laura contributed.

She hoped inwardly that A. B. Onslow was paying no
attention to the conversation.

"Shall we have some tea? I think it's in the library."

Laura's subconscious self, that exercised its powers of
observation entirely independently of her wishes, and even
her principles, rather resentfully noted the faint suggestion that Lady Kingsley-Browne hadn't even ordered
her tea in advance, and couldn't be perfectly certain
in which of her five sitting-rooms the servants might
have placed it.

The library was a panelled room, with a log-fire burning on an open hearth, and a number of very comfortable
armchairs.

Tea was on a gate-legged table by the fire, and neither
the cakes, the bread-and-butter, nor the bowl of vio-
lets presented that amateurish appearance associated by
Laura with her own tea-table.

"Are you going to the Point-to-Point next week?" she
heard Bébée enquire, and Alfred's slow-spoken reply.

"I daresay we shall. I'm afraid I hadn't realised it
was next week. The twenty-second?"

"Do let's go. I always love the Quinnerton Point-to-

Point," Laura exclaimed. She was partly genuine, and partly desirous of sounding ready to do anything that everybody else did.

"This dreadful girl attends every race-meeting in England," proudly declared Lady Kingsley-Browne. "Darling Bay-bay, who's taking you to the Point-to-Point?"

"I can't remember, mummie, but whoever it is will turn up in time for lunch, I expect."

"Isn't she *terrible!*"

Everybody flatteringly agreed that Bébée was terrible, and Bébée ate sandwiches and looked blasée and contrived to make everybody understand that in a district where young women and men were in a proportion of about twelve to one, it was positively difficult for her to make a choice amongst the escorts that offered themselves to her on every possible occasion.

It was not until tea was over that Onslow spoke to Laura, as he offered her a cigarette.

"When are we to have the pleasure of reading another story of yours in the *London Century?*" he enquired.

Laura flushed faintly, and smiled uncertainly.

Now, if ever, was the moment to impress A. B. Onslow, his wife, Alfred, Lady Kingsley-Browne, and the insufferable Bébée, with the fact that one might live in the country all the year round and be a wife and a mother, and yet remain a woman of the world, and one in touch with the interests of modern literature.

"I don't know," she heard herself reply, inanely.

"Soon, I hope," A. B. Onslow persisted gallantly.

"I hope so, too," said Laura feebly, and, overcome with

self-consciousness, dashed into an irrelevant reference to a book of memoirs. Had Mr. Onslow read it?

Yes, he had.

After that they were able to talk, and Laura found it the easier because Bébée had disappeared, and Lady Kingsley-Browne was talking to Alfred and Mrs. Onslow about pageants—evidently a link between country life and the artistic interests of Highgate.

It gave Laura acute pleasure to listen again to talk about books, although she would have preferred not to have had to say "I haven't yet read that" quite so often.

At last Mr. Onslow—evidently a man of infinite tact —again approached the subject of Laura's own contributions to literature, with all the air of one whose suspense was urgent.

"If I may say so, Mrs. Temple, that story of yours in the *Century* was a considerable advance in technique over anything that you've given us yet. I believe I've read everything of yours, and I've been wondering very much when another collected volume would appear. Soon, I hope?"

Laura laughed, flushing.

"I hope so, too. You can't imagine how encouraging it is to hear that from *you*. It makes me feel that I must go on writing at all costs."

"You must, indeed," Onslow assured her earnestly.

"And may I say how much I loved your last book?"

They talked about A. B. Onslow's last book until they were interrupted by Bébée drifting in again, her hands thrust into the pockets of her jumper suit, a cigarette between her rouged lips.

"Not that it doesn't suit her," Laura admitted to herself with reluctant honesty, gazing at that young, unnaturally-crimson mouth.

It was at this point that Mr. Onslow's attention to his conversation with Laura, although it did not waver, gave her an impression of being, as it were, nailed to the mast, by courtesy and kind-heartedness.

Mrs. Temple, as an instant result, ceased to be either entertaining or responsively intelligent, and their duologue petered out.

"I'm afraid," said Laura, looking at her husband, "that we ought really to be thinking——"

"Oh, must you really?" Lady Kingsley-Browne rose as she spoke. "How are the children? Mrs. Temple has two such perfectly delightful children."

"Have you really?" Mrs. Onslow asked—but Laura's maternal instinct knew very well that she required no reply, and would not perceive the absence of one.

The Temples were escorted to the door, their Morris-Oxford—looking strangely battered in the middle of the square, gravelled terrace, flanked by stone jars of geraniums—was politely extolled, and farewells were exchanged.

"Remember! I shall look out for that volume of stories," said Onslow.

"Do come and see us when you're in London," Mrs. Onslow begged. "We're in the telephone book."

"We'd love to," Laura returned smiling.

"Switch on," directed Alfred, and cranked up the car. The Temples, in Laura's opinion, were the only remaining couple in England whose car was not fitted with a self-starter.

As they drove away, she saw Bébée, with a familiar and nonchalant gesture, thrust her hand through the arm of her parents' distinguished guest.

"That girl is, with no single exception, the worst-mannered and most conceited little fool that I've ever set eyes upon," Laura remarked, in what she believed to be a detached tone of impartial scientific interest.

Alfred, more indifferently, but with Shakesperian outspokenness, coldly applied one single, racy epithet to Miss Kingsley-Browne.

"I daresay," said Laura, her feelings relieved by a small laugh. "What did you think of the Onslows?"

"Oh, all right. Did you notice her pearls?"

"Of course I did."

"You ought to go and see them when you're in London, Laura. I like to hear you talking about books," said Alfred simply.

Her heart glowed suddenly.

"Do you, darling?"

Occasionally Alfred said things like that, and invariably Laura sought to draw him on further, although seldom with success.

"Why ——?"

"Oh well, you do it very nicely, and I know it's a pleasure to you. Did you notice those hyacinths in the hall?"

"No—yes—yes, I think I did."

"They were very fine. That head-man of theirs is good. A Scotsman, of course. Did I tell you that I'd had a talk with him about sugar-beet growing the other day?"

How odd it was, Laura reflected, that her desire to hear Alfred talk about sugar-beet—although a loyal and a genuine one, if not absolutely indigenous to her own mentality—should so seldom coincide with Alfred's desire to talk about it!

Well, at least she could attend to it now, which she couldn't simply do at home.

"Of course, the trouble with these farmers ——" said Alfred.

Laura listened very attentively, and hoped that Alfred wouldn't remember to ask her if she'd yet read the article in the *Agricultural Journal*. It was on her writing-table still. She visualised it, and the small packet of letters that was just beside it . . . answered, thank goodness, but not quite finished with yet. Surely, surely, out of five addresses collected from the Quinnerton Registry Offices and one advertisement taken from the *Morning Post,* a house-parlourmaid would materialise. If one engaged them too long ahead they always seemed to fail at the last and most inconvenient minute, and if one left it too long, then there was no chance at all, and a terrible and expensive system of "tiding over" came into force. It entailed the presence of a woman from the village, at a cost of three shillings and several meals a day, and a great deal of uncongenial and personal hard

work on the part of Laura herself. And Alfred didn't
like it. And one couldn't have anybody to stay. And
it made extra work for nurse, because the boys were on
her hands at times when Laura habitually had them
with her. Worst of all, a prolonged period of tiding
over always caused the remaining servant to give notice.
So that by the time one had a new one, the old one was
just leaving, and the vicious circle went on.

"In fact it's actually a more profitable crop than
wheat," said Alfred conclusively.

And Laura replied with great emphasis, "Yes, I see it
must be. It's wonderful."

As the Morris-Oxford turned in at the white gate,
Laura forgot the existence of the A. B. Onslows, of the
Kingsley-Brownes, and of sugar-beet. She glanced at
her watch, and saw that there was still half an hour to
elapse before the boys need go to bed.

"Mummie!"

Johnnie dashed down the stairs and met her in the
hall, but, as usual, he eluded her kiss.

Edward followed more slowly.

"Mummie, will you play with us?"

"Will you read to us?"

"You're always out, aren't you?" said Johnnie pathetically, and quite untruly.

His mother contented herself with giving him a look.
She knew that Johnnie knew that she knew when he
was merely playing for effect.

"Have you been good while I've been away?" Laura

enquired, sincerely anxious for reassurance, and remembering too late that all the modern books on education stressed the importance of always taking for granted that no child ever had been, could be, or would be anything but good.

"Yes, very," said Edward glibly.

"Not so very, at tea," his brother reminded him. "I only upset my milk by an accident, and we wouldn't finish our crusts."

"Well," said Laura, and took them into the drawing-room. "What shall I read? It's Edward's turn to choose."

Edward looked timidly at his mother. He liked the Peter Rabbit books, and Tales about Bad Little Kittens, and even Nursery Rhymes with plenty of pictures. Laura did not smile upon her elder son's taste in literature. She read the Bad Little Kittens when he asked for them, in rather a chilly voice, for fear of creating a repression in Edward, but she kept her enthusiasm for Johnnie's favourite Tales from the Classics and Stories from English History. Both her children were well aware of this, as Laura guiltily realised.

"Hercules, please," said Edward rather faintly.

She saw that he was making a great effort to conform to his mother's standards, and felt both remorseful and impatient.

"I'll just take off my hat ——"

Laura threw off her hat and coat in the hall, noted with a passing distaste in the oval looking-glass on the wall that her hair always emerged untidy from under any hat, and that her nose required powdering, and went straight to the drawing-room and began to read.

Edward did not listen at all, and Johnnie listened intently, but earnestly bit his nails.

"Johnnie—your fingers—'So Hercules went to the marshes where those terrible birds ——' Johnnie, dear —and Edward, don't kick the furniture—'these terrible birds lived. They were called the Stymphalian birds.'"

"They had brass beaks," from Johnnie.

"Yes, don't interrupt, darling, and *don't* make me speak to you again about your fingers, or I shall stop reading."

" 'Now before he went, Hercules had taken the precaution ——' Do you know what that means, Edward?"

"Yes," said Edward hastily.

"What?"

"I don't know."

Laura, who was almost always mysteriously tired after quarter of an hour spent in the undisturbed company of her children, suddenly felt too jaded to point out Edward's failure, alike in intelligence and in truthfulness, with that pleasant, gentle reasonableness recommended by all her little modern books. So instead she said wearily and injudiciously, "Tell him, Johnnie." And Johnnie did so, and received in return a sulky look from his senior.

"It won't do to let Edward get jealous, poor darling," thought Laura, as she had thought a great many other times.

She resumed the Labours of Hercules.

At half-past six there was a knock at the door.

"Here's nurse," said Laura—too brightly, as she her-self felt. "Now I'll put in a marker, so that we shall know the place to-morrow. Good-night, darlings."

"*Must* we go to bed, mummie?"

"Certainly you must. I'll come up and say good-night to you."

"What about five more minutes?" Johnnie coaxed, his pleading far more nearly effectual than Edward's whining.

Laura glanced at nurse, a modern, efficient-looking young woman, not much over thirty.

Nurse had on her offended face.

Laura did not know the cause of this not infrequent catastrophe, and in all probability never would know it, since nurse was of those who "prefer not to say" when interrogated. But she did know that this was no evening for a display of maternal weakness.

"Not to-night, darling. Now say good-night—you can go and find daddy in the study before you go up, and don't keep nurse waiting."

A display of consideration which left nurse quite un-moved, as Laura noticed out of the corner of her eye.

Johnnie elected to be naughty.

He cast himself upon the floor, shrieked, and clung to the legs of the furniture.

Edward took the opportunity of shooting out of the room and disappearing from view.

Laura, exhausted, exasperated, and apprehensive lest

Alfred should hear from the study, sought to speak with calm.

"Johnnie, that's not like a big boy—that's like a baby. Don't make that dreadful noise. Go along, now ——"

("Never meet opposition with opposition," said the little book.)

"You're making my head ache, Johnnie dear. Please don't scream."

Johnnie's screams appeared instantly to redouble in intensity. Laura looked despairingly at nurse.

"Stop that now," said nurse in no uncertain tones, and advanced to where Johnnie lay. By a form of ju-jitsu known only in nursery circles, she miraculously jerked him to his feet again.

Laura could not help reflecting how effective physical violence always seemed to be, although so much opposed by every enlightened modern authority. If she were really true to her principles, she would certainly forbid nurse to employ it—but Laura knew only too well that her whole life was one continual compromise between her principles and her sense of expediency.

"Come along and stop that nonsense," said nurse, and Johnnie followed her, enveloped in a sudden and complete indifference.

"She can just find Edward for herself," thought Laura childishly, and sank back into her chair.

The house-parlourmaid, Nellie, entered.

"If you please, 'm, Mrs. Raynor is at the back door and would like to speak to you."

"You'd better ask her to come in here. And Nellie, if she hasn't gone at the end of a quarter of an hour, please come and say that I'm wanted."

Two minutes after the organisation of this inhospitable manœuvre Laura was saying pleasantly:

"Good evening, Mrs. Raynor. Come in and sit down."

Mrs. Raynor periodically worked and periodically had a bad heart. She had now come to ask if Laura ever wanted a day's cleaning done.

"Because, if so, Mrs. Temple, I'd be glad to oblige. I've given up the washing."

Laura reflected that the scrubbing and turning out of the two nurseries, by hands other than her own, always gratified nurse.

She engaged Mrs. Raynor to come early in the following week.

A vague feeling of uneasiness, connected with Mrs. Raynor, lurked at the back of her mind, but it was not until later that she remembered a certain rather anxious week in the previous year, in the course of which Mrs. Raynor had come daily to fill a gap, and had nightly departed with a small bundle under her arm.

(Alfred, when Laura had told him at the time what serious misgivings the bundle roused in her, had replied with an air of matter-of-fact common sense: "But you can easily find out. Just stop her one night and ask her what's in the bundle.")

"Well, anyway, I should have had to have her when Nellie leaves. Unless I've got a new one by then," Laura thought.

She had not yet found a house-parlourmaid. Her own advertisement remained unanswered, except by newspapers and agencies, the Registry Office assured her that girls wouldn't look at the country, and the faint possibilities heard of through the friends of friends who were losing theirs at the end of the month had always evaporated by the time that Laura had persuaded her husband to motor her some forty or fifty miles in search of them.

"Mum-mie-ee!"

"All right, darling."

She went upstairs, and exchanged prolonged goodnights with the hilarious Edward and Johnnie, that left her barely five minutes in which to change into her faded, friendly velveteen tea-gown that had served her for years when she and Alfred had no one staying at Applecourt.

"They are darlings when they are in bed," she thought, with a little glow at her heart.

The gong rang.

Laura and Alfred went in to dinner, and Nellie waited upon them with that alert efficiency displayed by a departing servant anxious to demonstrate to her employers that they are losing a treasure.

"The boys were having a pillow fight when I went in just now."

"Were they?" said Alfred. He smiled kindly, if without enthusiasm.

"It's extraordinary how much better balanced on his feet Johnnie is than poor little Edward. Why, he can bowl him over like a ninepin every time."

"Can he?"

This time Alfred hadn't smiled, and the absence of enthusiasm was rather marked.

Laura recollected herself with a start and began to talk about the League of Nations.

Chapter IV

ALFRED had been persuaded to drive Laura and the children to the dancing-class at Quinnerton. There was no security that he would repeat this concession weekly, but Laura had thankfully taken advantage of it, with reference in her own mind to the thin end of the wedge. She now sat in the Quinnerton Town Hall, on an uncomfortable seat placed in a draughty position, in the company of half a dozen mothers, a couple of nurses, and three governesses.

In the middle of the room ten little girls and five little boys waved their arms and legs about, with varying degrees of grace, more or less in time to the emphasised rhythm that proceeded from the piano at which sat a chilly-looking but decorative young woman in orange georgette. The senior teacher also wore orange georgette, that stopped short just above her knees, and gave place to pale stockings and heelless orange satin shoes.

She stood gravely facing the class, directing their movements with suave and superior gyrations of her own, and saying from time to time:

"Arms upward raise—knees outward bend—*one*, and two, and—on the toes, Cynthia—Edward—four, and one, and —— *Stop*, please."

The piano abruptly became silent.

"Johnnie Temple, you're not attending. Nor is Mary Manners. Now I can't have the whole class interrupted like this. You must pay attention, or go and sit down. Resume, please."

The piano and the class resumed.

Laura talked to the mother of Mary Manners, who was sitting next to her, wearing a grey squirrel fur coat.

"I always admire Miss King's appearance so much, don't you?" said Laura. "So very unlike the dancing mistresses of our day."

"Yes, isn't she? And really she gets them on very well. Mary has improved tremendously."

"Mary has such a good sense of rhythm," politely said Laura. "I've always noticed it."

"Oh, I don't know. She doesn't pay attention to what's going on, or she could do much better."

"So could Johnnie."

"What I feel about Mary is that she *could* do better, if she'd only concentrate. It's all there, but she doesn't *try*."

"It'll come, won't it? Though, of course, in some children concentration seems to be the natural thing. Now Edward will give his whole mind to anything that interests him, but then, unfortunately, he's not in the least interested in anything educational, except perhaps mechanical toys. Johnnie, who's really much cleverer ——"

"Mary! Mary dear!"

Mrs. Manners was shaking her head, and hissing in a distressed way through her teeth, and Laura perceived that her conversation was no longer receiving attention. She knew, however, that it had been directed to her own gratification rather than to that of Mrs. Manners, and was not surprised.

On her other side was a very earnest mother whose Cynthia was the star performer of the class.

Mrs. Bakewell, unlike Mrs. Manners, wore no furs, but always wore very plain tailor-made suits, small felt hats that seemed to be poised on the extreme top of her head, and immense chamois-leather gloves.

She had a very bright smile, a large nose, and a large, alert glance.

She turned them all upon Laura and said, with a strange effect of restrained ardour in her manner:

"I think dancing does so much for the little people, don't you? It helps them to express themselves, I feel."

"Yes," said Laura doubtfully. Cynthia Bakewell was beautifully poised on the tips of her toes, although she looked interested and conscientious, rather than spiritually uplifted, but Johnnie was expressing himself by means of trying to make Miss King rebuke him publicly once again and Edward was blowing his nose with great earnestness.

"They teach eurythmics everywhere now," said Mrs. Bakewell. "My elder girl is at a wonderful school, where the pupils dance in a wood, like nymphs, every evening in the summer."

"Shall you send Cynthia there? She dances so beautifully already."

"All my children have always danced, from the time they could walk. I used to play the piano, after tea, when they were wee babies, and they used to get up and dance, without any suggestion from anybody. Cynthia invented a dance when she was only three. It was a Butterfly Dance, and she did it beautifully."

Laura, as usual, wondered why her children were so unlike other people's children. If she played the piano at Applecourt after tea, Edward ran out of the room, because he found it boring inside, and Johnnie either wished to thump a humorous imitation beside her, or begged her to leave off and come and play. Never had either shown the slightest indication to invent a dance, or even to dance one which somebody else had invented.

"Of course, girls are so different. My two little sons ——"

"But Theodore dances quite as well as his sisters," said Mrs. Bakewell, interrupting.

Laura had forgotten about Theodore. He was at school, and no longer attended the class.

"He said to me the other day: 'Mama, do the angels dance? If they don't, I don't think I want to go to heaven.' "

"Did he? How sweet," said Laura, in a depressed way.

"It was rather sweet, wasn't it? He's only seven, you know. But of course he's danced ever since he could walk."

Laura said, "Oh, of course," as though all the children of her acquaintance, her own included, had danced ever since they could walk—and then felt that her words had sounded inane.

"Cynthia, of course, is much the best of them all," she

added, indicating the class, and in atonement for her tepidity about Theodore.

"It's very nice of you to say so, but then," returned Mrs. Bakewell more brightly than ever, "Cynthia has danced ever since she could walk."

Laura thought: "I wonder whether the mere fact of being a mother does really reduce one, conversationally, to the level of an idiot." Aloud she said: "Yes, of course."

"*Rest*," cried Miss King smartly, and all the children sank back on to the soles of their feet with relieved expressions on their faces.

Edward rushed to his mother, and Johnnie, whom she wished Mrs. Bakewell to have a good opportunity of looking at, on account of his superiority in good looks to the talented Cynthia and Theodore, walked to the far end of the room and made hideous faces at himself in the looking-glass.

"Is that your little fellow?" said Mrs. Bakewell with a tolerant smile, as Johnnie further distorted his features.

"I can't think what he's doing," murmured Laura, trying to return Mrs. Bakewell's smile while at the same time shaking her head violently and frowning in the direction of Johnnie.

"Showing off, I daresay," Mrs. Bakewell observed, more tolerant than ever.

"That was very nice, darling. You're getting on," said Laura to Edward, regardless of accuracy.

"I simply hate dancing," Edward replied gloomily.

"My little children love dancing." Mrs. Bakewell

turned her large, bright gaze upon Edward. "When Cynthia and her brother Theodore were tiny they used to invent dances. You ask Cynthia to tell you all about it. They had a Windmill Dance and a Butterfly Dance, and all sorts of other dances. They liked dancing better than anything."

Edward gazed indifferently at Mrs. Bakewell's smile. When his silence became embarrassing, Laura gently prompted him.

"That *was* clever of Cynthia and Theodore, wasn't it? That's why Cynthia is so good at dancing now, I expect."

"Is she good at it?" Edward chillingly remarked, and strolled away without waiting for an answer.

Mrs. Bakewell, her smile as indomitable as ever, said that children were so delightfully quaint, always, but Laura felt that it was time for her to turn again to Mrs. Manners, who now had Mary seated on her lap.

"What are you doing about Mary's lessons now, I wonder? I know you were finding it all so difficult a little while ago."

"It always is difficult, when one lives in the country. My husband says it's quite out of the question to drive her to and from Quinnerton every day."

"So does Alfred."

"It's with great difficulty that I've persuaded him to let me have the car and bring her into the dancing-class once a week."

"I can't even do that regularly."

"Oh well, of course, I drive myself. And unless they're going to attend regularly, it's no use at all, is it?"

"It's better than nothing," said Laura firmly. "And we're lucky about teaching. Miss Lamb comes every morning and gives them their lessons."

"That really is excellent. I," said Mrs. Manners, "am teaching Mary myself."

"And do you find it answers?"

"Oh yes. I simply, for the time being, become a teacher pure and simple. We're perfectly regular—perfectly punctual. Mary knows that the lessons have got to be done, just the same as if she was at school. And of course I always keep a little ahead of her, preparing the lessons."

"How do you find the time?"

"I make the time, Mrs. Temple," replied Mrs. Manners, not without superiority. "But of course, I'm not clever, like you. I know you write. Naturally, in the case of a gift like that, one hasn't the same time to devote to one's husband and children."

Laura reflected that, whether the time was there or not, one did devote it to one's husband and children, although ineffectually. It seemed impossible to do otherwise, in a small household. But, owing to the gift, it seemed that one got no credit for it.

"Now, please take your partners for the fox-trot."

Miss King was at the piano, and the youthful and charming assistant teacher had taken her place in the middle of the room.

"Will you come and dance with me, dear?" she said, patting Johnnie's curls.

Laura wondered whether this distinction was a tribute

to Johnnie's charms, or an indication that his steps required attention.

"Is that your other little one?" Mrs. Bakewell enquired of Laura benignantly.

"Yes, that's Johnnie. He's only five."

Laura tried to say this in a matter-of-fact, indifferent voice. In reality, it seemed to her to be almost inevitable that anyone in the world, seeing Johnnie for the first time, should be struck by his good looks, his curls, his intelligence and his size.

"Miss Thompson is always so good with the less advanced ones. So patient," said Mrs. Bakewell kindly.

"Long, short-short, long, short-short," intoned Miss Thompson firmly, bearing Johnnie with her as she skimmed up the room.

"He's really not doing it too badly, considering that he doesn't attend regularly," Laura remarked, trying to sound coldly impartial.

"Not at all badly," Mrs. Bakewell agreed. And Mrs. Manners, on the other side, said that it really was a pity that Laura's little boys shouldn't attend the dancing-class regularly. The elder one—Edward, wasn't it, was getting on quite nicely with his dancing.

Edward was dancing with Mary Manners, who was taller, older, and a good deal more skilful than he was.

At the end of the hour's lesson, the class departed. Alfred Temple, in the two-seater, came for Laura and the children. The boys climbed to the little dicky seat at the back, and their mother took her place beside the driver.

"I just want to stop at the Home and Colonial and go to the greengrocer's, Alfred—the one at the bottom of High Street, and change my books at the Library. You don't mind, do you?"

"I don't *mind*. But I should have thought, I must say, that you could have done your jobs while the boys were at their dancing. You're not obliged to stay there the whole time."

"You don't understand, dear. I must. They're not really old enough to trust by themselves. They'd take advantage of my not being there." It was one of Laura's most resolute convictions that her children behaved better when she was with them than when she was not.

(Many mothers cling to this theory, in spite of the immense inconvenience that it entails upon themselves.)

At the library, Laura encountered Lady Kingsley-Browne.

"You've come to get the new volume of the *Life of Disraeli*, I feel perfectly certain," declared Lady Kingsley-Browne. "So have I. It only came out yesterday, but I couldn't wait for it another day. Could you?"

Laura, who did not buy books, and was still waiting for the first volume of Disraeli from the Circulating Library, insincerely replied that she, also, wanted dreadfully to read it, but that she was only just changing the books, and could not contemplate any purchase.

"What are you going to get? Have you read *this*?" said her neighbour tiresomely, thrusting upon Laura's attention a novel with a title that she disliked, by an author whose works she never read.

"Is it good?" said Mrs. Temple doubtfully.

"Delightful. I'm sure you'd like it. And have you read this?"

"Yes, I have," hastily said Laura. "Have you anything on my list?" she added to the assistant.

"Only one, I'm afraid, madam. Would you care for this new detective story? It's in great demand, and people say it's excellent."

Lady Kingsley-Browne uttered a faint, protesting cry.

"How truly dreadful! *The Murder in the Old Mill*— what a name! And to offer it to you, of all people, my dear!"

The flattering implication of Laura's eclectic taste made it rather difficult to accept *The Murder in the Old Mill*, but Laura did so.

"Alfred always likes a good murder story," she apologetically explained; aware that in this case her likings and Alfred's were identical, but not having the moral courage to say so.

"Men!" ejaculated Lady Kingsley-Browne, in a tone of indulgence. "What about the Georgian Poems for your other choice?"

Laura did not get very frequent opportunities of changing her books at the Quinnerton Library, and from motives of economy she did not subscribe to a London one. She had no wish to take Georgian Poems in place of the many new novels that she wanted to read. Nevertheless she presently found herself leaving the shop with this unwanted addition to her stock of literature.

"Delighted to have met you," said Lady Kingsley-

Browne. "Do come out and see us again one of these days. The bulbs are quite nice just now."

"We'd love to ——"

"Bébée will be home in a day or two. She's been having a wonderful time at Nice. You know she dashed over there for a flying visit with another girl—just the two of them. Really, girls do have the greatest fun nowadays! When I think of what *our* mothers would have said if *we'd* suggested doing half the things they do ——"

Laura assented, hoping rather indignantly that Lady Kingsley-Browne realised at least approximately the number of years that separated them.

"You must come when Bébée's at home." And Laura repeated, with a final, valedictory smile: "We should love to," and hastened with relief into the greengrocer's shop. When she came out with one dozen bananas in a paper-bag, Laura found Alfred, the boys and the two-seater waiting for her outside.

She climbed in.

"That's all. I'm quite ready now." She turned her head. "Are you all right, darlings?"

"Mummie, look, I've got my overcoat on," said Edward, who had had his overcoat on ever ¬ince the end of the dancing-class.

"I see, darling," said Laura.

"Are we going home now?" Johnnie enquired.

"Yes."

"We're going home now," Edward echoed. "Now we're going home, aren't we, mummie? Aren't we, daddy? We're going home, we're going home now, aren't we, daddy?"

"*Ont-ils été sages?*" hissed Laura at her husband as the car started.

"O wee," said Alfred resignedly.

By the time they got home the second post had been delivered, and Laura found two letters waiting for her.

One was to say that the house-parlourmaid engaged a week earlier by Laura to enter her service at the end of the month had accepted another situation, and the other was a bill.

"That girl has failed me," exclaimed Laura, with as much pain, indignation, and surprise as though no servant had ever done such a thing before.

"What girl?"

"The house-parlourmaid—the one I definitely engaged —from the Registry Office."

"Have you any other possibilities?"

"Only the girl they wouldn't keep at the Vicarage because she broke things, and had a fit or something in the middle of the night—(she sounded to me epileptic)— and the one who wrote from Stockport, and said she was willing to learn. She's only eighteen, and asking thirty pounds a year, and it was a most illiterate sort of letter."

"It's a long way to get her down on approval. I suppose we pay the fare?"

"Oh yes, we pay the fare. And besides, now I come to think of it, I've had her letter nearly a week, because

I thought I was fixed up with this Jones creature—and she'll probably have been snapped up by now."

"I believe you'd do better with a married couple."

"They're much more expensive—and besides, Gladys is staying on as far as I know, and if I give her notice, we may find ourselves left without anyone. I wish I knew what to do."

"How long before Nellie goes?"

"A week."

"Then there's time, still, after all. And worst come to the worst, there's that woman—Mrs. Raynor."

"Yes, we can have her. Only it's unsettling for nurse and Gladys, and you know how they never will put up with anything nowadays."

Alfred did indeed know, and Laura felt that it would be fortunate for them both if he received no further demonstration of the state of affairs that she deplored.

"I'll go out to the Vicarage to-morrow and find out if that girl there is absolutely hopeless. There's nothing else I can do."

Nevertheless, Laura, as though fascinated, studied the columns in *The Times* headed "Domestic Situations Wanted," and before she went to bed that night wrote three letters, in which she conscientiously set out the disadvantage of a quiet place, right in the country, with oil lamps, and every other Sunday afternoon and evening out, in turns with the cook-general.

Laura held to a theory that by means of this preliminary candour she eliminated the possibility of subsequent reproaches and discontent on the part of the servant engaged. But it discouraged her when none of them answered her letters, not even when a stamped addressed envelope was enclosed.

At the end of the following week, Nellie went, and Mrs. Raynor made spasmodic appearances in the passages and the bedrooms, and Laura "helped with the beds," and Alfred changed the plates and handed the vegetable dishes at meals, and nurse said it seemed as though one pair of hands being gone put double the work on everybody else without getting it done, so to speak, and Gladys said it was unsettling and gave notice.

Then Laura, at great expense, secured a temporary house-parlourmaid, and by that time Gladys's month was up and she went away.

Laura heard of a man-cook, an old soldier. The temporary house-parlourmaid said that it would be quite impossible for her to stay when there was only a man in the kitchen.

A possibly permanent house-parlourmaid, with whom Laura was negotiating, said the same thing.

The man-cook had to be relinquished.

The possibly permanent house-parlourmaid was very sorry, but if things were unsettled at Applecourt, she'd prefer not to take the place. She'd rather go to a lady at Bath, whose cook had been with her for five years and whose house-parlourmaid had only left to be married.

Laura felt that nothing in the whole world mattered, except the solution of the domestic problem.

She relinquished her resolution of not talking about the servants to her husband, and talked about nothing else.

The days seemed to be entirely occupied in small dustings and cleanings, and the evenings in lighting the lamps, drawing the blinds and the curtains, and clearing away the things from the dining-room table.

The cooking was done by Mrs. Raynor, in the middle of the day, and the food at night was cold. This, in itself, served to depress the atmosphere.

Then, as had happened before, just as Laura felt that even the unendurable can become endurable by mere force of habit, one state of affairs merged almost imperceptibly into another. Laura acquired two servants, a man and his wife.

They asked, and received, wages that Laura, six months earlier, would have said emphatically, and with perfect truth, that she and Alfred could not afford to give them.

The man cooked well, although extravagantly, and the woman was obliging, but unpunctual and untidy in her work.

"There'll always be something," Laura said, indicating a determination to be satisfied with any state of affairs that should imply the presence, and not the absence, of domestics. Nurse, who at one moment had shown grave signs of becoming unsettled, now became settled again, and Laura was able to turn her attention wholly to the children, the meals, and the question of expense, instead of dividing it between the servants, the children, the meals and the question of expense.

Life continued to be uneventful, full of slight harassments, trivial satisfactions, and harmless, recurrent anxieties.

Spring gave place to early summer.

At the end of May, Laura's younger sister came to stay at Applecourt.

Christine was twenty-nine, but she looked much younger. Every time that Laura saw her, she looked younger. This time, her fair hair was bobbed—a thick, straight bob with a short fringe, that suited her square, boyish face and wide-apart hazel eyes.

Christine, when she was fifteen and Laura twenty, had been accounted plain, and indeed she was still plain. But she was now accounted pretty, and charming, and extremely amusing.

Laura was proud of her, and fond of her, and very often annoyed by her.

Christine was entirely independent. She, like Laura, had inherited a yearly income of two hundred and fifty pounds from their father, but, unlike Laura, she had only herself to spend it on. She earned money, too, by her writing. She lived in London, in a very small flat, by herself. Every year, and sometimes twice in one year, she went abroad.

Laura felt that it would be good for Bébée Kingsley-Browne to meet Christine, for Christine, also, knew many young men, and was inclined to talk about them a good deal, and Laura was forced to believe in the reality of their devotion, if only because of the number of letters that Christine received.

But there was always one—a different one every year

—of whom Christine talked most, and from whom she heard oftenest.

This year it was somebody called Marmaduke Ayland, who was musical, and composed settings for other people's songs.

"I should like you to meet him," Christine said, on her very first evening at Applecourt. "If he's anywhere in this neighbourhood, may he come over to lunch?"

"Of course," said Laura. "Hark, was that one of the children?"

"I didn't hear anything. You see, Duke wants to spend a week some time right in the country, where he can make as much noise on the piano as he likes, for this new musical comedy score, and not feel that he's disturbing anybody. So I suggested this neighbourhood. He could lodge for a week at that farm—you know ——"

"Yes, I know. Mrs. Sefton's. We can go and see about it. I wonder whether—you know, Christine, I really believe Johnnie is going to be musical after all."

"Oh, do you?" said Christine, and something in the way she said it recalled Laura to herself with a guilty start.

Chapter V

HAVING Christine at Applecourt was delightful, and she was a great help with the children, and her amusing conversation enlivened the evenings. But she made Laura feel very middle-aged indeed.

From sheer force of habit, Laura, who was no gardener, said something to her sister about the past glories of the bulbs, and Christine simply, candidly and unprecedentedly, replied:

"For pity's sake, Laura, don't talk about anything so deadly as the bulbs. I don't mind looking at them, when they're actually there, provided I don't have to walk through wet grass to get to them, but I do bar hearing about them. Let's talk about people—grown-up people, I mean—or books, or clothes or something."

"Everybody talks about the bulbs here."

"How very distressing! But I suppose you needn't answer. Then they'll guess you aren't interested, won't they?"

"They may or they may not. In any case, it won't make any difference."

Christine looked slightly awestruck.

"But aren't there any people here? Besides the Kingsley-Brownes, I mean. Are they all bulb-fiends?"

"There are some new people at Marchland. I shall have to call on them. Shall we go while you're here? Their name is Crossthwaite and he's been with Melsom's

Publishing Company, and now he's retired. Rich, I suppose—Marchland is pretty large. They may be useful for tennis."

"D'you suppose they've got an eldest son, or anything amusing?"

"Much more likely they've got three unmarried daughters, like every other family in this part of the world," said Mrs. Temple with the cynicism of experience.

"Well, it seems worth trying. Aren't you proud, Laura, to think you've actually had two boys and not any girls at all? I know it's supposed to mean some sort of sex-complex, when mothers want their children to be boys and not girls, but whoever started that theory couldn't ever have lived in England, in the country, or he'd understand."

"Of course, it's not as bad as it used to be, when unmarried daughters all lived at home together," Laura pointed out. "I wouldn't mind having just one girl, either."

"I shouldn't, darling, if I were you. It's expensive, and you'd have to start a nursery again just when Edward and Johnnie are ready for school, and it would be a pity to risk spoiling your figure. Three often does."

Laura wondered whether Christine was talking for effect. She knew, theoretically, but could not realise, that unmarried young women did talk like that. But not in the Quinnerton neighbourhood.

"I'm getting provincial, Christine," said Laura abruptly and desperately. "I don't know what it is exactly, but sometimes it comes over me suddenly, and I realise ——"

"You ought to go away more."

"It's very difficult to move Alfred."

"So much the better. Go by yourself."

"I couldn't leave him alone with the servants and the children. I know you think that's absurd, of course."

Miss Fairfield committed herself neither to assent nor contradiction.

"You don't understand how absolutely necessary it is to be there all the time, in a small house, especially when there are children. Everything goes wrong immediately if I go away for any length of time."

"Well, then, of course you can't," said Christine reasonably. "Let's hope the Marchland people will be assets, and have amusing friends to stay with them. And I'm certain you'll like Duke Ayland."

"What sort of aged man is he?"

"Six years older than I am."

It was a great relief to Laura to hear that he was not six years younger. It was nowadays her depressing experience that anybody who had achieved artistic success invariably turned out to be younger than herself.

Laura would have liked to know whether Duke Ayland was in love with Christine, but Christine volunteered no information on the point. She and Laura visited Mrs. Sefton at the farm, engaged a bedroom, and sent for the piano-tuner from Quinnerton to tune Mrs. Sefton's piano.

Then Christine wrote to Ayland, and two days later he arrived, and was bidden to lunch at Applecourt.

"Laura, this is Duke Ayland. My sister, Mrs. Temple."

He was tall and dark, looking a great deal younger than his thirty-five years. His best feature was a sensitive and well-cut mouth, with admirable teeth. He was clean-shaven. His hair was brushed straight back off his forehead, but Laura noted with approval that it was cut reasonably short.

She hoped that he was comfortable at the farm. Mrs. Sefton was a nice woman.

A very nice woman, and he was perfectly comfortable. So grateful to Christine and her sister for arranging it all.

And the piano? It had been tuned two days before. The piano was all right.

Alfred came in, Mr. Ayland was introduced, and shaken hands with. Alfred hoped that he was comfortable at the farm. Mrs. Sefton was a nice woman.

"Very nice indeed. Perfectly comfortable."

"The piano was tuned two days ago," said Alfred.

They went into the dining-room for lunch.

On the whole, Laura decided, she liked Ayland. He was quiet, and seemed to lack self-confidence—both unusual characteristics in a friend of Christine's.

She enquired whether he played tennis. They hoped to have some tennis on Saturday afternoon, and would be so pleased to see him. Ayland accepted at once.

"Who else is coming?" Christine enquired.

"Bay-bay, and one of her young men—someone who's staying there—I haven't met him and I forget his name—and Major and Mrs. Bakewell."

"Is that the mother of a child who dances? A woman with a nose?"

"Yes," said Laura, tacitly admitting the justice of this description.

"Oh my God!" said Christine pleasantly.

"You remember her, then?"

"Quite well. I saw her last year, that time you sent me to the dancing-class with the boys. She told me that all her children had danced before they could walk."

"How very unpleasant," said Ayland gently.

"And do you mean to say she can really play tennis?" Christine enquired with insulting incredulity.

"She plays quite well. So does her husband."

"Poor devil!"

"What is he like?" said Ayland. "Does he dance, too?"

"I've never seen him," Christine admitted, "but anybody who'd married that woman would be a poor devil. Well, it'll be great fun to see her again. I remember the first time I met her, thinking her utterly unlike any other human being on the face of the earth. I hope Saturday will be fine, Duke, and that they'll all come. Especially the Bakewells."

Saturday was fine.

Laura gave the servants final and reiterated instructions about the lemonade, the tea, and the necessity for postponing dinner, if necessary, in the event of any of her guests remaining on after half-past seven.

She went to the nursery to see whether Edward and Johnnie were resenting the preparations for a festivity in which they would have no share, and remembered too late that it was unwise to suggest discontent to them by begging them to be good.

"I wish you didn't have visitors. You won't be able to read to us this evening," said Johnnie, making his mother feel remorseful.

She kissed them both and went to her room to change her frock as quickly as possible. Christine was already on the lawn, with Alfred and Duke Ayland. She was wearing pale green linen, knee-length, with inserted squares of drawn-thread work. Her fair hair was uncovered. Laura thought how young she looked.

Her own frock was of cream-coloured sponge-cloth, and she knew that it became her. But she had to wear a hat, because her hair otherwise became so untidy, and the blue brim made her look pale, she thought, and gave an effect of dark semi-circles beneath her eyes.

Or was her face always rather pale, nowadays, and were there always semi-circles under her eyes?

Laura frowned at herself in the mirror, and went downstairs without answering her own question. It had left a faint tang of bitterness behind it.

The Bakewells arrived in a large Armstrong-Siddeley car, Mrs. Bakewell smiling largely under a small and precariously-perched white felt hat, and waving a tennis-racquet. Her husband was a small, sunburnt civil engineer, with an expression that seemed oddly harassed in conjunction with his wife's eager brightness.

"Howdydo, I'll just turn the car round," he said at once. "She'll be all right in the shade—sure I shan't interfere with anybody else here, Mrs. Temple? Flossie, you get out, will you, dear, and I'll just turn the car round."

Mrs. Bakewell descended, shook hands with Laura and Alfred, assured Christine that she remembered her very well indeed, and made the acquaintance of Mr. Ayland.

The same preliminaries were then gone through by Major Bakewell.

"Christine, won't you take Mrs. Bakewell on to the court, and start playing at once? Let me see——"

Laura had arranged the sets carefully in her own mind, but she was not very good at remembering anything of that kind, and the alert readiness of Mrs. Bakewell's eye was confusing her.

"Alfred and Mrs. Bakewell against Major Bakewell and me," said Christine briskly. "Duke doesn't mind waiting. Come on."

"Do you really not mind?" Laura enquired of the young man left obediently standing beside her.

"Not at all," he said gently. "I'm not a good tennis player. Tell me, is Mrs. Bakewell very good? She looks as though she were."

"She is, rather," admitted Laura.

"Please," said Mr. Ayland, "*please* don't put me in the same set with her. I could play with you and your sister, but not with her. That sounds uncivil, but I'm sure you know what I mean. She'd expect me to be a rabbit and I should be one. I'm very suggestible."

"I know that feeling."

"You don't, do you? I should have thought you were always self-possessed, and strong-minded, and composed."

Laura, who had in the past few years felt more and more conscious of being none of these things, was at this enveloped in an unwonted glow.

She looked responsively at Ayland, and found his dark eyes fixed upon her with an air of being positively and actively interested in what they saw that Laura had long missed from the eyes of her male acquaintances.

"You are not what I imagined you'd be, in the very least," Duke Ayland said.

"Didn't Christine tell you anything about me—about us?"

"A little, yes—but I meant your writing. I've always admired your work so much, you know."

"But I don't know!" Laura exclaimed, a little breathless. "Christine never said—I never even knew that you knew that I wrote."

"I've wanted to tell you—only I didn't dare—that one of your short stories ——"

The Kingsley-Browne Humber swept into the drive, with Bébée Kingsley-Browne at the wheel and a tall young man in flannels lounging beside her.

Laura, from being a deeply interested and rather gratified woman, became a hostess, and a privately censorious one.

She saw in a moment that Bébée Kingsley-Browne was in the midst of an access of affectation—although, indeed, in the opinion of Mrs. Temple, her young neighbour was never at any time devoid of affectation. But this objectionable attribute was always increased by the presence of an admirer, and it was but too evident that the tall young man was an admirer.

His name was Vulliamy and Bébée addressed him as Jeremy. Surely, thought Laura, such a combination was unthinkable.

Jeremy Vulliamy.

"Shall we come and sit down? They've just begun to play, so if you don't very much mind waiting for the second set ——" She led them to the striped black-and-orange canvas chairs set under the elm trees that prettily bordered the lawn, and as she moved forward something impelled her to exchange a glance with Duke Ayland.

The expression of interest was still there. . . .

Laura, that afternoon, played tennis better than she had played it for a long time. She played better than anyone, excepting the indomitable Mrs. Bakewell—(who impressed everybody by exclaiming, when she missed a very fast ball: "Dear me, it seems I can't volley to-day!")

"You're playing awfully well!" Christine murmured to Laura. "What an ass Bay-bay looks trying to serve over-hand!"

Laura was conscious of deriving gratification from both

these asides, although she refrained from verbal agreement with the latter.

Her tennis party was being a success. She did not, in so many words, tell herself that she, also, was being a success, but she was aware of it, and it inspired her. She caught sight of herself in the mirror in the hall on her way to tea, and was agreeably surprised to find that the blue hat, now that she was flushed and animated, suited her after all.

Miss Kingsley-Browne was telling everybody that she was to be bridesmaid at the wedding of a minor Balkan royalty in London.

"Rather a bore, in a way," she declared, with preposterous affectation. "I've already been a bridesmaid seven times—no, eight, I think."

"It's expensive, isn't it?" said Christine stonily. "My friends, I'm thankful to say, either get married in a Registry Office, or else just live in sin together."

Young Vulliamy burst out laughing, and then glanced rather nervously at Bébée.

"I'm surprised to hear you talk of a Registry Office, Miss Fairfield," said Mrs. Bakewell, tactfully ignoring the latter half of Christine's speech, although Laura felt that it had probably surprised her a good deal more than the first. "It's such an odd mistake, I always think, to talk of Registry for Registrar's. And yet how many people do so!"

"Don't let's mention the word registry at all," Laura begged. "It reminds me too much of hunting for a cook and never finding one."

She was grateful to Duke Ayland, Christine, and Major Bakewell for laughing.

Mrs. Bakewell remarked instructively: "What I always say when people talk to me about the servant problem is—there *is* no servant problem."

"How very unsympathetic!" said Christine.

Mrs. Bakewell's indulgent smile veered round upon her.

"But not at all. Now look at me. I have no difficulties with servants. I never have had difficulties with servants."

Alfred and Major Bakewell, unobtrusively, began to talk about the Government. Bébée and Mr. Vulliamy, more stridently, discussed plays.

It was left to Laura, Ayland, and Christine, to appear intelligently interested in Mrs. Bakewell's method of ensuring efficiency in her domestics.

"The secret is very simple. *They know that I'm not dependent on them.* If the cook leaves: well and good, I go into the kitchen and cook the dinner. If the parlourmaid leaves, I clean the silver and lay the table, and even little Cynthia, mite as she is, can help me. If the housemaid leaves, why, let her leave is what I say. I can make the beds, and dust and sweep, and it doesn't disturb me in the least. They know it. I say to them from time to time: 'I'm not dependent upon any one of you. Make no mistake,' I say, 'I can do without any of you quite easily if I want to. The house will be clean and tidy, the Major's meals well cooked, and served nicely, and everything will go on just exactly as well as usual, and rather better.' And they know it's true. It has a wonderful effect upon them."

"May I ask, then, how long you've had your present servants?" said Ayland in a tone of respectful enquiry, that Laura hoped and believed to be gently ironical.

"Dear old Cookie has been with me—let me see, is it fourteen or fifteen years?—fifteen it is. The housemaid five years and the parlourmaid about the same."

Christine's eyes turned wildly to her sister, plainly demanding: "Is she speaking the truth?" and Laura gave a slight, reluctant nod.

Mrs. Bakewell, having thoroughly and successfully taken the wind out of everybody else's sails, began competently to chew seed-cake.

The others, actuated by a common impulse, violently discussed Italy.

The Bakewells did not travel.

Italy led to music.

"I hear that you're quite a musician, Mr. Ayland," said Mrs. Bakewell suddenly and brightly.

Laura rose.

"If no one will have any more tea ——" she murmured —and they returned to the tennis court.

Duke Ayland, lighting a cigarette for his hostess, said to her in an undertone that gave a curious intimacy to his words:

"Don't ask me to play with Mrs. Bakewell. Please. She paralyses me. Can't I play with you?"

Laura smiled at him confidently.

"If you want to."

"Of course I want to."

He was behaving to her as though she were a young girl, and it made her feel as though she was a young girl. They played together as partners, and Laura played brilliantly.

She only faltered when both the little boys, in clean holland smocks, appeared on the lawn.

Laura, looking out of the corners of her eyes to see whether they shook hands politely with the visitors or not, missed an easy shot, and forgot to apologise. Then Christine, who was not playing, appeared to be taking her nephews under her charge, and Laura, relieved, turned her attention to the game again.

But she played less well than before, and was relieved when the set came to an end, and she could hasten towards the deck chairs under the trees.

Johnnie, who had been behaving with quiet and decorum, immediately began to show off, breaking into a refrain that he knew, from agreeable experience, always caused a flattering commotion in the nursery.

> "Oh, what a little short shirt you've got!
> You'd better pull down the blind."

On a second, and louder, repetition of the engaging refrain, Johnnie achieved his object.

Major Bakewell laughed, Edward imitatively began to sing also, and their mother turned pink and said, "That will do, boys. Where do you pick up these things?"

"*My* little children," said Mrs. Bakewell, "have been

taught how to sing. They can sing prettily, and in tune."

"Can they sing, 'Oh, what a little short shirt you've got'?" Johnnie enquired, quite unmaliciously.

"Certainly not. They sing pretty songs about the little squirrels, and the birds, and the great blue sky."

Alfred Temple, at this, invited Mrs. Bakewell to play tennis again. She agreed to do so, but as she stood up remarked to Laura that one could never be careful enough, which Laura rightly interpreted as an oblique condemnation of the society that she permitted her children to frequent.

"Johnnie is a born actor," she remarked unconvincingly, on the spur of the moment.

"Johnnie is a graceless young ruffian," Ayland declared, coming to her assistance and sensibly lightening the atmosphere.

She threw him a grateful glance.

"Come on," said Christine, "let's play."

For the rest of the evening, Laura's attention was divided between her guests and her children. But underneath her pre-occupation, she was conscious of a faint, but wonderfully stimulating, glow of pleasure and excitement, because she saw that Duke Ayland was attracted by her.

He remained to dinner, when her other visitors had severally expressed appreciation and gratitude, and gone home.

"Don't let's change, of course," Christine said.

They sat agreeably under the trees, with a new and

sudden sense of intimacy as they discussed the departed visitors.

"Do you think Bébée Kingsley-Browne pretty, Duke?" said Christine suddenly.

And Duke replied promptly and sensibly:

"Not in the very least."

Laura's already soaring spirits mounted perceptibly higher at this ungallant and unjustifiable verdict.

"Her young man was a prize ass, wasn't he?" Christine went on, demolishing her fellow-players with whole-hearted thoroughness. "Only a prize ass would allow himself to be dragged round the country at Baybay's chariot-wheels like that. She always has someone or other in tow, but they never last long."

"Is she engaged to Vulliamy?" said Alfred.

"Good heavens, no. We should have heard of it fast enough if she had been," declared Christine derisively. "It's my opinion that Baybay would give her eyes to be seriously engaged, and no one has ever yet been fool enough to ask her."

Laura, who found the conversation strangely exhilarating, realised, as the gong sounded from the house, that she had forgotten to go and say good-night to the boys.

Remorseful, she ran upstairs.

Afterwards she took off her hat, arranged her hair before the looking-glass, and powdered her nose, and went downstairs without a single misgiving about her own appearance, the appearance of her dinner-table, or the probable reactions of her servants to an extra place in the dining-room.

And all was well, from the cold chicken, the salad, and the junket and cream, to the complete absence of any interruptions from Johnnie.

After dinner, Duke Ayland played the piano, at Christine's request.

She and Laura listened to him, and Alfred appeared to listen also—but after a little while he began, by degrees, and with a certain effect of absent-mindedness, to obtain possession of *The Times,* behind which he gradually vanished, presumably still listening, but perhaps less intently. Laura had the curious feeling that the player would not care if neither Alfred nor Christine paid any attention whatever to his music.

It was not to them that he was playing, but to her.

She felt sure of it.

At first she gave, or supposed that she gave, her attention to the music, but she was not sufficiently familiar with modern composers to feel at her ease in listening to their works, and it made her nervous to feel that at any moment she might expose her ignorance.

Then Christine took up a book.

And Duke Ayland looked round at his hostess.

It was a grave, almost enquiring look, and it established spiritual intimacy between them.

Laura had met similar looks, before, although never after, her marriage, and they had been the almost certain preliminary to emotional adventures.

Was it conceivable that Duke Ayland—Christine's friend—sought to embark upon emotional adventure with her now?

Laura remembered her own reflections in the looking-glass that evening, and decided that, after all, it was not incomprehensible that a man should admire her.

She hoped, complacently, that Christine would not mind.

Then, invaded by a sudden recollection, she hoped—wistfully, indignantly, nervously and not even wholly sincerely—that Alfred would not mind.

Chapter VI

THE relations between Laura and her husband were as contradictory and unbalanced as those between most husbands and wives. They had been reasonably in love with one another. Alfred was—or so Laura supposed—incapable of being unreasonably in love, and she herself had expended most of her capabilities for romance in purely imaginary directions. She had, in her maiden days, composed speeches to an ideal lover that would have astonished and disconcerted Alfred to a considerable extent, had she ever spoken them aloud.

But she never had, and had never seriously wished to, and in the course of seven years of child-bearing and rearing, housekeeping, writing stories to augment her income, and talking about the bulbs to her neighbours, Laura had almost forgotten that she had once thought herself destined for a *grande passion*.

It was obvious, beyond question, that Alfred was not destined for a *grande passion*, and, once married to him, with the children, the house, the furniture, and the weekly books, all alike depending on their combined union, Laura had not considered the possibilities of romance any further, in regard to herself.

She did, however, very frequently wish that Alfred would make love to her, or even, if that was too much to expect, that he would make personal remarks to her.

But Alfred did neither. As an English country gentleman, he preferred out-door pastimes, and he did not make personal remarks because he was not particularly interested in persons, and in any case preferred silence to speech.

Laura, occasionally, and desperately, forced discussion upon him. But the results were never really satisfactory.

"Alfred, have I changed much since we were married? I don't mean to look at—of course, I know I look older ——"

Alfred withheld either assent or dissent, and gazed thoughtfully at his wife over his spectacles.

"Do you think that I'm less—enthusiastic—less alive about things?" said Laura wistfully.

"I shouldn't think so."

"Sometimes I feel as though my mind had lost its spring."

Alfred, obviously from pure kindness, did not pick up *The Times* again and go on reading it—but it trembled slightly in his hand.

"What would you do if I suddenly said I was desperately unhappy?"

"I suppose that I should ask you what the matter was," Alfred replied reluctantly, and this time he raised *The Times* about six inches from his knee.

"Well, I'm not," Laura admitted with a small laugh. "But I'm not sure that I don't sometimes wish I were. It's better to feel anything vividly than to feel nothing."

"Is it?"

"Don't you think so?"

"I haven't thought about it."

There was a pause, in which Laura faintly hoped that Alfred was thinking about it now, and might presently inaugurate a mutual exchange of opinions by the expression of his own.

Alfred slowly raised *The Times* altogether, and began to read it.

"I'm not as enthusiastic as I used to be. I don't get roused in the same way," cried Laura wildly. "Should you call me adventurous nowadays?"

"Not particularly, I daresay," said Alfred, who had evidently forgotten having once applied this epithet to Laura in the days when he sought to persuade her to marry him.

"Alfred, do you love me?" Laura insanely demanded, not because she doubted her husband's affection, but because her desire to talk personalities had now passed the bounds of reason and decency alike.

"I shouldn't have married you if I didn't," said Alfred, and he now, without compunction, opened *The Times* extensively and became absorbed in its pages.

Such dialogues had occurred not infrequently, in seven years, and after each one of them Laura had tempestuously decided that it should never take place again. It was undignified—degrading even—and it was bitterly unsatisfactory.

But she could not check the cravings of her nature for romance altogether. She lavished an exaggerated affection on her younger son, who greatly resembled her, and she read an immense number of novels, half unconsciously identifying herself with the central figure in each.

She had never, since her marriage, attracted the amorous attention of any man, and had, indeed, met few men at all.

She had supposed that Duke Ayland was in love with Christine.

On the evening of her tennis party, she knew that he was not.

To her mingled shame and exultation, Laura was unable to go to sleep that night for quite a long while.

It was the first time for years that she had been kept awake by anything unconnected with the children, the servants, or the need of money.

It bewildered her, and made her happy. She rehearsed a drama, in which she and Duke Ayland fell victims to an uncontrollable passion for one another, and then parted after a long scene, in which . . .

"Oh my heavens—and I'm thirty-four years old!" moaned Laura, pressing her face into the pillow until she was nearly stifled, as the early-adolescent nature of these fantasies was borne in upon her with sudden, intolerable clarity.

Viewed in the morning, they seemed so very much more ridiculous, that it became impossible to view them at all, and they were added to the long list of things that Mrs. Temple would not permit herself to remember.

"To-day," she said to Christine, "I shall call upon the Crossthwaites at Marchland. Will you come, or not?"

"I'll see what Duke is doing," Christine returned, with simplicity and candour.

In the course of the morning, Duke came up to Apple-court.

Laura saw him from the drawing-room window.

"Go out to him, Christine," she told her sister. "And I think you'd better not ask him to lunch. It's only the mutton, cold."

"He won't mind that," said Christine, and she went out.

Laura sat at her writing-table, her back to the window, and wrote steadily:

"Please let me have two pounds of scrag-end by mid-day to-morrow, also three or four kidneys."

And her mind, entirely unbidden, put to her the strange question:

"Does he ever kiss her?"

In Laura's day—that Grecian-nymph period that now appeared so remote—to let oneself be kissed was something that classed one. There was the sort of girl who did let herself be kissed, and the sort of girl who didn't—also, although not officially recognised, the sort of girl who didn't, but who pretended that she did. Laura, herself, had spiritually hovered on the borderland between the first and the last of these.

In her years at Quinnerton, she had come to realise that this distinction was no longer a recognised one. But never had she understood it with the vivid apprehension of that morning, when Christine went out to meet Duke Ayland under the apple-trees.

They did not come into the house, and Laura remained motionless, with her pen transfixed immediately above the word "kidneys," for some time.

There was a tap at the door.

"Come in!"

Miss Lamb, the daily governess, came in. She was a brisk, plain young woman, with a *faux air* of efficiency. In reality, she acted from intelligent impulses rather than from reasoned principles, and could attack a difficult situation better than she could sustain it.

"Do come in, Miss Lamb."

"I'm so sorry to disturb you, Mrs. Temple," said the governess, with a respectful glance at the writing-table. She was one of Laura's rather limited number of admirers in the world of literature, and Laura instinctively drew the blotting-paper across the postcard to the butcher.

"It's—I'm afraid—about Johnnie. I told him I should come to you. His disobedience, Mrs. Temple, really is beyond everything. Simply, he's flatly defiant. And he makes Edward naughty, too."

"He has so much more character than Edward," Laura murmured.

"Oh, he has plenty of *character*."

"But of course," said Laura, rousing herself, "it won't do. I'm so very sorry, Miss Lamb. I know how tiresome he can be. What was it this time?"

A long indictment followed, in which Fauntleroy figured ". . . and fond as I am of animals, Mrs. Temple, a dog is a dog, and naturally has habits ——" said Miss Lamb incontrovertibly. "So I told Johnnie I should give him extra lessons for that, and the result is that I have been able to do nothing with him all the morning. And it is such waste of time."

"Shall I punish him?"

Miss Lamb's face grew pink.

"I know one hates the idea. Perhaps if you spoke to him," she suggested.

"Very well. Would you send him here, at once?"

"Thank you, Mrs. Temple. And I'm so very sorry to have to worry you like this."

Laura was sorry, too. She laid down her pen and assumed an expression of severity. Would Johnnie be cross, or injured, or tearful, or simply indifferent? In any case he would be what Laura's little books spoke of as "difficult."

The door opened.

Laura's severe expression became more pronounced.

"Good-morning. Am I interrupting you?" said Duke Ayland. "Of course, I can see I'm interrupting you— but what I really mean is, mayn't I go on doing it?"

His eyes, as well as his mouth, smiled at her.

Laura smiled in return, and felt her preoccupations mysteriously drop from her. Johnnie came into the room, with his most casual air.

"Did you want me, mummie?" his infantile tones guilelessly enquired.

Laura, unable to summon back her expression of severity, could at least dismiss her smile, and did so.

"Go and wait for me in my room upstairs," she directed.

It was against the principles of the little books to let

a child feel itself disgraced by rebuke in the presence of a stranger—but it was not this consideration only that prompted Laura's forbearance.

She wished neither to drive Duke Ayland from the room, nor to appear before him in the light of a mere mother and housewife.

"In your bedroom?" said Johnnie with interest.

"Yes," said Laura, disregarding the interest.

Her son departed with alacrity.

Ayland had seated himself upon the window-sill.

"I hope you're writing, although if you are there's even less chance of my being allowed to stay and talk—but I've always wanted to see a real live author at work."

"I'm anything but a real live author," Mrs. Temple declared, with the utmost sincerity. "I am writing to the butcher, if you want to know. Figuratively speaking, I always am writing to the butcher. My other sort of writing I have to do when I can—generally in the evenings after the children have gone to bed."

"Do you mind?"

"I do, rather. When I meet people like A. B. Onslow, it makes me realise that there's a world where books, and writing, and art, are things that matter. But, of course, you live in that world yourself."

"That's why I like the other better. One gets bored with people who take themselves, and their work, so terribly seriously all the time. Your sense of humour seems almost too good to be true."

At this tribute Laura felt her sense of humour, which

had certainly lain torpid most of the previous night and all the morning, reviving again.

She smiled.

"What was A. B. Onslow like?" enquired Ayland.

"His hair was dyed," returned Laura thoughtfully.

"Was it?"

"Yes."

Duke Ayland looked serious and even interested, but Laura suddenly woke to the inadequacy of her appraisement.

"He was very nice really, and a delightful conversationalist, and took the trouble to talk to me."

"Do you know," said Ayland abruptly, "that you have an inferiority complex?"

It was such a very long while since anybody had talked to Laura about herself, that she would have admitted to any complex in the world in order to prolong the process.

"Have I?" she said with great interest. "Tell me what makes you think so."

They discussed Laura's inferiority complex at some length—thereby considerably diminishing it.

"So that it's perfectly absurd of you," said Duke Ayland gently, in conclusion, "to speak of A. B. Onslow as though he was on some eminence right above your head. He ought to think himself extraordinarily lucky to have had the chance of meeting you."

At this extravagance, Laura looked in sheer amazement at its originator, but he went on calmly:

"Where did you meet him? Does he often stay down here?"

"At Lady Kingsley-Browne's. I thought he admired Bébée, the daughter—the girl who was here yesterday."

"The six-foot high girl, who couldn't take your service?" enquired Mr. Ayland.

"Yes," said Laura shamelessly.

"And A. B. Onslow admired her?"

Ayland's tone was reflective merely, but Laura deduced that his own predilections were not likely to follow the direction taken by those of the novelist.

She changed the conversation.

"Where is Christine?"

"She said she was going to the village."

"Oh, didn't you want to go with her?" exclaimed Laura ingenuously.

"I wanted to talk to you."

This time their eyes met, and Laura, her heart suddenly beating faster, saw that Ayland's were ardent, earnest and compelling.

She looked away again, after a long, strange moment, and said with great abruptness:

"I liked what you played to us last night."

"I wanted you to like it. I'm glad you did."

"Tell me something about your music, won't you?"

She really wanted to hear, and she also wanted time to recover her own composure, severely shaken by a recrudescence of emotions that she had supposed herself to have long outgrown.

The clock struck twelve times, and Laura did not hear it.

But she heard the opening of the drawing-room door,

and saw the rather timid, apologetic entrance of her elder son.

"Mummie," said Edward—"How do you do, Mr. Ayland? I'm quite well, thank you—Mummie, Miss Lamb says, is Johnnie still being punished or can he come out with us?"

Laura leapt to her feet.

"Oh dear—I'll be back in a minute—I've forgotten——" Dismayed and incoherent, she hurried upstairs.

For the first time in several years, Laura had suffered a temporary amnesia, and had ceased to be aware of her own motherhood. She was forcibly reminded of it as she entered her bedroom, where Johnnie, decked in the slender contents of his parent's jewel-case, disposed of at random on his fingers, on the front of his holland overall, and round his legs and arms, sat absorbed in a small volume of Dr. Marie Stopes, that had been bestowed by Laura beneath a pile of her more intimate underwear at the back of her chest of drawers.

"Johnnie! Where did you find that book?"

"In a drawer," said Johnnie negligently.

"You shouldn't open my drawers, as you very well know," said Laura, restraining her violent inclination to snatch Dr. Marie Stopes away and merely detaching Johnnie's grasp very gently.

"You were such a very long time coming. Need I be whipped now?" said Johnnie pathetically.

Laura found herself trying in vain to recall what his offence had been. At last she said:

"I never said I was going to whip you, Johnnie. I

hope you've now had time to think over how badly you've behaved, and that you've made up your mind to be sensible and obedient for the rest of the day."

"Yes," said Johnnie, looking a good deal surprised and relieved.

"Then run along. Wait—take off those brooches and things."

Johnnie obeyed, his fumbling gestures a good deal accelerated by his mother, who felt a nervous desire to have her duty accomplished, so that she might return downstairs.

When she did so, however, the spell was broken.

The atmosphere had altered, and Christine was leaning in at the open window, hatless and sunburnt and smiling.

"I've just told Duke that we're going to pay calls this afternoon, and that he can do some work for a change. But couldn't he stay to lunch, Laura?"

"I hope so," said Laura, all gracious hospitality.

"Thank you, I'd love to."

"It's a cold lunch—if you don't mind ——"

"I don't mind ——" Duke Ayland assured her—and' he said it very convincingly indeed.

Just before the gong was sounded—Laura had never had a parlourmaid of the kind that announces lunch at the drawing-room door—Alfred Temple came in, glanced unfavourably at Ayland as he greeted him with a sound rather than a word, and went, as usual, to wash his hands as the clock struck one.

All through lunch, Laura had the unwonted feeling that she was being amusing, pretty, and thoroughly competent.

Even after Ayland had gone away, it persisted, and was not impaired by Alfred's sardonic enquiry, addressed to Christine:

"Wouldn't your young man like to come and live here, and save himself a daily walk?"

"I daresay he would," said Christine. "But he isn't my young man, Alfred."

"Does he really make a living out of this piano business?"

"More or less."

"Poor chap!" said Alfred cryptically.

Both sisters abstained from asking for elucidation.

"I'll get the car," Christine said.

She had a two-seater, and always professed that she enjoyed taking Laura out in it.

Her complete mastery over it always aroused a rather unwilling awe in Mrs. Temple, who had that entire lack of a sense of machinery so often, and so justifiably, associated with the literary mind.

"Have you looked at your tyres?" said Alfred, and performed the ceremony for them.

"You're all right. Don't forget that you turn to the left after going over the new bridge on the Quinnerton road, Laura."

"No, all right."

"Have you got your cards?"

"Yes, all right, they—Oh Alfred! *Would* you mind, darling, they're in the top left-hand drawer of the hall stand ——"

"Now are you all right?" said Alfred after he had brought the cards.

"Quite."

"Petrol?"

"Not a drop," said Christine. "Goodbye." And she dashed out at the white gate and into the lane without sounding her horn.

"You ought to check Alfred's fussiness, really and truly."

"I don't think he means to be fussy."

"That's all the worse. I don't mean that he isn't very nice, you know ———"

"Oh, I know," said Laura.

"He's such a typical Real Grown-up Person," said Christine, employing an idiom of their childhood.

"Do you think I am, too?" asked Laura rather timidly.

"Not really. You try to be, poor darling, but I shouldn't think anyone was taken in—not even the children."

"Sometimes I wonder if it's a mistake to try so hard, and if I hadn't better make up my mind to be my natural self."

"Oh, far better I should think," declared Christine. "Duke is frightfully smitten with you, by the way."

Laura's heart performed a strange acrobatic feat in her diaphragm.

"Nonsense. He belongs to you, doesn't he?"

"I was getting rather sick of him, to be quite honest. We never went to any lengths at all, of course—I'm not really his sort, and he certainly isn't mine. I really mostly had him down here to see if I did like him very much, and, fortunately for me, I find that I don't."

"Oh," said Laura.

"If you could bear to encourage him a tiny bit, truly I think it would be the very best for you, Laura. You said yourself that you thought you were getting into a rut, down here."

"I certainly shouldn't embark on a cheap flirtation by way of getting out of it," said Laura priggishly.

But an extraordinary feeling of exhilaration had taken possession of her.

She found herself laughing as she had not laughed for years, at jests and allusions of which the only merit was their extreme antiquity, and the number of times which they had already passed between Christine and herself.

They forgot Alfred's directions, and lost their way, and Christine stopped the car whilst Laura earnestly interrogated an old man, but omitted to listen to his information. They pursued a narrow lane, in which it was impossible to turn the car round, for what appeared to be hundreds of miles, and when they at last turned in at the lodge-gates of Marchland, Laura knew that she had gone back to being eighteen years old again.

"The house is pure Georgian," said Christine delightedly. "What a heavenly place! Be sure and find out if they have an eldest son, won't you?"

On this last delicate aspiration, Mrs. Temple and Miss Fairfield were shown into the Crossthwaite drawing-room.

The butler departed in search of his mistress, and

Christine and Laura instantly looked at themselves in the mirror that hung on the wall.

"Plenty of books," said Christine encouragingly. "And no water-colours in gilt frames. So far so good. Do any of these photographs look like an eldest son? A woman in a presentation frock taken about fifteen years ago, I should say—I wonder if that's Mrs. Crossthwaite. If so——"

Christine's voice died away, as she became obviously absorbed in calculation as to the probable age of her hostess.

"Some of the books are French," said Laura.

"Anything that's been banned over here?"

"Not that I can see."

"What ages she is!"

"I wonder if she has any children."

"Not children as young as yours," said Christine firmly. "This isn't a young person's drawing-room, to begin with, and besides, young people are never rich, nowadays, and never live in a large house. They're perfectly penniless, and live in a two-seater."

"*La voilà!*" hissed Laura, assuming—as one does, without grounds—that Mrs. Crossthwaite would fail to understand French.

Chapter VII

MRS. CROSSTHWAITE was tall, good-looking when she remembered to breathe through her nose and not through her open mouth, and with the figure of a slim, flat-chested girl. Her hair was fair and her complexion pale pink-and-white. She might have been some fifteen years older than Laura. She was wearing a tweed skirt and woollen jumper of a strictly neutral tint.

The customary tepid interchange of disconnected observations then ensued.

Laura touched upon the garden, Christine upon the architectural beauty of Marchland. Mrs. Crossthwaite smiled very amiably, and said successively to each:

"It is ravver jolly, isn't it?"

Perhaps Mrs. Temple was a gardener?

No, Laura's husband did more in the garden than she did herself. The children took up time.

Oh, had she children?

"Two boys, seven and five."

"Ravver fascinating ages," said Mrs. Crossthwaite. "One's always so sorry when they stop being babies."

"Yes, isn't one?" Laura rejoined eagerly, without for a moment considering that she was not speaking the truth.

Then Mrs. Crossthwaite politely included Christine in the conversation by asking if she was a Girl Guide enthusiast.

"I live in London," Christine explained.

"Oh, really. Oh, I see. My girls are so very keen. The eldest does Guides, and the other one does Wolf-Cubs."

Laura and Christine both declared that this was splendid.

"It's ravver jolly for them," said Mrs. Crossthwaite.

"Are they at home now?"

"I'm so sorry, they're bofe out. Playing tennis at Lady Kingsley-Browne's. I expect you know her?"

"Quite well—they're neighbours of ours."

"What a charming girl the daughter is. We all took such a fancy to her. Quite delightful, isn't she, and so amusing."

Mrs. Temple's mendacious murmur of acquiescence would have been even more mendacious than it was, but for her sister's presence.

"It was so nice of you to come," said Mrs. Crossthwaite, after tea had been refused, and she was escorting her callers through the hall.

"So glad we found you at home," Laura rejoined, and she and Christine got into the car again and drove away.

"Why does one do it?" Christine asked, after a silence that lasted the length of a whole mile of avenue, bordered by spruce firs and hydrangeas.

"I don't know," said Laura thoughtfully. "I don't know at all. Why *does* one do it?"

"Living in the country, I suppose—doing in Rome as the Romans do. How can you stand it, Laura?"

"I like it very much," said Laura, with her usual veracity.

"And I suppose you liked Mrs. Crossthwaite very much. My heavens! what a woman! I wonder if anyone has ever squeezed a sponge full of cold water over her as she lay in bed?"

"I should think it extremely unlikely."

"Oh, so should I—but it would have been very good for her."

"She might only have said that it was ravver jolly."

They both laughed.

"Seriously, Laura, you ought to go to London much oftener. Or Timbuctoo, if you prefer it. Anywhere that isn't Quinnerton. Duke said to me this morning that it was perfectly frightful to see anyone like you running to seed down here ——"

"Running to seed!" ejaculated Laura, hurt.

"Well, he may not have used that expression—I don't think he did, it sounds much more like one of my own—but that's what he meant. Aren't you ever again going to meet people whose interests are the same as your own, or people on your own level of intelligence and receptiveness? It seems to me that all the time down here you're moving heaven and earth to conform to standards that are considerably below your own. It's absurd."

"It's not a thing that I can argue about," said Laura, preparing to do so. "Alfred would be perfectly miserable, anywhere but here, and the country is good for the children—and besides, I like it myself. Of course, if you think my outlook is getting provincial, you'd much better say so."

"I do say so," Miss Fairfield affirmed, with an emphasis for which Laura had not been altogether prepared. "And it's worse than provincial, Laura. It's so completely domestic. You've got the house, and the children and the servants completely on your nerves."

"Everyone has servants on their nerves nowadays, and naturally one thinks about the children."

"I don't think your whole life ought to revolve round them—or, rather, round Johnnie, since poor wretched little Edward hasn't a look in. It's bad for you, and it's bad for them, and it's even bad for poor wret—for Alfred," said Christine, controlling in time the repetition of her former obnoxious phrase.

"Alfred," said Laura, after a long pause, "Alfred is inarticulate."

"You don't say so!"

"But that doesn't mean that he isn't, in his own way, absolutely devoted to me and to the children."

"The only thing is," Christine said, "wouldn't it be more satisfactory, in a husband, if he was devoted in *your* own way, and not in his?"

The almost blinding intensity of Laura's agreement prevented her from voicing it. Christine went on speaking:

"I'm certain husbands don't realise what a lot they'd gain just by making a personal remark from time to time." Laura winced inwardly. "Honestly, Laura, wouldn't you like it if Alfred, once in a blue moon, said that you were looking pretty, or even asked if you had a headache—when you really have one, I mean, not when you've just put on your best clothes?"

"Of course ——" said Laura. ("I'm not speaking personally, you understand, because nothing would induce me to criticise Alfred, even if there was anything to criticise, which there isn't ——") "Of course, one likes a little notice, I suppose, though I daresay it's very childish . . . but men aren't like that."

"You mean husbands aren't. Because ordinary men, unmarried ones, I mean—always seem to notice things, and speak about them. Personal things."

"Husbands notice things, too," murmured Laura, with a certain gloom.

"But only unpleasant things. Anything wrong with the food, or anything one's forgotten. Honestly, darling, has Alfred ever once, since you married, noticed when you'd been crying? Now don't say you've never cried, because everyone does sometimes, if only for the sake of being asked why."

"Fortunately, I've never cried for that reason," said Laura rather drily. "I should have been disappointed if I had. But, of course, I knew when I married Alfred that he wasn't wildly demonstrative. I shouldn't have liked it if he had been."

"Well," said Christine kindly, "I can't say that I believe you. And any decent analyst would tell you that you're doing yourself a great deal of harm by this constant pretence. It's bound to create the most frightful repressions. What sort of dreams do you have?"

But Laura, even though she did live in the country,

knew all about Herr Freud and his theories, and declined to commit herself in any way upon the subject of dreams.

She abruptly wrenched the conversation back to Marchland and Mrs. Crossthwaite.

"Did you notice that she spoke of 'my son from Uganda'? I got the impression that he was on his way home."

"So did I. With any luck he'll have arrived by the time she's returned your call, and then you can ask the lot of them, Girl Guides and all, for tennis. Though I suppose they'll cram Baybay down his throat as soon as he sets foot in the place."

The remainder of the drive was happily spent in dissecting, in strophe and antistrophe, the undesirable qualities of Miss Kingsley-Browne.

When they reached Applecourt, Laura, gazing round such portions of the garden as could be seen from the front entrance, without at the same time permitting herself to know for whom she was looking, followed her customary practice of going up to the nursery.

Nurse was sitting sewing by the open window, delightfully appropriate in her white uniform and clean apron.

"Where are the boys, nurse?" asked Laura, with the smile that she always instinctively assumed in the frail hope of propitiating the servants.

"Mr. Temple took them down to the orchard, madam."

Laura was divided between gratification at so unusual a mark of attention to his sons from Alfred, and serious apprehensions as to its probable results, when the atmosphere was shattered into fragments around her by the sound of the fatal words:

"I was wishing to speak to you, madam."

Knowing well that no amount of smiling would now avail anything, Laura gazed speechlessly at nurse.

"I shall be wanting to make a change at the end of the month," remarked nurse, in a monotonous voice, and not looking at Laura. "I don't wish to spend another winter in the country."

"I thought you *liked* the country."

"It's very nice in the summer," replied nurse temperately.

"And I did think, nurse, that you were fond of the children. But, of course, if you really feel like that, there's no more to be said. But if there's any other reason—any little thing that you'd like altered ——"

"Thank you, madam. But I think it's time I made a change."

Laura, with a sensation of black despair, repeated that there was no more to be said. She then entered into a very earnest conversation, in which she sought to extract the real reason of her decision from nurse, but in this she succeeded quite as ill as she had expected.

The conversation ended as it had begun, with the formula: "At the end of the month, then."

Laura, from sheer consternation, turned down the stairs instead of along the passage, and walked into the drawing-room as though walking in her sleep.

Christine was there, and Alfred stood at the window.

The two little boys could be seen at the far end of the tennis-lawn.

"Nurse says she wants to leave."

"I hear you found Mrs. Crossthwaite at home," observed Alfred, evidently continuing the train of thought engendered by conversation with Christine. He never easily shifted from one train of thought to another.

Christine was quicker, but still not wholly adequate.

"What a bore for you!"

"I can't think what I shall do," said Laura tragically. She felt herself to be absurd, but had to go on.

"I don't know what's the matter with her—she won't say. And a change is so bad for Johnnie and he'll be so difficult with a new one—and it unsettles the servants, too. It's *maddening* ——"

"But, Laura, there must be other nurses. Or why not let them have a governess?"

"A decent governess is expensive and she wouldn't sleep in the night nursery—and what about carrying up her meals? Maids will never wait upon a governess. And dusting the nurseries—well, she might do that, perhaps, but the turning-out ——"

Laura's incoherency was degenerating rapidly towards the hysterical.

"Has nurse given notice?" said Alfred, in the tone of one determined to get to the bottom of things.

"Yes, and she won't say why, exactly."

"I daresay you can easily find a better one. Or, as Christine says, a governess."

Laura with great difficulty restrained herself from rehearsing all over again the reasons why she could not agree to this suggestion.

"Come up and stay with me, Laura, and interview nurses in London. It'll save you any amount of writing."

"It might be cheaper in the long run—one has to see them, of course. Well, I've got a month, and I suppose I could advertise. . . ."

"Of course you could."

Christine began to talk about Marchland, while Laura, in her own mind, weighed the comparative merits of "Excellent references essential" and "Must be excellent needlewoman." "Young, bright, and genuine child lover," she discarded at once since young must always be relative, bright may very well mean bumptious, and all nurses, of necessity, are obliged to call themselves genuine child lovers, at any rate when speaking or writing to parents.

"But I must put 'Very quiet country place,'" was her final decision, as the air was suddenly rent by brassy yells from Edward and Johnnie, in violent dispute.

Laura sprang to her feet.

"Better leave them alone," said her husband.

Laura remained uneasily hovering between the open window and the inside of the room.

"Boys! It's time for tea!" called out Christine, and Edward immediately trotted towards her. Then he caught sight of Laura.

"Mummie's come home!" he shouted joyfully, breaking into a run.

Laura received him kindly into her arms, but her eyes

were fixed upon Johnnie, crawling morosely across the lawn.

He was annoyed because she had not come rushing out to see what was the matter when he had been screaming.

How could any new nurse, Laura resentfully wondered, expect to understand so complex and intelligent a child as Johnnie?

Quite impossible.

The boys went up to their nursery tea, Edward apparently quite satisfied by his mother's conscientious but absent-minded pattings, and Johnnie still unmollified by her ardent caress to the top of his curls and her whispered promise of a story after tea.

In the dining-room tea was a failure.

Alfred was in that frame of mind in which nothing would serve him but to ring the bell—an act of despotism disliked at least as much by his wife as by the servants whom it was designed to summon.

"Dear, what do you want?"

"Haven't we any jam in the house?"

"Has she forgotten the jam?" said Laura coldly. "I suppose that as none of us ever eat it, she didn't think it worth while."

"Ring for it."

"Please do ring, if you really want jam," Laura replied icily.

"How is she to learn, if we don't tell her?" was the indirect retort of her husband.

The house-parlourmaid appeared, looked quite as sulky as Laura had expected her to look at being disturbed in the middle of her tea, and replied impeccably that, if you please, sir, the jam was finished, and there was no more put out.

"Then there's nothing more to be said."

Laura sketched a movement of rising from her chair.

"I can get the key and go to the store cupboard," she said, with a perfectly genuine sense of martyrdom, to which she allowed full vent in her voice and expression.

"It doesn't matter," replied Alfred, with slightly raised eyebrows.

How trivial, and yet how infuriating, was life, with recalcitrant nurses and husbands and children, and nothing to look forward to ever, and at the back of everything an eternal sense of one's own inadequacy.

"I thought it would be rather fun to go to Brussels for a week this autumn," Christine was saying. "An exhibition I want to see. . . . Some of us may make up a party. I think Duke is going."

With an inward start of mingled astonishment and gratification, Laura realised that she had forgotten all about Duke Ayland and his very existence.

Perhaps after all it didn't matter about Alfred, the nurse, and the jam.

There might be something to look forward to, although Laura didn't quite know what.

"Duke is coming up on the chance of some tennis, after tea," observed Christine.

"I daresay you can give him a game if you don't mind singles. I must do a little weeding, and Laura will want to be with the children."

Alfred's agricultural proclivities led him to derive actual enjoyment from the process of weeding, to Laura's ever-recurring amazement.

"You'd better play tennis, Alfred," said Christine. "Four is much more fun than a single. The children can pick up the balls. And Duke gets so very few chances of playing tennis. He's always in London and always at work. He's got to be, to make a living."

"Is he very badly off?" Laura asked.

"Oh, very. But he's only got himself to think of—no wife or anything like that, so it's not so bad really. Duke hasn't even got a mother or a sister to support."

Laura, obscurely, was glad to hear it.

She was glad, too, that Duke Ayland was coming.

And after that, when he did, they played no tennis. Alfred continued intent upon selecting what appeared to Laura to be small green plants growing in the midst of other small green plants that exactly resembled them, and then throwing them away, and Christine took the two little boys away into the paddock.

Ayland sat down by Laura under the apple-trees.

"Don't let's play tennis. You look tired," he said in a voice of concern.

Laura turned to find his eyes as full of concern as had been his voice.

"Why are you tired?"

She wanted to tell him that it was wonderful of him to have noticed her tiredness, but the sheer unexpectedness of his sympathy held her silent with surprise and gratitude.

"I think you do far too much for other people, you know."

"I'm not tired now," said Laura suddenly, smiling at him—and indeed she felt miraculously rejuvenated and entirely unfatigued.

"The things that tire me are the things that bore me."

"Of course. Like all artists, you're most terribly sensitive, aren't you? One felt that directly."

Laura yielded to the insidious rapture of talking about herself exactly as she wished herself to be talked about.

"If I'm sensitive," she said slowly—"and I suppose you're right—I can't afford to own it to myself, far less to anybody else. I used to think that I could kill it altogether, by never giving in to it, and to a certain extent I've succeeded."

"Instinctive self-protection. Don't you see that if you, of all people, let yourself feel things as you could feel them, you'd go mad?"

Laura did see. But her seeing was as nothing compared to the blinding, ecstatic satisfaction of knowing that Duke Ayland saw.

"You're putting into words things that I haven't dared to let myself think, for years ——" she faltered.

It was true. One didn't dare let oneself think about emotions that one never had the chance of experiencing. But now, all of a sudden, Laura not only dared to think and speak about them, but she wished ardently to speak and to think of nothing else.

It appeared that her desires were shared by her companion.

When a conversation of this description is embarked upon for the first time between two people, there is no reason, perceptible to themselves, why it should ever stop. Any interruption from without comes as a complete and unwelcome surprise. Laura had just said, "I don't know why I'm telling you all this, quite—I've never told anybody else ——" when the two little boys came running up to say good night.

Laura felt herself violently jerked back into the atmosphere that she had for years thought of as "real life."

Duke Ayland roused in her a fresh, silent access of appreciation by standing up to receive the good night handshakes of Edward and Johnnie.

His manners *were* wonderful. . . .

At the sight of nurse, in her grey-and-white, competently escorting the boys into the house, Laura's latest anxiety took possession of her again. But even that remembrance held possibilities of alleviation.

"Christine wants me to go to London at the end of the month, to see about a new nurse, as this one is unfortunately leaving."

"Oh," said Ayland, "I was going to ask you if you ever came to London. I'm so awfully glad. Would you—if you haven't got every minute booked up—is there a chance that you'd let me take you out to dinner one night?"

"I'd love it," said Laura, trying to sound kind, rather than enchanted.

"If there's anything you specially want to see, perhaps you'd come to a show afterwards?"

"I'd like to very much indeed. I hardly ever see anything nowadays."

"If you'll let me know what you most want to see, I'll book seats directly I get back. I wish to goodness I wasn't going on Monday, but I'm afraid I must."

"I wish you weren't going. But you make me talk about myself a great deal too much. I haven't done it for years," Laura declared with truth.

"Next time," said Duke Ayland smiling, "I'm going to talk about myself, if you'll let me."

It was curious, the extraordinary sense of intimacy the words conveyed.

Or perhaps it was his tone.

He stayed to dinner again, that evening, and afterwards they played paper games—tolerated, rather than enjoyed, by Alfred, who served, indeed, merely as a foil for the skill of the other three players.

Playing at paper games was Laura's only genuine accomplishment, and the environments of Applecourt had never offered any scope for it. She went up to bed feeling clever, and successful, and when she gazed earnestly at herself in the glass she felt, as well, that she was still pretty.

"What is thirty-four, after all, nowadays?" Laura found herself recklessly enquiring.

She would go to London.

To look for a nurse, certainly, but also to enjoy herself.

She would go and see the A. B. Onslows. After all, they'd asked her to. It would be good for her writing.

Laura began to take off her clothes—it distressed her

to know that she usually wore at least three more garments than any other modern woman, but her circulation was poor, and it was a choice between that and a faint violet tinge to the tip of her nose—and as she did so, unconsciously fell under the obsession of a complex medley of thought, wherein improbable sartorial triumphs mingled strangely with encounters between intellectual affinities gathered together at the house of the A. B. Onslows.

"A crinoline hat of very palest yellow, and yellow organdie and lace—a slim silhouette—the long amber necklace. 'Mrs. Temple, I've always loved your work so much ——' Duke Ayland standing by the door, watching her." "She looks so absurdly young!" Would it be out of the question to go to a decent place, and get a really *lovely* hat? After all, it'd come in for weddings, afterwards. And for yellow organdie and lace—Bond Street —Duke Ayland and the theatre. No one wore any sleeves at all nowadays, but no one—except Laura—had vaccination marks that showed. She looked her best by artificial light, provided that her hair had been properly cut, shampoo'd and waved. "Don't you see that if you, of all people, let yourself feel things as you *could* feel them ——"

Laura snatched up her hand-glass, and examined her own reflection with passionate intentness. Whatever she might have looked earlier in the evening, she didn't look tired now.

Neither tired nor sleepy.

Always, she was both at the end of the day. A strange,

quivering excitement made her feel as though she might lie awake, to-night.

"Simply a passing gratification of my vanity. I'd better face it," Laura told herself, with a pseudo-candour that was the height of disingenuousness.

Her method of facing it was to get into bed, blow out the candle, and lie with her hands clasped beneath her head, recalling over and over again phrases and words and intonations, in her conversation with Ayland.

To the apparent interminableness of this exercise the entrance of Laura's husband put a check.

He seemed surprised, not without reason, to find her wakeful.

"Alfred, I've been thinking. Shall I go to London and stay with Christine, for a few days, at the end of the month?"

"Why not? To look at nurses, I suppose?"

"Yes. And I thought I'd go and see the A. B. Onslows."

"Is that the man with dyed hair that we met at Lady Kingsley-Browne's?"

"The author."

"That's what I meant."

"Duke Ayland suggested my dining with him one night and going to a play."

Alfred made no reply, and Laura's heart seemed to leap into her throat.

The silence became tense, unbearable.

"Alfred," said Laura faintly.

He got into bed.

"You don't *mind*, do you?"

"Mind what, dear?   I'm afraid I didn't hear what you said."

"Duke Ayland taking me to a theatre in London," murmured Laura.

"A very good idea," said Alfred.

In a spasm of relief, self-reproach and impatience, she leant across the bed and kissed him passionately.

Chapter VIII

Before Laura's visit to London, that she now looked forward to with a tremulous fervour that seemed to increase in proportion to her own conviction of its irrationality, there stretched a domestic track of more than habitual tediousness.

Christine left Applecourt on the same day as, and in the company of, Duke Ayland.

"I shall see you in a fortnight, darling," she said to Laura. "It's been lovely here. The only thing I'm sorry about is that Mrs. Crossthwaite and the son from Uganda didn't return your call while I was still here. Be sure and follow them up, if she does, and have him to tennis next time I come."

"Good-bye," said Duke Ayland in a low voice, gripping Laura's hand and at the same time looking at her with the kind of look that should—but more often does not—accompany the gripping of a hand.

"Only a fortnight before I see you in town," said Laura, compromising with her conscience, that officiously smote her at the words, by giving them a jaunty intonation that disgusted her as she heard it.

"I'll write to you about time and place," said Ayland, as eagerly as though he had not already said exactly the same thing five times within twenty-four hours.

"Yes, do," said Laura, with equal fervour and equal lack of originality.

He went.

"If you please, madam," said nurse, "could I take a day off next week to interview a lady in Bristol?"

"Certainly," said Laura dejectedly.

Nurse's day off was no longer the hectic affair that it had been in Johnnie's babyhood, when Laura had, as it now seemed to her, pushed the pram for hours and hours, in the hope of inducing slumbers that remained elusive, and the clothes of both the children had had to be changed again and again until neither the night-nursery wardrobe nor the linen closet would yield any further contributions, and Laura's head had ached only less than her back, and from being a bright young mother in the morning, she had degenerated into a whining victim by the evening.

But although that disturbing phase was over, it still remained a fact, partially acknowledged by Laura, that to be in sole charge of Edward and Johnnie, for one entire day, reduced their mother to spiritual pulp and physical exhaustion.

Sometimes Laura addressed herself rhetorically in sentences beginning: "How about the village mothers, with half a dozen tiny children, and all the cooking and cleaning to do as well?"

The picture appalled her—but her own inadequacy remained unaltered, whereas the village mothers went competently through their days.

Nurse went to Bristol.

The lady who wished to interview her chose a Saturday, the only day of the week upon which Miss Lamb did not come to give Edward and Johnnie their lessons, and the house-parlourmaid's afternoon out. In the morning, the boys played in the garden, and in the afternoon it poured with rain.

"We'll play with the bricks in the nursery," declared Laura cheerfully. This was a success for some time, until Fauntleroy, the terrier, dashed gaily into Johnnie's elaborate construction and reduced it to a jumble of wooden bricks and blocks.

Johnnie's immediate reaction was to fly into a temper with the blameless Edward, whom he kicked and pummelled viciously.

Edward, who was naturally quite a brave little boy, had learnt by experience that the onslaughts of his younger brother were entirely beyond ordinary methods of self-defence, and exasperated Laura by rushing behind her for protection.

"Johnnie, you can go outside till you—Edward, don't be such a little coward, stand up to him like a man—go outside till you're quiet again, Johnnie."

Never meet opposition with opposition. Always speak quietly and calmly when dealing with a passionate child.

Excerpts from Laura's little books crowded in upon her mind, but however quiet and calm she might be, it was necessary for her to raise her voice almost to a scream in order to make it heard at all, and this produced the very opposite effect to one of quiet and calm, even to her own ears.

Fauntleroy barked madly.

At last, by exerting considerably more physical force

than she herself, let alone the little books, thought really right, Laura got Johnnie and Fauntleroy both outside the door.

Then, as not unusually happened, she vented her disappointment and anxiety about Johnnie in severely rebuking Edward.

Edward sulked mildly, contrived, by a great and obvious effort, to shed a few tears designed to make Laura pity him, and characteristically defeated his own object by suddenly catching sight of a candle-end in the wastepaper basket and exclaiming with enthusiasm:

"Oh, look what I've found, mummie! May I have it?"

"What for?" said Laura, listening to Johnnie's shouts and kicks, now becoming perfunctory and spasmodic.

"To use for my cooking."

"*What?*"

"Miss Lamb makes us say 'Pardon' when we haven't heard."

"Never let me hear you say 'Pardon,' Edward. Say 'I beg your pardon' or 'What did you say?' Or even 'What?' But *not* 'Pardon.'"

"I'll tell Miss Lamb," said Edward, much interested in this conflict of authorities.

"No, you needn't do that. It'll be enough if you remember what I've said."

Then Johnnie returned, declared himself perfectly good, was thankfully absolved by his mother, and lured by her into exchanging a tepid handshake with his brother as a symbol of renewed friendliness.

The remainder of the afternoon was peaceful in so far as personal relations were concerned.

Laura, dishevelled, unpowdered, and exhausted, shepherded the boys down to the dining-room as the gong rang for tea. As they crossed the hall—Edward and Johnnie vociferous, and Laura limply silent—a shining and completely noiseless car drew up before the open front door.

"Look, a car," said Edward.

An elegant head was visible, and beyond it another head—less elegant but still unmistakably a head wearing the kind of hat suitable to paying calls.

The elegant head turned in the direction of Edward, and a still more elegant hand waved at him in a beautifully new chamois-leather glove.

Laura caught Johnnie by the shoulder, and said through her teeth:

"Visitors have come. Go and tell cook to put extra cups and plates through the hatch, and anything there is to eat ——"

"Visitors!" echoed Johnnie in dismay. "Then can't we have tea with you after all?"

"Yes, you can—there's nowhere else—only be very good. Go and tell cook, like a darling."

Laura's urgency communicated itself to her son and he rushed obediently away.

"Go and wash," hissed Laura at Edward, and herself turned, with determined smiles, and a *faux air* of astonished welcome, to greet Mrs. Crossthwaite and her elegant friend.

"We're much later than we meant to be," apologised Mrs. Crossthwaite. "The chauffeur was so stupid about finding the way—we've just been to the Kingsley-Brownes', and I felt I couldn't go home without returning your call. May I introduce my friend, Mrs. La Trobe?—Mrs. Temple."

"Do come in, won't you?" said Laura, thankfully remembering that at least she had "done" the drawing-room flowers the day before. "I'm afraid you've come in for a nursery-tea, my two small boys are on my hands this afternoon."

"Dear little people!" cooed Mrs. La Trobe in a contralto voice. "I'm so fond of little people."

Laura, ungratefully, took a violent dislike to Mrs. La Trobe.

"We really mustn't stay to tea," said Mrs. Crossthwaite, without very much conviction.

Laura exclaimed as though in dismay, the visitors protested, were over-ruled, yielded. Laura, with every appearance of graceful cordiality, conducted them to the dining-room where Edward and Johnnie waited for tea.

"How do you do?" cried Mrs. La Trobe without delay. "Dear little people!"

The dear little people, Laura was thankful to see, had reduced their persons to something approaching cleanliness, although neither had remembered the use of a hair-brush.

Tea was laid in the meticulously incorrect fashion peculiar to the house-parlourmaid's afternoon out, with the milk-jug standing in the slop-bowl, and the brown and the white bread-and-butter jostling one another on the same dish.

"You have ravver a jolly view," said Mrs. Crossthwaite, politely glancing from the window, whilst Laura made the tea and sharply parted the milk-jug from the slop-bowl.

Conversation was rather spasmodic.

Edward, who indiscriminately enjoyed any form of notice, marked his appreciation of Mrs. La Trobe's advances by becoming slightly noisy and boastful, encouraged by her contralto laughs and ejaculatory praises.

Johnnie, more critical and less susceptible, was nevertheless determined to assert his own claims to attention, and attempted humorous interpolations.

Laura endeavoured to suppress both her sons without embarrassing the visitors, to talk politely to Mrs. Crossthwaite about the Women's Institute, and to convey to Mrs. La Trobe that it was injudicious to exclaim openly upon Johnnie's curls and Edward's quaintness.

She heartily wished that Alfred would come in, and at last he did so.

At least, the children became quiet, although Laura, for the first time giving her full attention to Mrs. Crossthwaite, could dimly hear a further tender-hearted outcry of "Dear little people!" from her other visitor.

Mrs. Crossthwaite was civilly enquiring for Mrs. Temple's sister.

Christine had returned to London, Laura explained. She was coming back to Applecourt later. By a natural transition of thought, she asked about the son from Uganda.

He was back. In London. He, also, was coming down again later in the summer.

"We hope to have plenty of tennis, when Jim is at home. You and your sister must come over. My girls would be so delighted."

It faintly pleased Laura to hear herself bracketed with anybody's girls, and she reflected with mild cynicism that Christine would certainly wish her to accept any invitation that led to "Jim."

She did so.

Alfred and Mrs. La Trobe were less successful in pleasing one another.

It always took Alfred a little while to establish any sort of *rapport* between himself and a complete stranger, and it was evident to Laura that he was still rather resentfully wondering what Mrs. La Trobe's name was, why she had come, and how soon she might be expected to go away again.

Mrs. La Trobe, on the other hand, was endeavouring to charm her host by an excessive display of purely feminine qualities. She said that she loved children, and she "was afraid that she wasn't at all clever. I hear your wife writes; now that, to me, is so marvellous ——" and that she didn't drive a car because her wrists were really not strong enough for the gears, and that she had a tiny little house, and no servant bothers because she simply loved housework, and was really fond of cooking.

"I'm afraid," said Mrs. La Trobe, with a smile, "that I'm just what the Americans call a home-maker."

Laura, who knew her husband's opinion of any conversation in which personalities played a part, felt sorry for the guest, producing an effect so different from the one that she intended and expected.

She hastily turned Mrs. Crossthwaite over to Alfred, and herself became the recipient of Mrs. La Trobe's confidences.

"Mummie, may I get down?"

"Not yet, Johnnie dear."

Alfred rang the bell.

"Let Edward go," said Laura hastily. "What is it—more milk?"

"Yes. No milk left."

"Hilda is out," Laura said, hoping that her husband would grasp the implication that the cook was neither willing, nor even desirable, as an answerer of bells. "Edward, run to the kitchen and get some more milk."

"Are you a useful boy?" said Mrs. La Trobe. "I'm sure you're mother's useful boy."

"Oh no," said Laura lightly and insincerely, in order to bridge Edward's smirking, but unresponsive silence. "Boys are never really useful, unlike little girls. One of them ought to have been a daughter. Run along, darling."

"Dear little laddies!" ejaculated Mrs. La Trobe.

"Mrs. La Trobe is so devoted to children. I always tell her that I wonder she cares to stay with me at all, where there are no children in the house."

Laura uncharitably surmised that Mrs. Crossthwaite's combination of stupidity and good-nature must be valuable to Mrs. La Trobe. It could be trusted to present her in exactly that obvious light in which she wished to be presented.

Edward came into the room again and said brightly:

"There isn't any more milk. Not a drop in the house."

"What can have happened?" unhappily ejaculated Laura, although well aware of what had happened, since, owing to her own bad house-keeping, it had happened more than once before.

"If it was on my account, please don't bovver. I really don't want any more tea."

Mrs. La Trobe, evidently anxious to display equal tact, glanced into her cup, which had unfortunately just been replenished from the teapot, and heroically declared that she liked it without milk, and had been told that it was far better for her, and that, in fact, she often did drink it like that.

"May we get down now?" wearily enquired Johnnie.

Laura assented, and almost immediately afterwards followed the example of her sons, unable to bear the sight of Mrs. La Trobe sipping gallantly, but with a wry mouth, at her milkless tea.

"Run upstairs, boys dear."

"Shall you be able to read to us presently?"

"Yes. Run along."

Alfred, at the open door of the hall, hesitated wistfully.

"One peep at the garden if I may, and then we really must go," said Mrs. Crossthwaite.

The rain had long since left off.

The peep was vouchsafed, and Laura, by the time the car had been brought to the door by the uniformed chauffeur, was able to smile, and murmur hopes that next time it wouldn't be quite so much of a picnic. . . .

"So lucky to have found you at all," Mrs. Crossthwaite replied.

"There's nothing I love like a nursery party. I'm devoted to little people," declared Mrs. La Trobe, consistent to the last. The car, entirely noiseless, moved away.

Alfred Temple gazed after it disparagingly.

Laura hoped that he was going to speak, and waited, but after a few seconds he merely tipped his hat further over his eyes, and went away into the garden.

Laura sighed, feeling how much she would have preferred reproaches for her inadequacy as a hostess to such complete silence, although she was aware that it did not denote anything more than resignation on her husband's part.

Then she saw that there was a letter from Duke Ayland lying on the hall-table.

Alfred's silence, the absence of milk, and the comments that she feared her visitors were exchanging on their way home, all receded into insignificance. Laura, becoming eighteen years old again, caught up the letter and turned instinctively into the quiet of the empty drawing-room.

"Mummie, have the visitors gone?"

"Can you read to us now?"

The boys dashed tumultuously downstairs.

Laura thrust the unopened letter into one of the pigeon-holes in her writing-table.

She read to the boys, and played a game of Happy Families with them, and pretended not to hear Johnnie addressing the coloured representations of Mr. Bones the Butcher and his family in a drawling contralto: "Dear little people, I *am* so fond of you."

Nurse, who might possibly have got back to Applecourt before six o'clock by catching an early train at Quinner-ton, had not elected to do so, and Laura put her sons to bed. Theoretically, this is one of the most joyful and natural events in the day of a young mother and her children.

Laura knew this, and loyally tried to make her own feelings correspond to the knowledge. But, at any rate on nurse's day out, it was never of any use.

Her back ached, the bath remained just too deep for her to bend over it comfortably, the boys seemed to have got out of hand, and she almost always found that it took her five-and-twenty minutes longer than it should have done to get them into bed.

On this occasion she wanted so dreadfully to read Duke Ayland's letter that she informed Edward and Johnnie that they might play in the bath, as a treat, until she came back. Then she fled to the drawing-room.

It was not the first letter that she had received from Duke Ayland. It excited her even more than if it had been, because she knew now that it would contain the personal note she desired.

He omitted the formality of a stereotyped beginning,

wrote mostly about books, his own work, and Laura's writing, and ended with: "I am saving up such hundreds of things to talk to you about. Please don't be even one minute late on the 27th.—Yours, M.A."

As soon as she had skimmed the four pages, and re-read the last sentence five times, Laura found herself emerging from a kind of trance to the sound of hilarious shriekings and splashings that caused her to rush upstairs and into the bathroom again.

At last Edward and Johnnie were dried, clad in their striped Viyella pajamas, and tucked up into their respective beds.

Edward said his prayers with conventional gravity, Johnnie was discouraged by his mother in an attempt at melodramatic intercession on behalf of various improbable trespasses, and Laura shut the door of the night-nursery behind her.

There was barely time to change for dinner before the gong rang, and Alfred, coming in from the garden, said: "I must just go upstairs and wash. I shan't change."

"There isn't time," returned Laura frigidly. "The gong has just sounded."

It annoyed her that Alfred should be unpunctual, it annoyed her that he should not change for dinner, and it annoyed her to realise that his not doing so implied an intention of returning to his gardening again as soon as dinner was over.

"I never used to mind little things," she thought, remembering the light-hearted indifference of the days when she had not known responsibility.

The soup was not hot by the time they sat down at the dining-room table, but Laura could tell that it wouldn't have been hot even if they had come in punctually.

"No one to change the plates?" enquired Alfred, raising his eyebrows.

"You know it's her afternoon out."

"Why do all the servants go out on the same day?"

Laura explained curtly.

"Must you ask people to tea on days when we have no servants?"

"Alfred, naturally I didn't ask them to tea. Is it likely, with Hilda out and the boys on my hands? Mrs. Crossthwaite aggravatingly chose to-day for returning my call, and I suppose that absurd woman is staying with her. Of course, at Marchland it doesn't make the slightest difference if two extra people turn up for a meal, but here it does, that's all."

"It doesn't make any difference to the amount of milk we're allowed, apparently."

Laura received her husband's small jibe with a joyless smile.

"I don't know whether you've noticed it, dear, but whenever nurse goes out for the day, and you have those two boys to look after, by the time evening comes," said Alfred impressively, "you're fagged out. That's what you are—absolutely fagged out."

Laura, who had so often regretted and resented the fact that her husband never commented upon her looks, received this exception to the rule in an embittered silence.

"Well," said Alfred as they rose from the table, "I shall do a little gardening."

Laura went to the night-nursery, gazed at the sleeping Johnnie, forgot Edward, and ascertained by the presence of nurse's hat upon the lid of the clothes-basket, that nurse had come back.

In the day-nursery she found her.

The information that nurse had accepted the situation offered by the lady at Bristol renewed Laura's anxiety-complex on the subject of finding a substitute.

Someone who would be able to manage Johnnie. A good needle-woman, because Laura wasn't. Fond of animals, because of Fauntleroy, and besides, the boys might have a pony one day. Young enough to run about and play.

Old enough to have a sense of responsibility.

Willing to do her own nurseries.

Laura snatched up *The Times*, and tore feverishly through the advertisement columns.

"Town preferred."

"Baby from the month preferred."

"Would travel."

"Wages £70 to £80."

At the last item, Mrs. Temple remembered what a very long while it was since any story of hers had brought in a cheque.

If she wrote more stories, and could sell them for better prices, she might be able to afford the wages asked by highly trained nurses and governesses.

By the time that her husband came in, Laura had not

thought of a short story, but she had answered Duke Ayland's letter, and two of the advertisements in *The Times.*

"I wish you'd look at what I've written in answer to two 'Situations Wanted,' Alfred," she said.

"That seems all right."

"Do you think I've said enough?"

"Too much, if anything."

"Oh Alfred! I'd so much rather tell them the drawbacks beforehand, and then they can't say anything afterwards. What do you think I ought to leave out?"

"I don't say you ought to leave out anything exactly," replied Arthur carefully. "I only meant that the whole tone of your letter was rather calculated to put them off, that's all."

"Oh, is that all?" said Laura satirically, and then they both laughed.

It was always a relief to her when they laughed at the same things, because it engendered a sense of companionship.

Laura was passionately anxious to believe that companionship played a large and important part in the married life of Alfred and herself. She put aside the facts that they differed upon the question of the children, that Alfred's main preoccupations lay in the vegetable kingdom, and her own in the realm of the emotions, and dwelt firmly on the interests they held in common.

Sometimes—but not often—these were reduced to Fauntleroy and lawn-tennis.

Duke Ayland had in a fortnight shattered her carefully-cultivated attitude of mind.

His society had forced upon Laura that which she had resolutely made herself forget, for fear of missing it unbearably: the meaning of mental and spiritual affinity.

She wanted to see him again with an intensity that secretly frightened her.

"Am I in any danger of falling in love with him?" Laura asked herself solemnly, from time to time.

She never asked herself whether Duke Ayland was in any danger of falling in love with her. Whatever the answer to this, Laura instinctively knew that it would dismay her.

She thought of the difference between herself and Christine.

Love affairs came naturally to Christine. She had had one, Laura knew, with a married man. But it had not been tragic.

"It's utterly out-of-date to take things seriously," Laura told herself, more seriously than ever.

Although less than ten years separated her from Christine she felt that she belonged to the generation that accepted, if it did not positively manufacture, tragedy, renunciation, and sublimity.

It was impossible to her to be genuinely flippant and detached where personal relations were concerned.

Laura, as usual obsessed by two conflicting emotions, despised and resented this peculiarity in herself, and at the same time admired and exulted in it.

In a frame of mind that entirely defied analysis she prepared to go to London. Nothing, to her surprise, happened to prevent it.

"Mind you enjoy yourself. Go to some plays, or something," said Alfred at the station. Laura, touched and strangely self-reproachful, hovered for an incredible instant on the verge of an insane offer to remain at home and not go at all—but fortunately remembered in time that there was nothing more justly disliked by Alfred than a change of plans at the eleventh hour.

Chapter IX

THE train sped onwards, and Laura held her library book open upon her knee, and supposed herself to be reading it, whilst a merry phantasy careered round and round her mind, in which she sustained a rôle not unworthy of an American film-heroine featuring the brilliant night life of Broadway. But of this she remained fortunately unconscious, with that part of herself that would most strongly have objected to it.

At the junction, Lady Kingsley-Browne was also awaiting the London train.

"How delightful, my dear—look, you're dropping your book—are you actually going all the way to town? We can travel together."

A discrepancy in the class of ticket purchased respectively by Lady Kingsley-Browne and by Mrs. Temple would, Laura well knew, defeat this amiable project, but she received it nevertheless with an assenting smile, which seemed simpler to accomplish than an explanatory refusal.

"My dear, I'm glad—positively glad—that you're going to have a change. You sometimes look to me quite worn out," said Laura's neighbour solicitously. "A rag! Neither more nor less than a rag!"

"Oh, I hope not!"

Lady Kingsley-Browne shook her expensively-turbaned head.

"A change is what we all need, from time to time,

141

though I know how hard it is to tear oneself from the garden. How is yours doing now?"

"If we could only get a little really hot sun ——" said Laura, who had learnt by long experience that this observation can almost always be made with perfect safety in an English summer.

Lady Kingsley-Browne met it with almost passionate sympathy, and rushed into horticultural details whilst Laura allowed her mind to turn once more to the anticipations that had held her imagination for the past fortnight.

Suddenly she realised that her interlocutor was no longer straying amongst begonias and petunias.

"I know you're really interested, or I shouldn't say one word, but after all, you've known Bébée ever since she was so high, haven't you?" Lady Kingsley-Browne's white kid glove appealed to an imaginary line somewhere about the level of Laura's knees. "And I always think it's such a joy to hear of a girl being *settled*."

"Yes," said Laura, thoughtfully rather than assentingly. "Married, you mean?"

"Engaged, and then married, naturally."

"It's wonderful how much they enjoy themselves nowadays, it seems to me, without any of the responsibility that marriage brings," murmured Laura. "Look at my sister!"

But Lady Kingsley-Browne had no desire to look at Laura's sister, although she paid her the passing tribute of an indistinct murmur from which the words "charming" and "tennis" disconnectedly emerged.

"One likes Jeremy so much on his own account," she mysteriously assured Laura. "The very best type of young Englishman, is what one always feels."

"She brought him to Applecourt—I remember. He's very—quite young, isn't he?"

"To us he may be, but of course he's exactly the right age, really. About twenty-nine. And I've always been so fond of Felicia Vulliamy."

"His mother?" hazarded Laura.

"His mother. They have such a lovely place in Norfolk. I've never seen anything like their azaleas—and the rhododendrons in June—they had the new variety before anyone else in England."

She was off again, Laura rather unsympathetically told herself, and waited for a pause in which to interject:

"Is he the only son?"

"The only child at all. As a matter of fact, he will be one of the richest commoners in England. Poor Felicia idolises him. One felt she could only endure to surrender him to a girl of Bébée's type."

Laura's astonished inward conjecture as to the discernment thus ascribed to Mrs. Vulliamy's maternity was cut short by the approach of the London train.

"We must meet in town, dear!" cried Lady Kingsley-Browne. "I suppose you'll be at the Chelsea Flower Show?"

Laura, who did not at the moment ever wish to see a flower again, except within the confines of a restaurant dining-room, waved enthusiastic agreement, and sought the far end of the train.

Her excitement was growing steadily, and, in a blind instinct of self-protection, she sought to mitigate it by seriously analysing, with the help of a pocket-mirror, the justice of Lady Kingsley-Browne's description of her as a rag. On the whole, Laura decided, it was unmerited, especially with a hat on.

She took out a new and unused lip-stick, and applied it to her upper lip, but in such a manner that she could not really be sure if it had or had not altered the colour of her mouth.

In the luncheon-car she had one more glimpse of Lady Kingsley-Browne, emerging from First Luncheon as Laura approached Second Luncheon.

"Now be sure and look up the A. B. Onslows," cried Lady Kingsley-Browne kindly and earnestly. "I know they really want you to, and he thinks your poems so delightfully clever. We must meet there."

"Does she really suppose," Laura rhetorically demanded of herself, "that one goes all the way to London for the sake of looking at flowers and meeting country neighbours?"

At Paddington Christine met her.

Unlike Laura, she had not been in the least half-hearted in the use of her lip-stick. She looked very pretty and very well dressed, and seemed enthusiastically glad to see her sister.

"Duke rang up, to ask what time you were arriving. I think he wanted me to ask him round to the flat to-night, but I didn't in case you wanted to get your hair waved first, or anything."

"I'm dining with him to-morrow night, anyway," said Laura, who had wondered for days how she was to explain this engagement to Christine and now found it as easy as though she had been eighteen years old again.

Easiness was in the atmosphere of Christine's flat, and was prevalent in everything that she and Laura said and did.

Domestic mishaps, if they occurred, did not matter. There were no servants, and the absence of them was not a calamity.

There were no children and ——

At that, Laura's mind jibbed suddenly and irrecoverably. She was incapable of allowing the thought to reach to its logical conclusion.

The next morning she went to the famous Mrs. Laidlaw's Registry Office, and was conducted to a small cubicle like a bathing-machine, where a chair with arms received her, in contradistinction to the upright and uncomfortable stool that awaited the candidates for her situation.

To each one of these, Laura, after a brief, dismayed inspection, made a short and faltering speech, describing the disadvantages of life at Applecourt, and the excessive quiet of the surrounding country. The candidates, for the most part, were scornful-eyed, middle-aged women, who asked curt and business-like questions.

Laura never got as far as, "My second boy, I ought to tell you, is a particularly highly-strung child ——" which was the preface that she had designed for the elucidation of her theories on education.

She said: "Well, nurse, I'll write to you one way or

the other, before the end of the week," and one by one the candidates withdrew.

"I don't think it's going to be at all easy to find the right person for the boys," Laura said to Christine at luncheon.

"How are the boys?" said Christine. "I'm afraid I forgot to ask yesterday."

But Christine's forgetfulness, Laura felt, was as nothing to her own, in having neither noticed nor resented the omission.

Whilst she dressed for dinner that evening, Laura dwelt with passionate earnestness on the thought of her own maternity.

It seemed a kind of safeguard.

For the first time in several years, she found her frock, her hair and her general appearance, adequate, and when Duke Ayland came to fetch her in a taxi, she was immediately aware that he, also, found her so.

"It's simply splendid to see you again," he said earnestly. "I've been so absurdly terrified that something would happen to prevent it."

"So have I," said Laura, quite involuntarily. "Where are we going?"

"I thought of the Roumanian Restaurant, unless you'd rather go anywhere else. It's generally quiet there, and we can talk."

A sudden panic seized upon Laura, and caused her to say:

"I haven't talked to anybody about books since you were at Applecourt."

"But it isn't only about books that we're going to talk," said Duke Ayland gently.

He looked at Laura, and Laura looked at the motorbus that was towering against the side of the taxi, and a breathless and significant silence descended upon them.

She heard Ayland catch his breath before he spoke again.

"You know, you don't talk about yourself nearly enough. It would be much better for you if you talked about yourself a great deal more. Of course, to most people one would—or, at least, could—give diametrically opposite advice. But what I feel about you is that you suppress such a tremendous part of yourself, always and every day. Please stop me if you think I'm being too personal—I don't mean to be."

Laura took no advantage of the opportunity thus offered her for checking a conversation that was causing her genuine and serious alarm, considerable excitement, and a variety of disconcerting physical emotions.

Instead, she replied in a slightly choked voice:

"It's true, of course. But don't you see that I can't let myself think about it? One goes on from day to day, and life is perfectly bearable, just as long as you don't stop to think about—about the part that's suppressed. I suppose my life is the same as that of thousands of other women."

"That's what's so wrong," Duke Ayland exclaimed. "It might be all right for those thousands of other women— but not for you. For a woman of your temperament, and your talents, and your sensitiveness, it's all so absolutely wrong."

"Don't tell me that," said Laura in a low tone. "My life is what I've made it, I suppose, and even if what you say is partly true—and perhaps it is—I can't—I don't—and in any case —— But the only possible way is for me not to think about things, far less talk about them."

All the evening, in the intimacy of a corner table, Duke Ayland and Laura Temple talked upon the topics designated by Laura as "things." There were not very many people in the restaurant—but of such as there were, Laura was entirely unconscious.

She knew only that she had come to life again. Duke Ayland looked at her across the small table, and as often as her eyes met his, Laura felt the blood racing through her body.

She ceased to analyse, to examine her motives, and the strange discrepancy between them and her actions, and she ceased entirely and unprecedentedly to view the whole of life in the rather austere light of her own wifehood and motherhood.

Duke Ayland said nothing that directly recalled either.

He only gave Laura to understand, in that language of allusion so wholly alien to Applecourt, and so congenial to its mistress, that she was wonderful, magnetic, lonely, desirable, talented, adorable and the gallant victim of uncongenial surroundings.

Laura found herself seriously believing that this was the

dispassionate, considered judgment of a man with a profound knowledge of women.

She wanted to ask him about his relations with women, and presently she did so, phrasing the question subtly, and not with directness.

"I've been in love, of course," said Duke Ayland quickly. "I've never asked anyone to marry me, and I don't think I've ever loved in earnest. It's almost always been a physical affair."

"The physical is bound to enter into it," pointed out Laura, who had for years suspected herself of being gravely deficient in sex-magnetism, and was secretly afraid of being thought passionless.

"Of course it is. But the ideal is to combine the two—physical attraction, and mental affinity."

"That's the rarest thing in the whole world."

"It is. When you've found it—well, you have the perfect union."

Marmaduke Ayland and Laura Temple exchanged another look—one even longer, graver and more charged with mutual understanding than any of their previous looks. And something that resembled liquid fire rather than anything else raced afresh through Laura's veins.

It was eleven o'clock before they moved from the corner table.

"Let me take you home in a taxi," he urged.

Laura retaining memories sufficiently vivid, even if not recent, of the probable results of proximity and intimately personal conversation combined, replied that she would prefer to walk back to Bloomsbury.

Something in the look that he gave her—rueful, faintly humorous, and wholly tender—touched her sharply.

"Duke, I do like you," she said, warmly and naturally.

"So do I like you—Laura."

He had used her Christian name for the first time. Laura was able to realise clearly and with sincere disgust, how out-of-date was the emotion roused in her by this so simple phenomenon.

But it was of no use. Her brain might function with all the clarity of 1927 but her emotional reactions remained those of 1912.

They walked through comparatively empty streets, and across crowded roads, and then into the large, dark Victorian square that held Christine's flat, at the top of one of its highest houses.

And all the way, they talked.

Laura was enthralled by the mutually incompatible convictions that in one evening she and Duke Ayland had revealed themselves almost wholly to one another, and that a million such evenings would hardly suffice them in which to learn more.

It was impossible not to surmise a similar attitude of mind in Ayland when he asked her urgently:

"How soon can we do this again? Couldn't you dine with me to-morrow?"

"Christine has some people coming after dinner."

"May I come too?"

"I'm sure you may. Ring up and ask her."

"Yes, yes, of course I will," said Ayland feverishly. "But it won't be the same thing as having you to myself.

You're not engaged every evening while you're in town, are you?"

"No, I'm not," said Laura truthfully. "I'd love to do this again. We'll settle a date to-morrow, if you come."

"I shall come all right."

Laura drew out the latch-key that she had assured Christine she would not come home late enough to require.

"Don't come up—no, truly. I'll ring down here, and the door will be open before I get upstairs. Good night."

She gave him her hand.

"I have enjoyed it ——" murmured Laura. And again they looked at one another.

"Good night," said Duke Ayland. "It's been the most wonderful evening."

Laura—dazzled, radiant, insanely exhilarated—went upstairs conscious only of the pressure that his hand had given hers and of words and phrases that he had uttered —reiterating themselves again and again in her memory.

Christine was sitting up in bed writing, when Laura knocked gently at her door and came in glowing.

"You look about eighteen. That is such a becoming frock, Laura."

On this agreeable assurance Laura, shortly afterwards, kissed her sister and went to bed.

It seemed a perversity of Fate that she should be entirely wakeful in her solitude, whereas on some three hundred odd nights of the year, Alfred invariably found her sleeping profoundly soon after eleven o'clock.

"Now, I've got to think this out quite steadily," Laura said to herself as she lay down.

Steadiness of thought, however, eluded her. She sought to induce it, and succeeded only in involving herself with a number of metaphors. She felt that she must steer between the rocks, swim against the current, stand by her guns, stay the course, and even—towards the dawn— follow the gleam.

Interspersed with her hazy conviction of these strenuous obligations, came one ardent recollection after another, of the way in which Duke Ayland had looked at her and the things that he had said. Then she went to sleep at last, and dreamt vividly, waking to an intolerably lively, if scientifically inaccurate, recollection of the less pleasing of Herr Freud's theories as to the nature of dreams.

"Good God!" said Mrs. Temple earnestly, and rose with unwonted vigour.

A letter from the children's nurse at Applecourt awaited her.

Dear Madam,

This is to let you know that the children are as usual. It rained yesterday but otherwise has been fine. Johnnie had one of his fits over his lessons yesterday and Miss Lamb requested for him to go to bed early but he seems all right to-day up to the present.

Both boys are well and send you their love.

Will write again in a day or two.

Yours faithfully,

Nurse.

Nurse, evidently, had dutifully covered two sides of a sheet of notepaper, and felt that no employer could reasonably require more. It mattered nothing to her—it had probably escaped her notice altogether—that her undecorated reference to Johnnie's "fit" over his lesson only served to awaken a never very-deeply dormant anxiety in the breast of his mother.

Laura visualised Johnnie in disgrace, punished, saddened, lonely, perhaps needing her. She knew herself to be absurd. Whatever the details of the "fit" it was now past and over, and Johnnie had very likely been the person in all his little world to be least disturbed by it.

There was also a letter from Alfred.

My dearest Laura,

I was very glad to hear that you arrived safely and found Christine flourishing. I hope she is making you comfortable and that you are having no difficulty in finding a suitable nurse.

It rained yesterday between three and five, but not enough to do any real good in the garden. Very close again to-day and I hope you are not finding London too hot. The boys are quite well, and send their love. Be sure to go to see the A. B. Onslows, or anyone else amusing. I hear Lady Kingsley-Browne is in London.

Your devoted husband,
A.T.

Laura reflected. "Very few men are really good letter-writers. Men do not like writing letters, nor even reading them. It's really an extraordinary proof of how much Alfred does care, that he should write to me at all."

It had long ago become instinctive with her to translate the inarticulateness of Alfred into terms of "caring."

"Are the children all right?" said Christine.

"Quite, thank you. Johnnie seems—but I daresay it wasn't anything. Alfred says that I must go and see the A. B. Onslows. They did ask me, in a way."

"How in a way? Surely they either asked you or they didn't ask you."

"They did ask me," Laura explained, "but I don't suppose they really meant it."

"That's your inferiority complex again, my dear, that Duke is always talking about. Naturally they meant it. Will you ring them up this morning?"

"No. But I might write a line to Mrs. Onslow. It would be interesting to go there."

"Of course it would. I'd love to go myself. Laura, what shall you wear for the party to-night?"

The conversation became animated to the point of feverishness, although exactly the same topic had been discussed between them twice already.

At ten o'clock Duke Ayland rang up and Laura heard Christine's assurances that he might certainly come to the party at nine o'clock that evening.

"Or any time you like, after dinner," said Christine. "What? Yes. Did you want to speak to her? Wait a minute, I'm not sure whether she's in."

Laura shook her head violently.

"No, I'm so sorry. She's just this moment gone out.

Any message? All right, we'll expect you to-night. Good-bye, Duke." Christine replaced the receiver.

She made no comment whatever on Laura's unaccountable shake of the head, and looked neither more nor less detached than she always did.

Laura secretly admired Christine's poise. She looked at her younger sister with impartial admiration.

Christine's short, stiff frock of *broderie anglaise* suited her fair hair, and the warm sunburn of her face and neck and arms. Her square-cut bob with its short fringe, was exactly right. So were her silk stockings and flat-heeled Charleston shoes.

She combined individuality, and conformity to prevailing fashion, in her appearance.

"What are you going to do to-day?"

"My literary agent is taking me out to lunch. If you want to have yours here, we can lay this table before we go out. Only don't touch any of the party food," said Christine earnestly.

"Of course not. I'll lunch at my club. I'm going to spend the morning at the Army and Navy Stores."

"You get much more exciting things at Selfridge's."

"I know," said Laura. "But they wouldn't do, in the same way."

As she put on her hat, she thought:

"I am like a curate's wife, doing a day's shopping in the market town, and going to the principal grocer's shop because she always has gone to it."

At the back of her mind, however, glowed the consciousness that no curate's wife had ever been taken out

to dinner in exactly the way that she had been taken out
to dinner on the preceding evening. The remembrance
of it coloured her day, aided by anticipations of seeing
Duke Ayland again that evening.

"But," thought Laura, with a recrudescence of her noc-
turnal frenzy, "I can't go on like this. I must face the
whole thing steadily, and not just let myself drift. Whatever happens, I've got to play the game, by the children
and Alfred and—and everybody." The feebleness of this
conclusion dismayed her. It was a great relief to find
herself amongst bath-mats, rubber sponges, and nursery
toilette appliances. Laura gave them her whole attention.

Her day, on the whole, was agreeable, although she
went to tea with an aunt who lived in Wilton Crescent,
and the aunt, as is the custom of so many relatives, gave
her to understand that she was making many mistakes
in regard to the upbringing of her children, the solution
of her domestic problems, and the selection of her clothes.

Laura could scarcely believe that she had once lived
with Aunt Isabel, during the war, and had endured her
with equanimity.

"After all—a home of one's own ——" thought Laura.

It was a wordless recognition of what Alfred had done
for her in marrying her.

For Christine's party, Laura put on a flowered chiffon
frock that she had bought that afternoon. It was mauve-
and-blue—a combination of colours that suited her. She
found herself prettier than she had been for some time,
and the conviction lent an additional animation to her
face and voice. She felt radiantly alive.

Christine's friends were people, mostly young, who wrote, or painted, or did secretarial work for celebrated authors.

The conversation, at first, was spasmodic. They drank coffee and smoked.

Duke Ayland arrived, and seemed to know everybody in the room. He sat down beside Laura, and on his other side was a medical student, whom everyone called Losh, who immediately began to talk to him.

Laura, in momentary isolation, studied the faces round her.

The girls, for the most part, looked overworked and over-strained, although three out of the four were pretty.

None of the men were in evening clothes, and the appearance of most of them was dusty. It would be difficult, Laura felt, to visualise any of them in the drawing-room at Applecourt, talking to Alfred about sugar-beet—or even about modern poetry.

Duke Ayland, alone, was different. She knew it, although she could not look at him.

In a sudden pause, the voice of the medical student rang out:

". . . and I said, 'My dear girl, there's nothing to be *ashamed* of! You're abnormal, that's all—simply and naturally, abnormal.'"

In an instant, the conversation had not so much turned upon, as rushed upon, the subject of abnormality. It seemed to be taken for granted that the only abnormalities worth discussing were those concerned with sex, and that these could not be discussed exhaustively enough.

Laura was thoroughly interested, quite determined that she was not shocked, and extraordinarily anxious to prove to Duke Ayland that she, also, could talk about sex with impersonal candour.

Words, hitherto met with by Laura only in the works of Havelock Ellis, hurtled enthusiastically through the room.

The atmosphere of Applecourt, and the nursery, and Alfred sleeping over *The Times*, seemed indeed remote.

Chapter X

Mrs. A. B. Onslow replied to Laura's note by an invitation to lunch.

"Remember that you're a writer yourself, and may be quite as celebrated as he is, one of these days," said Christine firmly.

Laura went to Highgate.

The house stood on the top of a hill, with the famous garden surrounding it. Pergolas and lead statuary met the eye. A fountain splashed. Laura reflected: "It's lovely—but it must look very cold in winter. Probably, however, they're never here to see it in winter."

She followed a rather austere butler through a square hall, a room that looked like a library, and into another, larger room, with French windows opening on to stone pavements and rock plants and a sundial and a plethora of roses.

Thus did the scene present itself to Laura, as she received the greetings of her host and hostess, and acknowledged introductions to people whose names she did not hear.

It was without enthusiasm that she saw detach itself from the background of confused first impressions a familiar maypole figure of slim and silk-clad arrogance, and heard the nonchalant recognition vouchsafed her by Miss Kingsley-Browne.

"Hallo, Bébée," said Laura coldly. "I travelled up with your mother the other day."

"Mummie always goes by train. I don't know how she can bear it."

Laura's host came up to her.

It seemed more natural to see him in a black coat and grey trousers than in tweeds.

Laura perceived in his eye a gleam of that interest which any man, however celebrated, is apt to bestow on a woman of attractive appearance, and to withhold from one who merely has a literary reputation.

With a skill that she felt was habitual, he contrived to let her know with his first sentence that he remembered the circumstances of their previous meeting, and retained a vivid an ineradicable recollection of invaluable contributions made by Laura to the conversation on that occasion.

Against all reason, she felt dimly flattered and encouraged. They talked about books.

Then lunch was announced.

Mrs. Onslow, at the foot of a black oak table with twisted legs, upon which amber-coloured glass stood on cobweb lace, begged Mrs. Temple to take the chair next to A.B.'s.

Bébée was on his other side.

("Her face is painted like a savage," reflected Laura, with her usual injustice, and employing a totally unjustifiable simile for Miss Kingsley-Browne's exquisite rose and vermilion.)

Laura's other neighbour was a small, quiet American gentleman, who asked, with sense and firmness, to be told her name, and in return informed her with a grave smile that his own was Jenkins.

"Montague Edward Jenkins."

"I have a boy called Edward," said Laura.

"Indeed! And is he in the Army?"

"He is in the nursery," said Laura, dashed. Mr. Jenkins looked disconcerted.

"Oh, of course, of course," he agreed. "That would be so. And does he come with you to London?"

"No. I left my two little boys in the country with their father."

In vain did Laura wish that she had not entered upon this familiar domestic vein. She found it impossible to abandon it.

Mr. Jenkins seemed anxious to make amends for his former tactlessness, and made minute enquiries into all the characteristics of Laura's children.

"I'm sure," said Mrs. Onslow with a kind smile, at a lull in the conversation, "that you're talking about the *children*. I hear you're such a wonderful mother."

"It sounds like an earwig," dejectedly replied Mrs. Temple.

She was considerably relieved by the laughter that ensued; and Edward and Johnnie were allowed to give place to a discussion on the latest volume of autobiography.

"You've read it, of course?"

"As a matter of fact, I saw it in manuscript," returned Onslow. "It's a stupendous piece of work. He had to go to Albania for six months to get the last half written."

"Why Albania?" Bébée enquired, voicing Laura's own curiosity.

"To get the right atmosphere. He can't write at all in England. He tried London, and Yorkshire, and Cornwall, and they were all hopeless."

"He came to us for a little while," said Mrs. Onslow, shaking her head. "I thought perhaps that if he had *perfect* quiet, and a room overlooking the river—and his meals, of course, whenever he could manage them—he doesn't touch anything except black coffee and stewed figs—he might be able to work. But he couldn't. He used to come down in the evenings looking ghastly, and say that he'd been in hell."

Laura instinctively glanced round the table, wondering if her own inclination to comment flippantly upon so poor a recognition of hospitality was out of place.

She could not doubt that it was.

Bébée was looking soulfully at her host, but every other face wore an expression of concern for the difficulties that had momentarily overcome genius.

"It's most curious, that inability to produce one's best work except in the right surroundings," said Onslow. "Personally, I can work almost anywhere, provided that I can get absolute quiet."

"He really is wonderful," his wife agreed. "I've known A.B. to sit down at Granada, and write in the hotel drawing-room or on the terrace of our tiny little villa at Capri. Surroundings make no difference to him."

A lady in round, tortoiseshell-rimmed spectacles spoke from the other side of the table.

"I prefer to write, or, rather, dictate, in bed. Many people, I know, find bed quite impossible. But I'm not strong, as you know"—Mrs. Onslow made a sympathetic sound of corroboration—"My wretched back won't let me sit up for long. So I simply stay there until lunch time every day and dictate for two and a half hours, sometimes more."

"Do you really?"

A. B. Onslow's intonation expressed an almost incredulous admiration.

"Do you *really?* That's extraordinary. And you don't find that the ordinary sounds of the house are intolerable?"

"They are, of course," said the spectacled lady quickly. "But I've trained myself to disregard them. It can be done, I assure you. There are double doors to my room, and no one is allowed to come near it until after twelve o'clock; I, of course, am invisible to everyone except my secretary, until I've finished the morning's work."

"To me, it's so marvellous that you should be able to work like that to order," Mr. Jenkins remarked. "Don't you ever feel that you lack inspiration, and must put off work till the evening, say?"

"No. No. I never feel that. In the evenings I need people. The interchange of ideas—conversation—people. They stimulate me."

"Wonderful!" said another lady, whom Laura had thought of as wealthy rather than talented, owing to her clothes and the fabulous size of her pearls. "I need complete silence and isolation. I often think of poor Carlyle, and his sound-proof room. And I've come to the conclusion that there is no such thing. I have a bungalow on the Sussex Downs, you know, to which I retire whenever I write. But even there, I'm sent nearly mad. A dog barks, or there's a fly buzzing in the room. Never *absolute* silence."

"Leave England," advised her neighbour, a fair man with enormous and prominent eyes, and an enormous and prominent Adam's apple, in whom Laura thought that she recognised a reasonably well known poet. "Leave England. It's the only thing to do. I was six months in the Sahara last year."

Laura's head was reeling slightly.

Evidently, she thought, none of these talented people were bound by any domestic ties whatsoever. The lady who was sent nearly mad by the bark of a dog and the buzz of a fly could never have produced a Johnnie or an Edward, and subjected her reason to the far greater strain of existence in their neighbourhood. The tortoise-shell-glassed lady, who was invisible to everyone but her secretary all the morning, either possessed a supernaturally efficient housekeeper, or else no servants at all. The Sahara—Albania—Granada hotels—villas at Capri— Laura contemplated for one hysterical moment, announcing that whenever she wrote a short story, she found it essential to cross the Pacific Ocean in a balloon.

But when A. B. Onslow turned to her with his charming air of finding himself in suspense until her answer came, she only said:

"Devonshire is very delightful, I always find."

"Ah, you get beautiful surroundings there, and quiet and solitude!" he replied in a tone of understanding. "How wise of you, Mrs. Temple! But you don't give your whole time to your work, do you?"

"No," said Laura with some feeling. "Not my *whole* time. No."

"That's wise, too. Every creative effort ought to be followed by a period of absolute rest. The mind ought to lie fallow for a time. You've found that out?"

"Yes," said Laura, and was preparing to say more when she perceived that Miss Kingsley-Browne was listening to her, with something faintly cynical in her meditative gaze.

The course of the discussion, stemmed by Laura's unnaturally curtailed contribution, turned into other channels.

It became incumbent upon Mrs. Temple either to remain silent, or to pretend that she was as much *au fait* with contemporary French poetry as was the circle of the A. B. Onslows. From prudence, rather than from conscientiousness, she chose the former course.

And the moment she became silent, she began to think about Duke Ayland.

It was better than thinking about her own inadequacy as a conversationalist which had always, on similar occasions in the past, obsessed her.

Duke had not found her at all inadequate.

Bébée Kingsley-Browne, so obviously enslaving her rather more than middle-aged host, had not attracted Duke as Laura had done.

For the first time in several years, Laura looked at her expensively-clad and elaborately-coloured young neighbour without resentment.

It seemed to her that Bébée was making a display of the flirtatious terms upon which she found herself with the celebrated A. B. Onslow. She addressed herself exclusively to him, and called him "A. B." with marked assurance, and made many allusions to a past and a present equally shared.

Mrs. Onslow, at whom Laura glanced, seemed to wear a very faintly harassed expression—that of one who sees the approach of a tiresome, but familiar, recurrent phenomenon.

After lunch, she took a seat beside Laura, in the flagged garden, to which coffee was brought by the austere butler.

"Bébée's mother is a neighbour of yours, I think? We met at her house, I know."

"Yes. They're our nearest neighbours."

"The girl is a pretty creature," said Mrs. Onslow, with, however, only a tempered admiration in her eyes.

"Very pretty. We always think her a little bit spoilt, though. I daresay it's natural."

"Oh, most natural. She's attractive, and certainly pretty, though personally—so much make-up—but then, they all do it, nowadays. I often wonder why. I don't think," said Mrs. Onslow artlessly, "that *really* nice men admire it, you know."

It seemed a little bit difficult to agree, and tacitly

brand her host as something less than really nice, or to disagree, and emphasise his already evident infatuation.

Laura murmured.

Without making any definite statement, she found herself obscurely hinting at the existence of the eligible Vulliamy, and at Lady Kingsley-Browne's high hopes that a safe anchorage would shortly receive the volatile barque of her daughter's affections.

Mrs. Onslow brightened, and said that she believed in marriages, especially for girls, and when Mrs. Temple rose to go away, she was cordially invited to come again.

"No one can say that I've been an absolute failure there," was the singular form of congratulation tendered to Laura by her own inner monitor, as she left the house.

She rehearsed to herself the witty and trenchant phrases in which she would presently, for Christine's amusement, delineate her fellow-guests.

(Alfred was very seldom amused by accounts of festivities at which he had not been present—and still less by those at which he had, since in these he found inaccuracy, which he disliked.)

Christine was as appreciative as her sister had expected her to be, and as unmaliciously satirical on the inexhaustible topic of Miss Kingsley-Browne's latest lapses from decent behaviour. Then she remarked:

"You'll hardly believe it, Laura—I always say I have the devil's own luck—but I have got an invitation for the theatre for us both. Do you remember Vulliamy?"

"Bay-Bay's young man? His nose is well out of joint, now."

"I do not personally believe that it was ever *in* joint," replied Christine imperturbably. "I was walking across the Park, and I met Losh—you remember that medical student who was here the other night—the one who's keen about sexual aberrations, you know—so we sat down under the trees, and he began to tell me about some unfortunate creature with Habits, and how perfectly splendid it was to think what a lot of cases there were simply waiting to be investigated, and presumably cured—when he said, 'There's a man I haven't seen for years! May I go and speak to him?'

"Naturally, I thought anybody in whom Losh took an interest would be a freak and a degenerate—and then I saw Vulliamy and remembered him perfectly."

"Let me see, was he good-looking?"

"Quite."

"Did he remember you?"

"He at least had the decency to pretend that he did. And we're going to do a theatre—you and I and Losh and him—he. It's his party, of course. Shall you mind, Laura? Losh is really quite amusing, in his own way."

"I'm glad you said 'in his own way,'" Laura remarked, remembering the conversation of Losh.

She was inwardly amazed at the purely fortuitous fashion in which Christine so frequently collected the invitations of young men.

At Quinnerton there were not, and never had been,

any young men, and Laura supposed—without realising that the supposition was now out of date—that since the war there had been no young men in London either.

"He's going to ring me up, about where we'll dine and what he can get tickets for. Tuesday—that's two nights before you go home. Though if you can stay longer, darling, I should simply love it."

"I can't—possibly," said Laura. "The children. And besides——"

"*I* see," said Christine.

Laura hoped, and believed, that Christine did not see, in any very extensive sense.

The days were passing, she was meeting Duke Ayland daily, and still she failed to achieve that dispassionate facing of the situation that she so frequently promised herself.

Duke Ayland's society had an effect upon Laura that she considered strange and unusual. His companionship stimulated her, she was happy and at her ease with him, prompted to an unreserve the depth of which constituted a spiritual luxury, and fully conscious that her own effect upon him was exactly similar.

His admiration gave her a sense of expansion. He thought her wonderful, and it was so long since anyone had thought such a thing, that any latent possibilities of wonderfulness in Laura had almost died, from sheer inanition. Duke had revived them.

She had been told the story of his life, in which actual events had apparently counted for little, and psychological reactions for much.

In return, she had unrolled for him the history of her days up to the year of her marriage, emphasising the two rather bloodless love affairs that alone could be mustered from the past—for Laura had been a person of romantic imaginings rather than actual contacts.

She wanted to speak of her marriage, she passionately wanted to be honest about it, but she had a sense of obligation to Alfred, and a Victorian conviction that Duke Ayland would think the better of her for conforming to its conventions.

One evening, dining with him alone, she fell.

"You've never told me about your marriage, Laura?" said Duke Ayland.

"No."

"I wish you would."

"It's so difficult," murmured Laura, her heart throbbing violently. "I've often thought of it——"

"Surely you can say anything to me?"

"Yes. It's only—I'm very fond of Alfred," said Laura, taking the plunge, and temporarily unaware that almost all wives begin conversations about almost all husbands in precisely the same way.

"I know you are."

"I don't think we were ever desperately in love with one another, but I know he's devoted to me, in his own way—and so am I to him. And there are the children, of course."

"Yes," said Ayland, with a different intonation. "There are the children, I know."

"I admit that if we hadn't had children, I might have felt rather—lonely, sometimes."

"You see," Ayland said, without looking at her, "you and he haven't really got very much in common, have you?"

"I suppose not."

Laura felt this simple statement of simple fact to be the crossing of the Rubicon.

"I can't possibly discuss Alfred, or my relation to Alfred, with you or anybody," she exclaimed unhappily.

"I think I know exactly how you feel about it. But do you think that so much repression is really good for you or for your writing—and after all, your work does matter."

"But does it?"

"It's your form of self-expression, besides being a thing that's valuable—because it's sincere—in itself. I should say it mattered very much indeed."

"It is really quite a new idea to me," said Laura, without any affectation, "that my writing matters anything at all."

Duke Ayland smiled.

"You're the only writer I've ever met who thought that about their own work. If it was anyone in the world but you, I should say it was a pose."

"It isn't."

"I know that. You're incapable of posing."

Laura experienced the double gratification of receiving a tribute, and of knowing it to be one that she did not always entirely deserve.

"It isn't even as though I'd married when I was very young," she irrelevantly observed.

"In some ways, my dear, you're very young now—and always will be. I don't know what it is, exactly—I can't find the word I want—not exactly 'unawakened'——" He paused, and Laura felt herself blushing. Partly because she detested so *démodée* and unsuitable a manifestation of her feelings, and partly from pure nervousness, she dashed into speech.

She spoke very low and rapidly, and with astonishing vehemence.

In something under seven minuutes, she had released what Duke Ayland called the repressions of more than seven years. She had put into words resentments, regrets, despairs, and madly romantic ideals that she had never yet had the courage to acknowledge even to herself. She had cast loyalty to the winds. She had, indeed, forgotten Alfred as a man altogether. He was one with her immense, her unique, grievance against life itself.

Ever since she had awakened to conscious values, Laura had wanted, and expected to find, such things as happiness, companionship, and perfect love. Her grievance was that she had not found them.

When, in the course of years, it had been borne in upon her that she was not destined to succeed in her quest, she had found it impossible to accept defeat. She had cast from her mind any recollections that could evoke the thought of happiness, companionship and perfect love.

She had immersed herself in domestic problems of which the solution brought her neither joy nor triumph.

Instead of suffering, she had developed an irritable temper, and the habit of waking daily to a mild depression. Instead of happiness, she had experienced a timorous relief on discovering new servants to take the place of departing ones, and a trivial satisfaction when her accounts showed a balance on the credit side.

Spiritually and mentally, she had remained static for years. Emotionally, she had ceased to exist.

Laura, in effect, told Duke Ayland everything of which he had himself made her aware.

There was silence when she had finished. A revulsion of feeling overwhelmed her.

"Whatever he says, I shall hate it," she thought, in despair.

Ayland, without saying anything at all, put his hand gently over her clenched ones, and looked at her.

He did not speak a word, and Laura translated his silence into the response for which any words must have been inadequate. It stood to her for the complete sympathy and understanding that her whole being craved. Rapture and gratitude flooded her soul, and in that illuminated moment, she acknowledged to herself, without shame or dismay, that she was in love.

It neither frightened nor surprised her when Duke Ayland that evening told her that he loved her.

It had become inevitable.

He took her back to Bloomsbury and Christine was out.

"May I come in and wait till she gets in?"

"Yes," said Laura, almost inaudibly.

Christine's small sitting-room was very quiet, high above such traffic as passed through the square, and lit only by the small, scarlet-shaded electric lamp on the writing-table. Laura, intolerably conscious of the emotional tension in the atmosphere, murmured something about another light, and broke the spell.

"Wait," said Duke. "Darling, you know I love you, and I'm going to tell you so."

She stood stock still on the instant, and faced him.

"Laura, Laura—say you love me."

The knowledge that romance had found her, after all, affected Laura so extraordinarily that she nearly fainted. Actually, she swayed slightly towards Ayland, and he caught her in his arms and held her to him.

Blindness and ecstasy descended upon Laura as they kissed.

Chapter XI

"WHAT are we going to do?" said Ayland, next day.

(He had previously been saying other things, far more agreeable to Laura than this inevitable, but difficult, enquiry.)

They were sitting in Kensington Gardens, within sight of the Albert Memorial, and Laura gazed earnestly at it before replying, as though seeking counsel of Albert the Good, so straightforwardly domestic.

At last she said:

"I've been trying to think. It's so difficult to be honest. I used to say that if ever I fell in love with anybody else, the first person I should tell would be Alfred."

"*I* used to say that if ever I fell in love with another man's wife I should either persuade her to come right away with me, or else go right away myself and never see her again."

"The first alternative," said Laura gently, "is obviously impossible."

"The second one is much more so, darling."

To hear such things said in Ayland's deep and agreeable voice, reduced Laura to an exquisite and breathtaking silence.

"Will you come away with me, Laura?"

"I could never do that. The children ——"

A pang went through her as she said the words, and an unbearably vivid image came before her mind's eye

of Johnnie and Edward at home. She could feel Johnnie's silky curls under her hand.

It was inconceivable that she should have got to a
stage where such a suggestion as that of her leaving them
could have been made.

If that suggestion were possible, what else might not
become possible? In a confused and irrational way, she
seemed to see herself deserting the children, less by an
act of free-will than by the working of some mysterious
and oppressive fate, for the existence of which she was
nevertheless responsible.

"You don't understand," said Laura violently, "that
Johnnie—the boys—are the most important things in the
world to me."

"I do understand."

"There could never be any question of my doing anything that would hurt them."

"Perhaps some day—a long time hence, when they're
both grown up ——"

"Perhaps," said Laura gently, avoiding any inward
calculation as to the tale of her own years at that remote
period.

She was, in fact, relieved to have softened the edges
of her impassioned negation. It reassured her, that
Duke should know how inexorable was her decision, and
his knowledge seemed to leave her more freedom. She
wanted to be made love to more than she had ever wanted
anything in her life.

"We could have had the most wonderful marriage if
we'd met years ago," she murmured.

Ayland's response was as ardent, as detailed, as she had wanted it to be.

Whatever happened, or did not happen, Laura's dreams had for a little while come true, and she knew it.

Ayland told her all those things about herself that she had most wished to believe, but had been forced to doubt since for so many years no one had appeared to perceive them. Under the magic of his words she could feel herself actually verifying them.

He found her beautiful, and courageous, and lovable and gifted—and she became so.

"I have never been alive before," thought Laura, her mouth trembling.

They talked for hours.

Nothing that they said was new, except to themselves.

At last Ayland returned to that aspect of the case which Laura, even in her own thoughts, preferred to shelve.

"You know what you said, just now, about telling your husband. You don't still feel that's necessary, do you?"

"I can't deceive him."

In the silence that followed, Duke's carefully unspoken retort seemed to become almost audible.

"You may say, what else am I doing now?—and you would be right. But I don't know what I shall do when I see Alfred again. I'm going home in two days now."

"But you'll come up again?"

"I don't know."

"Laura, darling! Don't you want to see me again?"

"I want to more than anything else in the world. Couldn't you come down to Quinnerton again?"

"It's very difficult for me to meet your husband," said Ayland slowly.

"He didn't dislike you, you know," Laura said, experiencing a strange moment of pride that this should have been so.

"I didn't dislike him, either. But of course he doesn't understand you—he isn't fit to be your husband. He has never known how to make you happy."

"He's very fond of me."

"That makes it worse, because, being what you are, it will prevent your ever having the courage to break away."

Laura shook her head.

"The children ——"

They were back at the children again.

As though knowing that, against that bulwark of Laura's virtue, there could be no assault that would avail anything, Ayland changed the subject. They talked, inexhaustibly, about themselves.

Laura, obliged at last to go back to the flat in Bloomsbury, felt that Christine must inevitably ask her what had happened. It was impossible, that the whole of life should have become transformed for her, and that she should show no sign of it.

But Christine, if she did see what appeared to her sister to be so unmistakable, made no comment.

She met Laura at the door and said, low and rapidly, in the domestic French employed by everybody and

supposed to be entirely incomprehensible to everybody
else:

"*Il y a une femme qui attend, dedans. Envoyée par
le Registry Office. Une nurse. Assez gentille.*"

"Oh," said Laura, startled.

It was very difficult, to be thus suddenly thrust back
into the atmosphere, so familiar and yet now so remote,
of nursery necessities.

"I'll go to my room. You'll see her in the sitting-
room, won't you?"

"Very well."

Laura instinctively took the little mirror out of her
handbag, powdered her nose, felt a moment's astonished
wonder at the shining of her eyes, and went in to interview the nurse.

She seemed much nicer than any other nurse that
Laura had interviewed.

Gentle and pleasant, with a ready smile.

The violent anxiety that, on previous similar occasions, had led Mrs. Temple to urge upon the applicant's
notice every possible deterrent to the situation, was ab-
sent. Indeed, a kind of spiritual haze seemed to have
interposed itself between Laura and reality.

She asked questions, she smiled, as though in a dream.
Unprecedently, she heard herself saying: "So long as
the little boys are kept well and happy, I don't really
mind . . . I like them to be happy."

Happiness, she felt as never before, was the only thing
that mattered.

It ought to be attainable by everyone.

The little books about Education, about Diet, and about Sex-Enlightenment of Children by their Mothers had faded away—insignificant ghosts of the past—she did not seek to extract the nurse's views on these so important points.

She said:

"Have you satisfactory references?"

"I have them here, madam."

Laura, still in a dream, read a letter on stamped blue paper, another one on expensive white with red lettering.

They seemed to be nice, enthusiastic letters.

Charlotte Emery was evidently a treasure.

She looked a treasure. Her kind, middle-aged face gazed at Laura as an older woman's face does sometimes gaze at a younger one's—with a touch of wistfulness, of un-envious admiration.

It was a very long while since Laura had met that look —but she recognised it unerringly. It was her own rejuvenation, her secret rapture, that had drawn it forth.

She engaged Charlotte Emery to come to Applecourt in a week's time.

The anxious quest of so many days had been brought to a successful conclusion in half an hour.

"Well?" said Christine, when the nurse had gone.

"I've engaged her. I like her very much."

"How splendid! You think she'll be able to manage Johnnie?"

"Oh yes, I think so."

Christine looked rather surprised at this unprecedented optimism.

"I never really think Johnnie is as difficult as you make out, you know. Of course, he's terribly precocious, but he can be a perfect darling when he likes, and any nurse is sure to get fond of him."

"They get fond of him more easily than he does of them. Johnnie has been so very much with me."

"How excited the boys will be to get you home again!" said Christine.

Laura said with sudden passion: "Not half so excited as I shall be," and went to her room. She wrote a letter to Alfred, telling him the things that she thought would interest him—there were not many of them—briefly announcing the satisfactory acquisition of Charlotte Emery, and giving the time of her own arrival at Quinnerton.

In three days more she would be home again. She would wake up in the morning without the thrill of knowing that the day was to bring a meeting with Ayland.

But she felt that never again would her first waking thought be of the servants, the stores, the ordering of a pudding. Her horizon could never again, surely, be bounded by such considerations day after day.

Her mood of exaltation dropping abruptly, Laura wondered whether perhaps instead she would open her eyes to problems less material, indeed, but also infinitely more painful. Would it be possible to see Alfred beside her and not to ask herself what justification she had for deceiving him?

"But then," reflected Laura, "if it comes to that, what

justification have I for enlightening him?   As Duke says, it would only make him unhappy or angry, or both."

She could not imagine how Alfred would receive the information that his wife loved another man.   She had never seen Alfred confronted with any emotional situation.   Emotional situations were things that Alfred did not attract.   They died still-born in his very presence.

It was inconceivable that Alfred should, like a husband in an old-fashioned novel, wish to shoot Duke Ayland, or even to horsewhip him.   It was equally inconceivable that he should, like a husband in a modern play, agree to discuss the whole problem dispassionately with his wife and the man who was in love with her.

What, Laura wondered, were the remaining alternatives?

She could find only two.

Either she must continue to see Duke Ayland and tacitly deceive her husband, or she must give up seeing Duke Ayland altogether.

Confronted by these two courses, each one of which appeared to her to be entirely incompatible with her own self-respect or peace of mind, Laura instinctively floundered her way into a morass of compromise.

She represented to herself that it might be possible for her to see Duke as often as they could arrange to meet, but that he should not make love to her.

Friendship.

Laura, like Mr. Twemlow, might be represented as saying to herself all that evening: *"Hold on to friendship."*

She was obliged to say it during the night as well, for she slept badly.

It is impossible to ignore the fact that Laura, at this juncture, was profoundly agitated by the unescapable consideration so deftly implied in a more reticent age, by the euphemistic reference: "The Woman Who Did."

Never, since she had outgrown the sentimental and supremely ignorant eroticism of early adolescence, had Laura identified herself with the type of Woman who Did. Marriage, indeed, had served to inculcate in her the chastity—than which there is none more rigid—of a romantic woman, married to a man with whom she had never been in love.

Duke Ayland had revolutionised many things.

Laura, refusing absolutely to be anything but truly modern, had the greatest difficulty in persuading herself that any decision she might come to on the subject, must be based upon the individual merits of the case alone.

Tradition, and the force of early upbringing—so much more powerful, always, at night than in the day-time—thronged in upon her. Quotations, every one of them in favour of renunciation, continued to distress her.

"The only thing," said Laura to herself, sternly, "the only thing is, what is least likely to hurt the children, and Alfred, and Duke. And myself."

But it still continued impossible to find any formula that should combine an absence of hurt for the children, Alfred, Duke and Laura.

"And in any case," said Laura wildly, " 'thou shalt not commit ——' "

She had been trying not to remember it, to think that it had no power over her.

But it had.

She got up, washed her face in cold water, fetched pen and paper, and wrote an immensely long and exhaustive letter to Duke Ayland, in which, like the compiler of the Athanasian Creed, she sought to define the indefinable.

The performance left her far from satisfied.

She put the letter into an envelope, sealed it, and placed it underneath her pillow—as a measure of precaution.

More wholly wakeful than ever in her life before, Laura told herself excitedly that she *must* get some sleep.

Lying down in the not very profound obscurity of the early summer morning, she closed her eyes.

Instantly, the letter, assuming gigantic proportions, began to torment her, suggesting to her mind terrible possibilities.

Letters read aloud in the divorce court—indiscreet letters in blackmail cases—letters, even, figuring sensationally in certain well known murder trials.

Laura's imagination, leaping every intermediate stage, placed her momentarily upon the scaffold. She jerked herself miserably back into the realms of comparative common sense.

Her letter, after all, was a work of supererogation.

She was going to see Duke, and she could urge her

point of view upon him—especially if she were only able to formulate it clearly in her own mind first. She would not be unfaithful to Alfred.

She put her children before every other consideration in the world. She could never leave them.

But she could not relinquish Duke.

A more than distasteful analogy rushed unbidden to Laura's memory.

"Hunt with the hounds and run with the hare," she muttered distractedly.

And, after that, she slept.

In the light of morning things—as is their custom—looked less desperate.

She was able to consider the value of her letter dispassionately and to apply a lighted match to it without compunction.

"And I shall see him to-day," thought Laura, and felt that little else mattered.

She was to see Duke in the evening at a small literary and artistic soirée, for which he had given her and Christine tickets.

"A totally insignificant kind of club," he had apologetically explained to her, "to which I've belonged ever since it started, over a mews near Southampton Row. It's quite prosperous, nowadays, and meets at quite expensive restaurants. Consequently I go there very seldom. Sometimes they get A. B. Onslow there."

Christine, on the morning following Laura's *nuit blanche,* reminded her of this festivity.

"Are you going to do anything special to-day? You'll

be going home, worse luck, in such a short time," Christine superfluously added.

"I know. This afternoon I'm afraid there's nothing for it but to go and see old cousin Louisa Temple at Queen's Park. I've been meaning to do it ever since I got here, and putting it off—and if I don't do it now, I never shall."

"And must you?"

"Yes."

A pilgrimage to Queen's Park was indeed something that no member of the Temple family, even though only a member of it by marriage, could omit. Almost all families are subjected to similar oppressions.

Cousin Louisa, strangely, lived at Queen's Park from choice, with a niece who would have been an old lady herself, if cousin Louisa had not been so much older. The extravagant senility of Cousin Louisa consigned her niece to a dim, perpetual middle-age. She was called by almost everybody Poor Selina, and sometimes, by those who knew her less well, Poor Miss Thingamy.

Laura had been aware ever since she married, that an expedition to see Cousin Louisa at Queen's Park was a moral obligation attached to every stay in London. It might be—and almost always was—inconvenient, but it could not be shirked. A tradition had been established, and only death could break it. She must, of her own free will, deliberately immerse herself in the atmosphere of pills, and Halma, and little grey shawls, diffused by cousin Louisa and Poor Selina.

Before she started, Duke Ayland rang her up on the telephone.

He wanted to take her out to lunch.

"But we shall meet this evening. You're coming to fetch us, aren't you?" said Laura, entirely for the sake of hearing his reply. When he had protested, she suggested going out to tea with him instead, for she knew from experience that a visit to old Cousin Louisa could not possibly take place within the confines of a morning.

"I ought to see a man about some songs, this afternoon," she heard Ayland's voice.

"Oh, then, please ——"

"But that'll be all right. I'll settle him somehow. Can I call for you anywhere?"

"But, Duke, the man sounds important. You'd better see him."

"He's not half as important as having you to myself for a little while. *Of course* I shall chuck him. What time, Laura?"

It thrilled her exquisitely, that he should think it worth while to cancel his appointment for the sake of being with her. Amongst her friends and acquaintances, she knew of none who would not resign cheerfully, and as a matter of course, any personal engagement that should clash with a business one.

After arranging a rendezvous with Duke, it was easy to undertake the Queen's Park expedition, although Laura disliked the atmosphere of the Underground and almost always lost herself in the Tube at Oxford Circus.

She had made up her mind to tell Duke Ayland that

he must not make love to her, that they would remain friends, and that she would see him whenever she possibly could, and write to him very often. This course would combine loyalty to Alfred with fairness to themselves, and to the claims of creative art, that surely demanded some emotional outlet for its depositaries.

Only too well aware that if she thought any more about this resolution, she would gradually be overwhelmed by its disadvantages and general impracticality, Laura in the train read the *Daily Mirror* from end to end, and did its cross-word puzzle.

Her visit to Queen's Park was exactly like all her visits to Queen's Park. Cousin Louisa was as old, as wonderful—from the point of view of what are called faculties —and as inquisitive as Laura had always known her, and Poor Selina as effusive, inconsequent, and tiresomely unselfish. Lunch, as usual, was an affair of pale boiled mutton and glutinous white sauce, unsuited to a hot summer's day, pink corn-flour mould, and tapioca pudding, followed by cups of strong tea. Laura, also as usual, inwardly criticised Poor Selina's housekeeping, and felt ashamed of herself for doing so.

The conversation concerned itself with relations whom Laura never saw, and whom Cousin Louisa and Poor Selina seldom saw, but in whose doings they nevertheless kept up a pathetic interest.

"I had a post-card from Annie last month."

"We hear that Bob Temple's second boy—the one who had rickets—is being put on to this new food—this milk extract."

"Barbara—(I don't think you know her, Laura, she's Alfred's third cousin, lives in Yorkshire)—she has such trouble with her servants. I hear she's going to try having all men."

Laura replied with suitable ejaculations, and as many comments as she could think of, and produced innocuous pieces of information about life at Applecourt in order that they, in their turn, might be retailed to subsequent uninterested visitors. Remorse at her own boredom, and relief at having accomplished her pious excursion, lent a spurious fervour to her farewells, and Laura plunged gladly back into the Tube, that seemed airy, light and gay by comparison with old Cousin Louisa's stuffy and congested atmosphere.

"And if Alfred hadn't married me," Laura, according to her wont, relentlessly informed herself, "Aunt Isabel and I might have come to that." But she did not say it with quite the old amount of conviction.

Since Duke Ayland had found her beautiful and desirable, Laura no longer really doubted that she could be both of these things, at least in flashes. She went and had her hair waved, in preparation for the literary soirée, and permitted herself to arrive with absolute punctuality at the tea-shop indicated by Ayland. (Another one of her mother's maxims had been to the effect that a Man should always be Kept Waiting a Little, but Laura was belatedly reaching the conclusion—long since urged upon her by Christine—that the maxims of parents are usually quite inapplicable to the adult existence of their children.)

Duke had so many things to say to Laura, and she so

much liked hearing them, that it was only with difficulty that she was able to issue her ultimatum.

Ayland did not appear to take it very seriously.

"How different things look in the daytime," thought Laura, unable to recapture any of the earnest frenzy that had possessed her thoughts throughout the night. She also, like Duke, felt that nothing mattered very much beyond the present.

In this dazed and happy frame of mind, that in itself had a mysteriously becoming effect upon her personal appearance, Laura went with Christine to the party that evening.

A. B. Onslow was there, as guest of honour, and almost as she recognised him, Laura heard Christine's disgusted comment:

"Will you *look* at Bay-bay! He isn't allowed to move an inch away from her. I've a good mind to tell her that a girl of her age must be hard up for an admirer, if she can't annex anybody but a man who already belongs to another woman."

"He's the most celebrated person here. That's why." Mrs. Temple curtly and elliptically explained her young neighbour's indecent display of her preferences. She was herself gratified, later on, when Onslow came up and talked to her, and as far as possible she ignored Miss Kingsley-Browne, still hovering at the elbow of the distinguished object of her favours.

With a self-confidence that was in gratifying contrast to her habitual attitude towards society, Laura was able to exchange literary opinions with Onslow.

"Mummie is here, somewhere about," said the insufferable Bébée, interrupting them. "She's been looking for you, Mrs. Temple."

"How nice of her! I must—but do tell me about the new Published Letters. I've always thought——"

"There she is!"

Laura continued to look at A. B. Onslow and A. B. Onslow to look at her, as though exchanging a mutual hope that by strenuously ignoring Bébée's officiousness, they might render it innocuous.

"There are only two letters, but they throw a wonderful light on the whole question. You're interested in it on the psychological, as well as the literary side, I take it?"

"Yes, I am. In fact, principally on the psychological side, I think."

Laura, without looking round, was aware that Bébée had successfully hypnotized her parent to her side.

"Mummie, here's Mrs. Temple. I know you and she are dying to talk gardening."

Lady Kingsley-Browne's quiescent rejoinder was such as to leave Onslow little alternative. He bestowed a valedictory smile upon Laura, and moved away beside his insolently self-satisfied disciple.

"Even the *cleverest* men seem to go down like ninepins before Bébée," murmured Lady Kingsley-Browne, with for once more anxiety than pride in her expression.

Laura thought of several excellent rejoinders, but was unable to make any of them.

"Well," said her neighbour, "it's very delightful to

meet you here. Somehow I never expected to. This"—
she waved a be-diamonded hand vaguely—"is all so unlike Applecourt, and so on, isn't it? I never somehow
quite realised this side of you before. You know, dear,
I always associate you—we all do, in fact—with the country and those darling children, and all the dear things
one enjoys in the garden so much."

Chapter XII

"LADY KINGSLEY-BROWNE wants to come and see me," announced Laura in a high key of astonishment two days after the soirée.

"Can't she wait until you're home again? Her back-door is next to yours."

"Apparently she can't. Look at this!"

Laura handed a pale coffee-coloured sheet with a heading in white lettering to her sister.

The Chesterfield Club,
W.1.

My Dear Laura,

Should I find you at home, if I called at your sister's flat this afternoon? I hope you and she will both forgive me for suggesting such a thing, but there is no quiet here, and I feel I must speak to you. If you would be kind enough to telephone a message, saying what time you are free, I can make any time convenient.

Yours,
Gertrude Kingsley-Browne.

A telephone number followed.

"After her iniquitous behaviour at that party, too! Perhaps she wants to apologise," said Christine. "What time shall you say?"

"Five o'clock—or six, then we needn't bother about tea. Six."

"All right. I shall be here, but if it sounds in the least private, I'll go out."

"It can't be private," Laura declared. "We aren't on those terms at all."

But the first sight of their visitor, at six o'clock, caused Christine and Laura to exchange a swift glance of horrified incredulity.

Lady Kingsley-Browne's habitual air of prosperity had given way to one of flushed agitation, her hat was one-sided, and her manner distracted.

"Forgive me for this—for coming like this. I've been so upset—and possibly you might help me—we've always been such good friends."

"I'll go," said Christine.

"Don't go, please don't go. I don't in the least mind your hearing—or, rather, I mind most dreadfully, but nothing can make any difference, and you yourself are a modern girl."

"Bay-bay!" Christine mouthed silently at her sister, who nodded in agreement.

Lady Kingsley-Browne sat in Christine's largest armchair and began to cry.

"Oh, dear, I'm so sorry. What is it?" Laura asked.

"You will find it perfectly impossible to believe."

"Yes?"

"I do myself," said Lady Kingsley-Browne.

"What has happened?"

"I hardly know how to tell you. I can hardly imagine what you'll say."

Laura gazed at her afflicted neighbour in a respectful silence.

Christine said firmly:

"You must tell us what it is. We can't say anything till we know, can we? But we'll do anything we can to help, whatever it is."

"You can't! Nobody, I am afraid, can do anything. If you had told me, a year ago, that I should find myself in the state I'm in to-day, I simply shouldn't have believed you. I simply should *not* have believed you."

"I daresay I shouldn't have believed myself," Laura declared sympathetically. "I can't imagine what can have happened. Is it about Bébée?"

"Indeed it is! Have you heard anything?"

"Not a word."

"But it can only be a question of time before you do," said Lady Kingsley-Browne, again in tears.

"Is she going to have a baby?" Christine suggested— giving Laura a slight shock.

But the distraught parent of Miss Kingsley-Browne appeared to have passed beyond shocks. "No, she is not going to have a baby, as far as I know. But nothing could surprise me now—nothing in the world. Could you yourselves ever have imagined that any girl could behave so insanely?"

"You haven't yet told us how she has behaved."

"It seems so dreadful, put into words. Bébée—you know how fastidious she has always been, and what a choice of men she had always had at her feet—Bébée has fallen in love with a married man."

"Is that all?" said Christine. "But heaps of girls do that nowadays. Nobody thinks anything of it, truly."

"Is it A. B. Onslow?" Laura asked.

"Of course it is. Why, I can't think. Of course I know he must be very clever, and Bébée has always been very clever too, but when she could have had a choice of *young* men ——"

"What has happened to Mr. Vulliamy?"

"What *could* have happened, except that he has gone away? He never even proposed. She let him see quite plainly that she cared for nobody but Onslow. She— I suppose one ought to admire her for it—but she seems to have no shame about it at all."

"I don't think one ought to admire her for it in the least," cried Christine. "It's preposterous of her! What about poor Mrs. Onslow, after all?"

"What indeed! Of course, being married to a writer, she may be used—but on the other hand, he's not young now."

"It must be very much his fault," Laura suggested, sacrificing both her fellow-writer and her own convictions out of pure compassion.

"The terrible thing is that it isn't. At least, not now it isn't, though I don't say he wasn't attracted by her in the beginning. Men are always attracted by Bébée instantly," said poor Lady Kingsley-Browne, with a reviving flash of her slaughtered pride.

"I know they are," Laura could afford to say.

"It's always been she who was the indifferent one. There have been times, I assure you, when I've begged her to be a little bit kinder to people, simply for fear of their blowing their brains out, or something like that. One never knows, does one?"

"Never," said Laura gravely, desirous only of calming the unhappy matron looking up at her with drowned eyes.

Christine was less single-minded.

"But about A. B. Onslow? Isn't he—doesn't he—you aren't afraid of his blowing his brains out?"

"Indeed no. He is much more likely to blow Bébée's brains out, from what I hear."

"What a good thing! I don't mean that, exactly, but surely, if he is being sensible, and not losing his head, it will put an end to the whole thing."

"You would think so, wouldn't you? Any rational person would think so. But Bébée, poor, poor darling—that I should live to say such a thing—is not rational. She says—she says that whether he knows it or not, they are necessary to one another, and—and that nothing will induce her to leave him until—she has made him realise it."

A scandalised silence descended upon the room at this outrageous quotation, delivered amidst floods of tears, by the unhappy parent of its originator.

"Leave him?" said Christine at last in low, aghast tones. "Do you mean, then, that she has—has gone to him?"

"She went to stay there a week ago. I—I don't think

they invited her, exactly. Certainly Mrs. Onslow didn't. But she went. And now they can't get her to go away again."

"I saw her there the other day, of course," Laura exclaimed. "I didn't know she was actually staying, in the house—but of course I saw her there."

"How—how did they strike you?"

"I didn't notice anything very unusual. Bébée was rather—rather inclined to sit in his pocket perhaps."

"Yes, yes—I know she was."

"She was very—very—in quite good spirits, wasn't she?" Laura hesitated, as the recollection of Miss Kingsley-Browne's unholy bloom and intemperate exhibition of her conquest rushed upon her afresh. "And he was more or less as usual—the fact is, I know him so little. Of course, one saw that they were on—on friendly terms, but, as you say, men are very apt to admire her."

"There is hardly an eligible man in London that she couldn't have had if she'd wanted him," Lady Kingsley-Browne exclaimed, in impassioned exaggeration. "And to think that she should lose her head about a man who is really old enough to be her grandfather, and who doesn't even encourage her!"

"I have never heard anything so dreadful in all my life," Christine remarked, with entire conviction. "Do you actually mean that she has foisted herself upon that unfortunate man—to say nothing of his wife—and that nothing they can do or say can rid them of her?"

The visitor winced.

"You are putting it rather crudely, perhaps," she said

unhappily, "but—yes—in effect, that is exactly what she is doing."

"She must be mad!"

"That is exactly what I said myself, when Mrs. Onslow —in despair, poor thing—rang me up on the telephone, to ask what they were to do."

"What they were to do!" ejaculated Laura in her turn. "What more can they do, beyond asking her to leave the house—and that you say she won't do. Can they—can he—possibly have made it clear to her that they had *rather* she went?"

"Perfectly clear, I gather," said Lady Kingsley-Browne in a low and most unhappy voice. "She insisted upon quoting to me exactly what she had said to Bébée—I did not want to hear in the very least, but she insisted on telling me—and I assure you that if she said what she told me she said, nobody in the world could have failed to understand what she meant."

"And Bébée wouldn't go?"

"She said that she could perfectly understand Mrs. Onslow's resentment, but that a—an admiration such as hers transcends anything like that, and that A. B. owes it to his work to—to—Her actual expression was, to take all that she has to give him."

"Good God!" said Christine.

There was another silence, in which more, and worse, implications seemed to multiply themselves every moment.

"I am more sorry than I can say, and so is Christine," said Laura at last. "Is there anything at all that we can do?"

"Yes—yes, I think there is. Of course, you must wonder why I've told you at all. It isn't a story that any mother would tell for her own amusement, is it? But I can't help thinking that you might possibly have some influence over my poor darling if only you would try."

Laura, in spite of herself, made a gesture of horrified protest at the suggestion.

"Don't, don't say you won't. You are my only hope, just now. You see, you're literary yourself, and so she can't say that you don't understand about that side of things, as she does to me, and A. B. seems to have told her that he liked you, and thought you so very clever. I know you go and see them, and I thought perhaps you'd be so very, very good as to see Bébée, and perhaps talk to her, and bring her to reason. Please, please don't refuse. I am in such despair."

It was evident that she was, and not indeed without ample cause, Laura reflected.

"But what will the Onslows think?" she temporised feebly.

"They would go down upon their knees to anyone who would get her out of the house," said the mother of Miss Kingsley-Browne, with the reckless outspokenness of sheer despair.

"I don't see why she should pay any attention to me."

"She might. Girls will almost always listen to anyone who isn't a relation. And she knows you're clever, and that you write, and yet—if I may say so—you are so—so—so *respectable*. Married, and in the county, and all that sort of thing. Oh, I am being so stupid—but if you only knew how much I've cried, you'd understand."

"I do understand. I'm so dreadfully sorry. I'll try, if you like."

"I can't ever thank you enough. No, don't come with me, please. I'd rather go down alone. I can pick up a taxi. I'm very grateful to you both."

She tottered from the room leaving Christine and Laura looking at one another.

At last Christine said in a hushed voice:

"How utterly and absolutely incredible!"

"I don't know. I've always felt that I could believe anything of Bay-bay."

"Oh, good gracious, yes, so have I. I meant, how extraordinary to see poor Lady Kingsley-Browne in such a state. Reduced to asking us, of all people, for help. Poor, poor wretch! Did you see how she positively fled, after you'd said yes, before you had time to change your mind?"

"She showed her sense," said Laura gloomily, "for if I'd had even one minute more in which to think, I should have said that nothing would induce me to take on such a job. What on earth am I to do?"

"You can only try, and if you do fail, there's an end of it. But I can't believe that even Bay-bay, if it's put to her in black and white, will insist upon staying on with people who would go down upon their knees before anybody who would rid them of her, as her mother so explicitly put it."

"I suppose that I had better go to-morrow morning."

"Don't let it spoil the theatre party for you to-night," Christine begged. "If you can't get it out of your mind, why don't you talk to Losh about it? He adores anything to do with abnormality—and you needn't say who the girl is."

"I might, perhaps. He's the one who told us about that—that unfortunate German, who had a complex about his grandmother, isn't he?"

"Yes. Losh always tells one about cases of that sort. You didn't mind, did you?"

"No," said Laura doubtfully. "Oh, no. Not at all. Why should I? Everybody talks about everything now. Not so much in the country, though. In fact, hardly at all in the country. I don't know what people will say about Bébée, at Quinnerton."

"Bébée, of course, is being perfectly preposterous. But apart from her, do you think people in the country are still as moral as they used to be? For instance—" Christine looked away from her sister—"does anyone who is married already, ever have any sort of an affair, or would the skies fall?"

"I think," replied Laura, with some deliberation, "that the skies would probably fall."

It was a positive relief to discuss with Christine, however obliquely, the question that had been in the atmosphere between them for days now.

"Of course, it might be worth while to let them fall— but one would have to be quite certain that it *was*," Christine said.

"Children and things."

"Oh yes."

"And exactly how much one could count upon the other person. It might so easily be a case of out of the frying-pan into the fire."

"Do you mean divorce? That kind of thing?"

"Yes, that kind of thing. I mean to say, one would prefer it to be one thing or the other, I suppose. Not just meeting at a pub half-way between London and Quinnerton and saying it was the dentist, or any hole-and-corner business of that kind."

Laura shuddered in entirely genuine disgust.

"What an extraordinarily offensive way of wording it!"

"Well, that's what it would boil down to," said Christine doggedly. "The only alternative that I can see, would be running away altogether, or else chucking the whole thing for good and all."

"Which would you do?"

"Chuck it," said Christine without hesitation. "If I did leave one man, it wouldn't be in order to go to another man."

"But if you loved him?"

"I should be more likely to stay loving him, if we weren't living together. Truly, Laura, I'm not being cheaply cynical. If one has married the wrong person, more or less—and after all, almost anyone feels like the wrong person after one's lived with them for a number of years, I imagine—surely it's better to go on, than to begin all over again with somebody else. It's such waste of all the adjusting that one has learnt to do. Because

the awful thing is, that one love affair is very like another. It gets to a certain pitch, and then—practically
always—it declines. And it seems to me it would decline
even faster than usual, if the woman knew all the time
that she'd given up, say, her children for the sake of the
man."

A revulsion of feeling came over Laura.

"When you talk about giving up children, it makes one
realise how utterly impossible and out of the question it
would ever be, to do anything of the sort."

"Of course."

"I'm not speaking personally, but simply on general
principles."

"Yes, I know."

"That sort of thing seems to be in the air, rather. What
with Bébée and A. B., and one thing and another."

At one thing and another, they left it.

But Laura knew that her younger sister, to whom she
had never denied both shrewdness and candour, and to
whom she was—more reluctantly—obliged to concede an
experience of men wider than her own, had pronounced
her verdict upon Laura's problem of the emotions.

Christine's theatre-party was a success, as her parties
almost always were, whether she was the hostess, or the
guest.

However improbable it might have seemed in advance
that a quartette composed of Mr. Jeremy Vulliamy,
Laura and her sister, and the psychopathic Losh, should
derive intense and lively satisfaction from one another's
society, it came to pass that they did so.

The dinner was delightful, the play was amusing, and before the end of it Vulliamy had begged them all to come on somewhere and have supper and dance.

"Impossible for me, worse luck," said the medical student. "I've got an abdominal at nine o'clock to-morrow. A chap with a ——"

"That will do, Losh," said Christine. "Laura, we could, couldn't we?"

"I think I'll go home, darling, if you don't mind. Thank you very much, Mr. Vulliamy, but ——"

"All right," Christine interposed promptly. "I'll go with you and we'll make a night of it. You won't sit up, will you, Laura?"

Laura's lips assented, while Laura's incurably Victorian mind recalled how she and Christine had learned, at their mother's knee, that nothing was more fatal than for any girl to let any man perceive that she liked being taken out by him.

Vulliamy, however—and Laura now recalled that Lady Kingsley-Browne—in days other, and for herself, happier—had once spoken of him as the future richest commoner in England—Vulliamy lost none of his evident enthusiasm for Christine and her society.

Losh took Laura home.

He was an unkempt, untidy-haired creature, with a ceaseless flow of technical conversation, but he was likeable, and possessed a sense of humour.

His first observation was of that outspoken character to which Laura was by now becoming entirely accustomed.

"Christine's got off with Vulliamy all right. He couldn't take his eyes off her. Well, I'm not surprised."

"She is attractive, isn't she?" Laura said, and immediately felt she was being like Lady Kingsley-Browne.

"She's a darling, of course. I've been in love with her for years—with interludes, naturally. But I always knew she'd end by marrying a fellow with money. Vulliamy has money, tons of money. And will have more."

"I believe so."

"Well, he's a good sort. I hope they'll be happy."

"But don't you think you're going rather fast?"

"No. No, I don't think so. I don't know Vulliamy at all well—in fact I hadn't seen him since we were at school together, I don't believe, till just the other day—but I can tell he's in earnest. You see, he was in love with a girl who let him down rather badly, and he'd got all keyed up about her, and then Christine came along, and got him on the rebound. Reaction. It's a well known psychological phenomenon. The other girl, from what I can gather, is a nymphomaniac. Neither more nor less."

"I see," said Laura hastily.

"I don't know whether you understand ——"

"Oh, perfectly."

"So it's quite natural that he should be attracted by Christine, who's an absolutely opposite type. So normal, sexually, as to be almost abnormal, in these days."

"I think this is us," said Laura, as the taxi stopped.

"Good night," said Losh. "I say, don't mind my saying so, please, and don't think me interfering—I don't mean to be—but I wish you'd read some Jung."

"But I have."

"Then read more. Talk about what you read. You know, you're afraid of your biological fate—so many women are—and the only way to get the libido into the right channel is to take out the whole question of Sex and look at it. You're not vexed with me?"

"No," said Laura forbearingly. "I'm not vexed with you. But if you had ever stayed at Quinnerton, which is where I live, you would understand why I don't take out the whole question of Sex and look at it. Good-night. Thank you for bringing me back."

"Good-night. The best thing for you to do, probably, would be to leave Quinnerton."

"I can't. I don't want to, either. Good-night."

"Good-night. Inhibitions—especially sexual ones—can be ——"

"Good-night," said Laura for the last time, and went upstairs.

Greatly perturbed, she went straight to the looking glass.

Why should everybody, even casual young men, assume that she needed advice, that she was in a fog of uncertainty? Did they also know what it was about?

Her eyes stared back at her from the mirror, large and full of alarm, and she saw that what she had been aware of all the evening as a slight pallor was in reality a sickly, greenish-grey shadow, round her mouth and under her eyes.

Laura, like Mr. Vulliamy, was suffering from reaction.

It was almost a relief to her that, on the following morning at least, her chief preoccupation should be, not with Duke Ayland, but with her own exceedingly distasteful embassy to Highgate.

"I should go early and get it over," advised Christine. "I'm frightfully sorry for you."

"Will you come with me?"

"How can I? I've never even met the Onslows. I can't walk in on perfect strangers and say that I've come to help my sister get rid of their incubus for them."

"I don't know that I shall get rid of her. Probably I shan't. I shall ask to see her—not the Onslows at all."

"Be sure to come back to lunch and tell me all about it; I shall be on thorns till I know. And Laura, if it's any help, you can tell Bay-bay that she's dished herself for good and all with the richest commoner in England. We had it all out last night. What he can't get over is her having said to him that polygamy is a necessary concomitant of genius, and one of its highest forms of expression."

"I shouldn't have believed that any woman on earth could be so lost to the most elementary sense of decency," said Mrs. Temple trenchantly.

"Or of common sense either," Christine remarked thoughtfully. "Jeremy is quite a difficult person to shock —he's thoroughly modern, and not particularly stupid, and she must really have gone out of her way to do it. I always said she was an ass."

"So am I, for ever having undertaken this ridiculous mission," said Laura.

Nevertheless, she went.

The austere-looking butler did not open the door to her, rather to her relief. A footman did so.

"Is Miss Kingsley-Browne staying here?"

"Yes, madam."

"I should like to see her, please."

"I don't think Miss Kingsley-Browne has left her room yet, madam."

Laura nearly exclaimed "All the better!" but substituted, "I would rather see her in her room. I should prefer to go straight up to her."

"Very good, madam."

Feeling more like a house-breaker than a caller, so fervently did she hope not to meet the owners of the house, Laura crept upstairs behind the footman, waited—resisting an inclination to flatten herself against the wall —whilst he exchanged murmurs with a housemaid, and finally was ushered by the housemaid into the guest room from which it had become at once so difficult, and so desirable, to eject the guest.

Bébée was sitting on the bed, in a pale-pink garment bordered with flame coloured feathers, smoking a cigarette in a long amber holder. Flimsy silk clothing, and tissue paper, lay over the chairs and on the floor.

"Do come in. Good-morning," said Miss Kingsley-Browne affably. "Can you find somewhere to park yourself? I hope you don't mind all this muddle."

"Are you packing?" asked Laura hopefully.

"Unfortunately, yes. A. B. has to go to America. It is quite unexpected, and he is in despair about it, of course, but his publishers have cabled most urgently."

Laura, although aghast at the extreme expedient to which her fellow-writer had been driven in order to escape from his admirer, felt relief surge over her.

"Do they go at once?"

"We sail on Saturday."

"*We?*" Laura echoed incredulously.

"I have offered to go as his secretary. He hesitated a good deal about accepting, but I simply said I was coming and that ended it."

"Your mother ——"

"Have you seen Mummie? Poor dear, she's taking such a distorted, exaggerated view of the whole thing. Has she talked to you at all?"

"A little. She is terribly upset."

"I'm afraid she is. Well, do try to persuade her that this is nineteen-hundred and twenty-seven. I have the greatest admiration for A. B., and I can help him in a way that nobody else can. His wife has never understood him."

"What does she say about your going to America?"

"She very ridiculously insists upon coming too," said Miss Kingsley-Browne morosely.

"And what does he say?"

"He will have to let her come. The truth is—you see I am perfectly dispassionate about it—he hasn't the courage to face a scandal. I should be perfectly prepared to go away with him. I make no secret of it—but he won't hear of it. He wants us to say good-bye to one another, in fact, but as I've told him, he owes it to his work not to turn his back on love."

Laura drew a long breath.

"My dear child, are you sure you haven't lost your head over this? I know he finds you attractive, and pretty, and he may have made love to you—but when it comes to breaking up his home, and leaving a wife to whom he's been married for years, and creating a considerable scandal—don't you really think it's expecting too much of a man of his age?"

The imperturbability of Bébée's reply, delivered through a cloud of cigarette-smoke, left Mrs. Temple, if possible, more entirely convinced than before, of the futility of her errand.

"I daresay it is. But I am determined not to leave him until I have made him see that I am as necessary to him as he is to me."

Chapter XIII

As THE train gained speed, and Laura gazed out of the window, she felt that she had been away for a lifetime.

Duke Ayland had come to see her off at Paddington, and so had Christine. The memory of Duke's eyes looking into hers, and of the grasp of his hand, had entirely obsessed her thoughts for the first half of the journey.

Later, she began to realise that she was coming home, and as the outline of flying fields and hedgerows on either side became familiar, the focus of Laura's imaginings altered.

At the junction, she changed from the express to the local train, and crossing the platform, was reminded of her encounter there with Lady Kingsley-Browne. She remembered with amazement that it had taken place less than three weeks ago.

"If anybody looks like a rag now," thought Laura, whose memory was as retentive as that of everybody else on certain counts, "it's probably that unfortunate woman herself. Bébée is dancing attendance on a man who has a wife of his own already and doesn't want her in the very least, and Jeremy—the richest commoner in England—is falling in love with somebody else. Shall I go and see her, or would it be more tactful to leave it alone?"

Laura's charitable speculations occupied her until the end of her journey.

Alfred was on the platform, the two-seater, dusty, shabby and familiar, in the lane outside, and the two little boys waving excitedly from the back seat.

"Oh, Alfred, how nice of you to bring the boys! How are you all?"

Laura, absurdly inclined to tearfulness, had kissed Alfred fervently before remembering that she had been certain that her first kiss would recall Judas to her mind, sped through the barrier, was recalled in order to produce her ticket, failed to find it, searched agitatedly, recovered it, and was free to exchange rapturous greetings with Edward and Johnnie.

"Darling—oh! how did you get that bruise?"

"I just fell off the banisters. I wasn't at all brave," said Johnnie, anticipating his parent's next inquiry. "I screamed and roared as if I'd been killed on the spot. Nurse said so."

"Never mind! It must have been a frightful bump."

"I've lost another tooth," said Edward. "Look!"

"I see, darling."

"Is this all?" Alfred enquired.

"That's all. Oh—no—wait a minute——"

"Have you got my engine, mummie?"

"Yes, darling, and Edward's football."

"Did you say there was something else, Laura?"

"My hat-box, I thought—Oh, it's there. Then that's all."

"What's in that basket, Mummie?"

"I'll show you when we get home."

"Well," said Alfred, "how are you? I think you look better than when you went away."

"I am. Have the boys been good?"

"Just as usual, I think."

"But nothing special? That's a frightful bruise on Johnnie's forehead."

"Mummie," yelled Edward from the dickey, "Fauntleroy caught a rabbit yesterday."

"Did he, darling?"

"How did you leave Christine?"

"She's very well, and oh, Alfred, you'll never guess who——"

"Mummie!"

"Yes, Johnnie."

"Mummie, will there be time to unpack our surprises before tea or shall we have to wait till after?"

"I think I can let you have them at once. I put them in on the very top of my suit-case on purpose."

"Have you heard anything of the Kingsley-Brownes, Laura? There's been a lot of chat going on."

Laura twisted her head round again from the unnatural angle at which she was obliged to hold it in order to converse with her sons.

"Have I heard anything of them?" she ejaculated. "I defy you, or any sane person, to guess what I have been doing. Will you believe it, that Baybay is more utterly lost to any sense of decency than we supposed, even, and has insisted upon——"

"Take care! They can hear every word——"

"Oh, I suppose they can." Laura lowered her voice.

"*Alors je te dirai plus tard*. Alfred, how is the garden looking?"

"Wants rain."

"It hasn't rained once all the time I've been in London."

"Mummie, do you see that a tree's been cut down there?"

"Yes, I do, Edward. Did you see it come down?"

"No, I didn't see it come down, but I saw it when it was lying on the ground, and I guessed someone had cut it down."

Laura's head came round again.

"How have the servants been, Alfred?"

"All right. I had to speak to Hilda the other day."

"You had to speak to her!" echoed Laura, aghast. "What about?"

"Only about her work. She wasn't doing it properly, so I had to speak to her."

A host of disquieting implications rushed into Laura's mind.

"Was she upset?"

"I don't know."

Laura thought to herself, "If Hilda gives notice, then we shall lose her and the cook."

Such possibilities had not presented themselves to her mind during the past ten days. Now they recurred with a tempestuous force that caused her to wonder how she could ever have permitted them to remain in abeyance.

She did not, however, comment upon Alfred's indiscretion. If Alfred was left in charge of the household, it was inevitable that he should exercise his own methods of ruling it. Laura's sense of justice admitted as much, in the midst of her forebodings.

Applecourt stood in the light of the afternoon sun, the purple clematis was out, Johnnie's scooter lay on the front step, and Fauntleroy rushed round the corner of the house, jumping up and down in an ecstasy of welcome.

"It's home," she thought and experienced an intolerable mingling of pain and joy.

"Isn't Fauntleroy excited?" said Edward, proudly. "Look, he's got his new collar on."

"And look," cried Johnnie. "Daddy's moved the cuckoo clock to the other side of the hall!"

They were joyful and preoccupied with all that they had to show her.

Laura permitted herself to kiss them once more, although aware that neither of them really welcomed the attention, gave them their presents, and sent them upstairs.

Through the open door of the drawing-room, she could see the excessive tidiness of books, magazines, bowls, and boxes, each scrupulously dusted and replaced on the wrong spot, and evidences of Nurse's zeal in the presence of a vase containing two spiky red geraniums on her writing-table and another one of delphinium on the mantelpiece. A rather depressing selection of correspondence lay on the table in the hall.

"I didn't forward things that looked like bills or advertisements," Alfred explained, "and these came this morning."

"Nothing interesting. The Bakewells want us to play tennis on the 10th; I suppose we can. The new nurse arrives the day before. Do you think it'll be all right to leave her with the children?"

"I thought that was what you engaged her for."

Laura laughed.

She had expected to feel guilty, remorseful and unhappy in the presence of her husband and children.

Sometimes she had wondered whether, like the heroines of novels read in her schoolroom days, she would suddenly discover, on returning home, qualities, hitherto unperceived in Alfred, and fall violently, passionately, and legitimately in love with her own husband. In that case, her London adventure would be as a dream, and duty and bliss—improbable combination!—would become one and the same thing. But no emotional reaction came to overwhelm Laura. In the presence of her husband and children she was happy, partly because it made her so to be with them again, and partly because of the underlying consciousness that never left her, of Duke Ayland's love and her own. She did not experience a new and emotional reaction towards Alfred, although it was a relief to be able to talk eagerly to him without being consciously obliged to avoid the fatal topics of the children and the servants through sheer paucity of subjects.

She did not—astonishingly—feel remorseful. It was already incredible to her that she should ever seriously have contemplated a confession to Alfred.

"I wrote to you about Duke taking me out to dinner?"

"Yes. I daresay a restaurant was quite a good thing,

after Christine's cooking. Is he doing anything with his music?"

"Quite a lot. He's finished the Operetta, and he's going to send it to me to look at." Laura had made up this speech beforehand because she wished Alfred to draw the deduction that she and Duke Ayland meant to correspond with one another.

She gave utterance to it with a self-consciousness that disgusted her.

It seemed to her that Alfred could scarcely fail to notice the unnatural lilt given by her voice to the end of the sentence.

"While you were away," said Alfred, "we had trouble with that cistern again."

Throughout Laura's first evening at home, they exchanged similar detached, but interesting, pieces of information. The presence of Hilda in the dining-room early laid an embargo upon the subject of Miss Kingsley-Browne, but Laura, between the soup and the boiled chicken, was able to remark feverishly:

"I can't tell you what a state poor Lady Kingsley-Browne is in—as well she may be! She actually came to us—Christine and me—for help, so you can imagine how reduced she is. As for Baybay, flogging at the cart's-tail would be too good for her."

"Would it? The whole neighbourhood would probably agree with you, I imagine. People have been talking about her quite a lot lately."

"What people? What do they say?"

"I can't remember any particulars. But I have a general impression that she is supposed to be going the pace, and that some young man or other, who was expected to ask her to marry him, hasn't done so."

"Oh, Alfred!" said Laura impressively, "I can tell you the whole story, practically."

She did so.

Alfred's comment was pithy.

Laura found that he was entirely correct in assuming that the amorous extravagances of Miss Kingsley-Browne were being discussed in the county. Even Mrs. Bakewell, at her own tennis party, subjected Laura to cross-examination on the subject.

"Is it true that the girl is positively living in the house of A. B. Onslow and that his wife has left him?"

"She hadn't left him when I was there. She was sitting at the head of the table, quite in the ordinary way."

"*Was* she?" ejaculated Mrs. Bakewell darkly. "Poor soul!"

"She talked to Bébée just like anybody else."

"Poor, poor soul!"

"She—they—are off to America, I believe."

Mrs. Bakewell shook her large head, on the very top of which a little white hat clung in a detached, independent-looking fashion.

"America is not the place to go to, in those circumstances," she observed. "Or, rather, perhaps, it *is* the place to go to, from one point of view. Sometimes one feels, does one not, that it is as though brains were a positive snare."

"I don't think that Bébée has any particular brains. In fact, I'm sure she hasn't."

"It was Mr. Onslow I was thinking about. His writing —and now this madness and folly! The Onslows have no children, have they?"

"None."

"Ah! Little feet pattering about the house—they keep one from so many, many dangers."

Laura felt a passing wonder as to the nature of the perils from which Mrs. Bakewell had been preserved by the pattering of Cynthia's and Theodore's feet.

"You and I, my dear," said her hostess, "may be thankful that we are just humdrum every-day wives and mothers, with little ones to occupy our thoughts, and plenty of work at home."

"What would she say," Laura enquired of herself, "if I told her that I am in love with another man, and that I have let him make love to me, and that he has asked me to run away with him?"

Her imagination was entirely unable to supply any reply to the question.

She looked unseeingly at the Bakewell tennis court, upon which two strapping Crossthwaite girls were partnering respectively a very young man indeed, and a stout, elderly clergyman.

The young man's mother and the clergyman's wife sat and talked spasmodically to Major Bakewell and Alfred. From time to time the mother of the very young man called out to him:

"Play up, Dickie dear!" and from time to time the

clergyman's wife ejaculated: "Quite like Wimbledon, isn't it?"

Presently Mrs. Bakewell's children appeared.

Cynthia and Theodore were plain, and Theodore wore spectacles, but their manners were beautiful. They shook hands, and they smiled, though rather joylessly, and they sat down upon a rush mat at their mother's feet.

"How are Edward and Johnnie, Mrs. Temple?" Cynthia politely enquired. "We haven't come across them at the dancing-class lately."

"It's getting rather hot for dancing, isn't it? I don't think they'll go again till September."

Cynthia looked surprised and said: "Theodore and I don't ever think it's too hot for dancing, do we, Theodore?"

"No, we never do. We dance in the garden sometimes. Shall we dance for you after tea?"

"Thank you very much," said Laura, not, however, committing herself to any assent.

"You must come over to tea with Johnnie and Edward one of these days," she added.

"Thank you, Mrs. Temple, we should like that very much. Do they play Mah Jongh?"

"Not yet."

"They are rather small, aren't they?" Cynthia said kindly. "But I daresay we could teach them."

"We are so fond of the tinies," said Mrs. Bakewell aside to Laura. "When we go to a party, we always have a crowd of babies round us immediately. Really quite wonderful, in that way."

A ball went over the net into a distant flower-bed, and Laura was forced to admire the alacrity with which Cynthia and Theodore leapt up unbidden in pursuit, no less than the efficiency with which they found the ball and returned it to the players.

"Theodore is such a regular boy," Mrs. Bakewell said confidentially to Laura. "Anything to do with a ball— it doesn't matter what it is—and just the same with machinery!"

Whatever Mrs. Bakewell's syntax, her meaning was clear.

"Johnnie cares more for books than anything else," Laura said firmly. "He really has quite a good memory."

"Has he—now has he!" Mrs. Bakewell absent-mindedly ejaculated. "I wonder where he gets that from. Up to seven years old, my treasures have always run wild. The doctor wouldn't hear of anything else. There are brains enough there, he used to say—*more* than enough. Build up the bodies first, and you'll find when they do begin, that they'll get on all the faster. And I'm bound to say that he was right. Lessons have never been any trouble to us. I taught each in turn to read, at seven years old. Not a day before."

"Johnnie could read quite well at five, but I don't think it's done him any harm."

"Perhaps not. It's difficult to tell, though. It's later on that these things—but, of course, one can't really say."

"One can only do one's best," Laura assented, since

the platitudes of a hostess are best met by platitudes from her guests.

"Indeed, yes, and that's where one feels that our poor, poor friend has perhaps failed. And now this terrible retribution! (Darlings, run into the house for mother and see if tea is ready). Bébée—unfortunate girl—was always spoilt, and this is the result. Her life ruined, before she is thirty."

Infinitesimal though Mrs. Temple's regard might be for the object of Lady Kingsley-Browne's over-indulgence, she found herself protesting at so trenchant a criticism.

"She is very foolish, of course—idiotic, and very badly behaved—but do you think that people's lives are easily ruined nowadays? It seems to me that they can do almost anything, especially girls."

"Everything is very lax, I quite agree, but I am not aware that tampering with the seventh commandment is ever looked upon lightly by decent people," said Mrs. Bakewell with great directness.

Laura felt herself beginning to blush, whether for the outspokenness of Mrs. Bakewell, or from her own sense of guilt, she scarcely knew.

"Probably Bébée will come home again when her mother does," she said hastily. "I daresay a great deal of it is only talk."

Mrs. Bakewell shook her head and looked doubtful, but Cynthia and Theodore, gracefully bounding across the grass, came to tell her that tea was ready, and Laura's tête-à-tête with her hostess came to an end.

For the remainder of the evening she played tennis very badly.

Such self-confidence as she could now boast had deserted her. The knowledge that her play was growing worse and worse, discouraged and disconcerted her, and discouragement and disconcernment, as usual, sapped her vitality, so that she felt herself becoming plainer and less attractive every moment.

It was a great relief to her when the Bakewells could be thanked, taken leave of, and left.

"I really think I'd better give up tennis altogether," Laura dejectedly observed, in the well-worn phrase that is heard so often and so regularly every summer in rural circles. "I get worse and worse."

"You were off your game to-day," Alfred agreed, leniently.

"I don't think I have ever been on it. If I ever have a daughter, I shall have her taught to play games, to dance, and to hold herself properly. I don't believe anything else in the world matters."

Laura's husband, according to his wont, made no comment upon so rational and feasible a scheme of education.

The days slipped by, and already Laura's stay in London had become dreamlike.

Duke's letters, although she would scarcely have owned it to herself, were faintly disappointing. She did not wish him to write indiscreetly, and she knew that it was principally for her sake that he never did so, but nevertheless only the most reckless of letters could really have satisfied her, after the nature of their conversations together.

He still wrote about books, and about Laura's work, and his own music, and he alluded—but guardedly—to their London meetings.

Laura, actually, sometimes found her replies difficult. As usual, she had not had any opportunity for reading books that everybody else was reading, until everybody else had nearly forgotten them, and she herself had done no writing at all since coming home. She found that her letters to Duke Ayland were becoming a patchwork of comments upon what he had written to her, and of humorously extravagant descriptions of domestic calamities and festivities at Applecourt. Rightly aware that this form of epistolatory wit is generally more amusing to the writer than to the reader, Laura bitterly assured herself that her letters resembled nothing so much as a most inferior imitation of Jane Welsh Carlyle's.

She urgently desired to see Ayland again, and had a quite irrational feeling that to do so would in some way clarify the whole situation.

"Anything would be better than to go on like this," Laura sometimes wearily thought, but she did not particularise "anything" nor really know what she meant by it, since her determination not to break with Duke was second only to her determination that she would never wrong Alfred or the children.

With a vague consciousness that she was only marking time until her next meeting with Duke Ayland, Laura returned to her accustomed routine.

It was diversified in precisely the usual manner.

"If you please, 'm, I don't think the new nurse quite understands about the nursery slops. It's her place to do them and not mine, I always understood."

"Mrs. Temple, I'm really very sorry to trouble you, but I think I ought to let you know at once that next term I'm very much afraid I shan't be able to go on teaching the boys. My mother's asthma . . ."

"I haven't been able to do anything with the kitchen stove this morning, 'm. I think it must be the *wind*."

Dear Madam,

We beg to inform you that your account is now overdrawn to the amount of Twelve Pounds Fourteen Shillings and Sevenpence . . .

Dear Madam,

May we very respectfully draw your attention to the enclosed account which is now considerably overdue? As our Annual Audit of Accounts commences this week, we shall be greatly obliged by your cheque at an early date.

Assuring you of our best attention at all times.

We are, dear madam,

Obediently yours,

Harker & Co.

£2 4s. 8½d.

Laura, though far from exhilarated by such communications, found them less overwhelming than she had once done, since she had now a major preoccupation to distract her attention.

At the end of the summer, domestic calamity again overtook her, and the married couple that constituted the staff at Applecourt, gave notice. Laura advertised, went to the Registry Office, wrote letters and sent telegrams.

It was all very familiar and unsuccessful.

The evenings, which had temporarily been animated by Laura's numerous accounts of her experiences in London, degenerated again, and Alfred read *The Times*, and later fell asleep, while Laura battled silently with the dismal phrases that kept on rising to her lips and that were concerned exclusively with the servants, the children and the question of expense.

Then Lady Kingsley-Browne returned home, and Laura, actuated by mixed motives of genuine compassion and still more genuine curiosity, went to see her.

Bébée's parent was in the rose garden, snipping off dead blooms and bestowing them in a large basket.

At the approach of Laura she raised a ravaged and exhausted, but composed face, and greeted her kindly.

"So nice of you to come, dear! Let's sit down on the stone bench—it's so wonderfully warm, isn't it—and tell me all about yourself."

"At the present moment, I'm, as usual, looking for a cook. I suppose you don't ——"

Lady Kingsley-Browne shook her head.

"I'm afraid not. And I'm so sorry you're in difficulties again. I know what it means."

From this, Laura silently dissented, the loss of a cook

in a house where a kitchen-maid and scullery-maid remain, not being in her opinion, comparable to the loss of two servants from a house in which only two servants are ever employed.

"One has so much to cope with, one way and another, but the only thing is to be philosophical. Things pass. When I find myself out here, amongst all these dear things," said Lady Kingsley-Browne, looking down at the dead roses in her basket, "I realise that it is so true that *Tout passe, tout casse, tout lasse!* The only thing, is not to let oneself be overwhelmed."

The melancholy resignation of her so materially-prosperous neighbour roused Laura to agitated pity. She murmured something entirely incoherent, that yet conveyed the suggestion of a question.

Evidently poor Lady Kingsley-Browne realised only too well that any question addressed to her at the present juncture by any intimate, could have only one bearing. Although her child's name had not been mentioned, she replied at once:

"Oh yes, she's gone. My one comfort is that Mrs. Onslow has gone too. Poor, poor woman! What a life! Standing between her husband and his infatuations! Though I can't possibly pretend that this is his doing, or anyone's except poor darling Bébée's!"

"Is she as—as determined as ever?"

"Quite, I think. I get letters from her, you know. She's always been sweet about keeping me informed of her movements. They are in New York."

"I wonder she wasn't detained on Ellis Island for moral

turpitude," was the sentence that sprang to Mrs. Temple's lips. But aloud she said:

"When are they coming back?"

"Before the end of next month, I think. Perhaps by that time ——"

Lady Kingsley-Browne's voice died away without completing the sentence, but Laura had no difficulty in deducing the unspoken conclusion. Perhaps by the time the celebrated A. B. Onslow returned to his own country he would have hit upon some efficacious manner of ridding himself once and for all of the unprincipled and immodest young creature who now persisted, with such unparalleled tenacity, in linking her existence to his.

Chapter XIV

SOME weeks after Laura's return from London, Duke Ayland wrote and told her he was obliged to come down to the West of England for two nights on business. Could they possibly meet?

Laura, profoundly agitated, suggested that he should come and stay at Applecourt.

Ayland, by return of post, was very sorry that this was impossible. He stated the fact without attempting to produce any explanation for it. Could Laura possibly come as far as Great Quinn and have lunch with him?

Laura honestly believed that she considered this suggestion carefully for hours.

Then she said to her husband:

"Alfred, Duke Ayland is very anxious that I should go and have lunch with him at Great Quinn and—and look at the new University Buildings."

"What's he doing at Great Quinn?"

"He's coming down on business."

"Ask him to come on here for a day or two."

"He can't."

"Do you want to see the new University Buildings?"

"I should like to go," said Laura, trying to be truthful.

"I can take you as far as Quinnerton in the car, and you can go on by the eleven o'clock train. Which day is it? Not the meeting of the Housing Committee, I hope?"

"Wednesday."

"That's all right then. I can manage that."

Laura wrote and told Ayland that she would come, and became the prey of an excitement that nearly made her ill.

"This will have to stop," she told herself solemnly. "I can't go on like this. I had better say good-bye to him and let it be over. If I were a young girl—and free ——"

A pang went through her for her irrevocably vanished youth and for the few and poor opportunities that it had ever afforded her of misbehaving herself.

Ridiculous and fantastic visions assailed her, just as she was going to sleep at night, of Alfred suddenly announcing that he had for years been in love with another woman, and that now he intended to leave Laura and the children and to marry her. Becoming slightly more wakeful, doubts assailed her even of the practicability of this solution.

Duke and the children seemed somehow a rather improbable combination, although he had been so nice to them. Edward, yes. You could give Edward a ball, or a Meccano set, or tell him that he should go out to tea with other children, and Edward was happy and generally good. But Johnnie—with his insistent demands for attention, his uncannily acute powers of observation, and his violent, incalculable temper! Impossible to suppose that Johnnie would ever endure the sight of his mother's absorption in anybody but himself.

And if Alfred objected to the excess of time and thought

bestowed by Laura on her younger son, surely Duke might be expected to resent it with equal intensity, and a great deal more articulateness?

"But it couldn't possibly happen, after all," the semi-wakeful half of Laura's consciousness murmured, and she was deeply and irrationally relieved by the thought.

For the two days preceding that of her expedition, many things conspired to discourage Laura from any very great exhilaration of spirits.

"Mummie, can I go with you to Great Quinn when you go?"

"No, darling, I'm afraid not."

"Then can I?" Edward, as usual, imitated his junior, in defiance of every law of probability.

"No, I can't take either of you."

"I wish you didn't go away so often, mummie."

"Darling, I don't go away often."

"You went to London the other day, for ages and ages. Shall you be back in time to have us downstairs before we go to bed?"

"I'm not— Well, I'll try to be, Edward. Don't kick the piano, darling!"

"Why not?" enquired Edward, looking astonished.

"Because it spoils it. I've told you often. Shall I see if Cynthia and Theodore Bakewell could come and spend the afternoon with you to-morrow?"

"No, thank you," said Johnnie, shuddering affectedly.

Edward looked wistful, but Laura's sympathies, as usual, were on Johnnie's side, and she did not press the offer.

"Run out and play, darlings."

Then Hilda, the departing house-parlourmaid, came in with a telegram between her fingers. Laura, who disliked correcting her servants because she imaginatively supposed that it must humiliate them, felt with relief that as she was to leave next day, it was not worth while to send Hilda back for the salver.

She opened and read the message.

Sorry cannot arrive before Wednesday same train Johnson.

Laura felt herself turning pale.

"No answer. It's from—It's—Oh, Hilda, please tell the boy there's no answer, and then come back here a minute, would you?"

During the brief interval in which this errand was accomplished, Laura re-read the telegram five times, and fully realised the extent of the calamity it implied. The new cook had elected to postpone her arrival. Instead of being "settled in," as the official, if optimistic, phrase runs, by her mistress the day before her own expedition, she intended to arrive on the very afternoon when Laura had expected and decided to meet Ayland in Great Quinn.

"Hilda," said Laura in a controlled voice, "the new cook whom I have engaged is unfortunately prevented from arriving to-morrow."

"Is she, 'm?" Hilda clicked her tongue against the roof of her mouth and looked amused.

"She is only delaying till Wednesday—at least I hope that's all."

"The day after to-morrow like," Hilda suggested.

"Yes. The only thing that's rather awkward is that I want to go to Great Quinn on Wednesday for the day."

"It's early closing day on Wednesday, 'm."

"Is it? But that wouldn't make any difference. I mean, I wanted to see the new University Buildings."

Hilda made no reply.

"I suppose your own plans are fixed up?"

"Yes, 'm, they are."

Of course they were. Laura reflected, not for the first time, how easy it was for servants to replace unsatisfactory employers, and how complicated the reverse process.

"I shouldn't at all wish you to alter your arrangements in any way on my account, but if you hadn't been actually settled, I should have asked you to stay on another twenty-four hours."

"Yes, 'm," said Hilda, simulating perplexity.

"Why not speak to Price about it?"

"If you like, I will, 'm."

Hilda went away to her husband in the kitchen. Laura, who knew the telegram by heart, read it again.

Quite impossible to let a new cook arrive, and find her mistress gone out for the day. Equally impossible to bid her postpone her arrival, and thus leave Applecourt without a cook at all—even such a cook as was Laura herself —for an entire day and a half.

Perhaps the Prices would stay on until the new cook could arrive.

But they would not.

Hilda returned, having accomplished her mission with a celerity seldom brought to bear upon her legitimate duties, and said:

"I'm sorry, m', but we've made our plans, and Price can't see his way to altering things."

"It doesn't matter at all," said Laura coldly, "I quite understand. I can easily get in someone from the village just for one day."

"Perhaps Mrs. Raynor could oblige you, 'm. It's only the one day."

"I know, but it happens to be the day I want to go to Great Quinn."

"Wednesday's early closing day at Great Quinn," Hilda pointed out all over again.

"Yes, I know. Well, that's all, thank you, Hilda."

Laura went up to the village to find Mrs. Raynor.

She did not like Mrs. Raynor very much, and she gravely distrusted her habit of always arriving with a smallish bundle in the morning, and going away with it, altered in shape and size, at night.

After all, it was only for one day.

Mrs. Raynor was at home, but informed Laura that her heart had come on again.

Laura, understanding that this meant a more or less complete inability to exert herself, condoled with Mrs. Raynor, explained that she had wanted to go to Great

Quinn on Wednesday, heard without surprise that Wednesday was early closing day, and took her leave.

"Perhaps they could have cold food on Wednesday. It would *only* be Wednesday. But there's laying the table and the clearing away and washing up afterwards—and the new house-parlourmaid won't like it."

Laura felt annoyed, and helpless, and impatient, but the more these emotions gained upon her, the more determined she became not to abandon her intention of meeting Ayland at Great Quinn on Wednesday.

"Early closing day or not," she added viciously.

On her way home she stopped at two cottages where occasional "help" could be found, but both Miss Weald and Mrs. Potter were already engaged. This exhausted the possibilities of the immediate neighbourhood.

"Could I get a temporary cook for a week—but if I put Johnson off she's certain not to turn up at all—and anyway, there never are any temporary cooks. Besides, the expense ——"

Indulging in such familiar arguments, Laura went home again.

"Alfred, I've had a telegram from the new cook. The tiresome woman isn't coming till Wednesday."

"Why not?"

"She doesn't say why not."

"Possibly she's taken another job, and doesn't mean to come at all."

"Oh no!" said Laura passionately. "I think it must be genuine. Otherwise, why Wednesday? It would have been simpler just to say she wasn't coming. But she does say Wednesday. Only, it's awkward, because that's the day I'm going to Great Quinn."

"Better put it off."

"I can't do that."

"Why not? Wednesday isn't a very good day— it's ——"

"Yes, I know. But I told Duke Ayland I'd meet him for lunch, and that we'd look at the new University Buildings."

"Better tell him you can't manage it. Unless the Prices can stay on for an extra day."

"They can't," said Laura shortly. "And Mrs. Raynor can't come, nor Miss Weald nor Mrs. Potter."

"If she comes on Wednesday, it practically only means a day and a half without anyone. I should think it could be managed, though I'm afraid the cooking is a great nuisance for you. Couldn't we have cold beef or something?"

"Oh Alfred!" said Laura.

"Well, well, well," said Alfred, in acknowledgment of her emotion.

He went into the house just as the gong rang, and when he and Laura met again at lunch, he spoke only of the political situation—and of that briefly, as was his wont.

Laura's replies were neither intelligent nor ready. She was thinking about Duke Ayland, and the new University Buildings, and the failure of the cook, and the surpassing difficulty of explaining to everybody why it was so important that she should get to Great Quinn, on an early closing day.

Aloud, she was interspersing her comments—such as they were—with injunctions to Johnnie and Edward.

Very soon, Alfred relapsed into silence altogether. Laura, in a worried, subconscious kind of way, was aware of this, and felt it to be her own fault.

But, on the other hand, it was surely important that Johnnie should not be allowed to drink with his mouth full, nor Edward to sit with his elbows on the table.

If only Alfred would talk about politics after dinner, instead of reading the paper and then going to sleep! (Although Laura knew well that their discussions were of no intrinsic worth, since Alfred never went very much beyond: "Look at Russia, if you want to see what the Labour Party is bringing us to!" and "The League of Nations idea may be all very fine in theory, but they can't put it into practice, while human nature remains what it is." Laura did not really agree with either axiom, but having long ago discovered that her husband disliked argument, she was weak-minded enough to differ from him very gently, and then gradually let herself be brought to the stage of repeating thoughtfully, "I see what you mean, of course," which indeed was true. Thus did the Temples contribute the Power of Thought to the contemporary problems of the world in which they lived.)

In the afternoon another telegram was brought to Laura.

"To say the cook isn't coming at all," went in cold despair through Laura's mind.

But this telegram had been sent off from Quinnerton, by the honorary secretary of an organisation in which

Laura took an active part, and a branch of which she had helped to found in her own village.

Reply paid Mr Mindy Headquarters speaker requires accommodation to-night original arrangements fallen through can you possibly put him up if so arriving six o'clock bus will be fetched to-morrow for afternoon meeting here many apologies short notice—Smithson.

Laura had known too many emergencies in her own career not to sympathise profoundly with those in Miss Smithson's.

She did not know Mr. Mindy, but outside contacts were good for one . . . and, in any case, she had assured Miss Smithson that her house would be available in such times of stress.

She telegraphed back, "Will meet six o'clock bus," and hoped that the brevity of her style might be a lesson to Miss Smithson.

Before five o'clock the spare room had been prepared, even to a bunch of sweet-peas on the dressing-table, and Alfred had been told of the impending visitor.

Laura went to the village to meet the bus. Mr. Mindy, carrying the little bag that all speakers carry, whether they have come for a night or for a week, was unmistakable—a tall, thin man, with a grey beard and a shock of pepper-and-salt hair in tight, irrepressible curls.

Laura, shaking hands with him, wondered vaguely if Johnnie's hair would ever look like that.

Before the slow pony had drawn Laura and Mr. Mindy, in the governess-cart, as far as Applecourt, she perceived that he would provide his own entertainment.

In a steady, pleasant, unfaltering way, Mr. Mindy talked, and talked, and talked.

He was profoundly interested in his organisation, and took it for granted that Laura was also, and he had recently toured the United States, and whilst there had stored and neatly tabulated an incredible number of impressions.

Laura listened to him in something that gradually became a minor form of hypnotic trance.

How interesting Mr. Mindy might be, if only he gave one less at a time, she reflected dreamily.

After a while, however, she ceased to feel this. Mr. Mindy's voice went on and on, and Laura said, "Did you really?" and "I see," and finally said nothing more at all, as she reverted in her own mind to the problem of the cook.

"What I said in Alabama, for instance, was quite different to what I said in Ohio."

"I suppose it would be. Yes."

"But this, Mrs. Temple, is one of the things that struck me most. In order to make myself clear to you, I must explain that the methods of organisation in the South, for instance, are not the same as those in the East. You're sure I'm not boring you?"

"Perfectly certain, Mr. Mindy. I'm most interested. Do please go on!"

Laura assumed a more animated expression, and Mr. Mindy, satisfied, went on talking.

No one, Laura supposed, had ever answered, in reply to such a question—"Yes, you are boring me, I am sorry to say. Indeed, I am only pretending to listen to you, and I therefore suggest that we should begin again, on a more equal basis."

Candour of that sort, and to that extent, would not be a success. People might occasionally be glad to say such things, but never would they be glad to hear them. Probably, also, they would always find them unbelievable, said to themselves.

"Forgive me," said Mr. Mindy, "but I'm afraid you look tired. I know from our friend Miss Smithson how very hard you work for the organisation."

"Do I?" said Laura, much startled.

"Surely. And what I feel about the way things are done over there, is that the *individual*—like yourself, Mrs. Temple—can get so very much more accomplished, by so much less personal expenditure of time and trouble. Efficiency seems to be the watchword of our friends across the Atlantic. Now take this——"

Mr. Mindy was off again.

"But how," thought Laura, "will Alfred like this?"

Alfred had a prejudice, entirely unreasonable and entirely ineradicable, against the whole of the United States of America.

At Applecourt, Laura took the bull by the horns.

"My husband, Mr. Mindy. Mr. Mindy has just come back from a most wonderful tour in the States, Alfred.

He's been telling me how efficiently they run things over there."

"I assure you that I was very much struck ——" said Mr. Mindy.

Laura went into the house, and left them at the front door.

Looking at herself in the glass, she felt that her visitor's personal remark was in a sense justified. She did look tired. Never once, in London, had she looked like this. Her face was pale, there were shadows round her eyes and mouth, her hair hung limply over her ears, and her clothes seemed to hang limply on her body.

"Forty years old, at least," observed Laura trenchantly to her own reflection.

From beneath her open window, fragments of Mr. Mindy's monologue, and of Alfred's occasional growlings, floated up to her.

"New York . . . Prohibition . . . the check system for luggage . . . telephone . . . telephone . . . TELE-PHONE. . . . Now, in Massachusetts, the organisation of the whole movement . . . I was greatly struck . . . efficiency. And again EFFICIENCY."

Finally, in antistrophe to a curt, inaudible word from Alfred, *"Hundred per cent efficiency*—neither more nor less."

At this, Laura felt impelled to hasten the powdering of her nose and to go downstairs again to Alfred's rescue, if not to Mr. Mindy's.

"Perhaps," said Laura, "Mr. Mindy would like to see his room."

"I'm in no hurry, Mrs. Temple, thank you. I was just telling your husband some of my impressions of America. There can be no doubt that it's a wonderful country."

"It must be."

"Just to give you one example of the efficiency of their methods of organisation," said Mr. Mindy.

When he had finished, Alfred walked away, and Laura asked whether Mr. Mindy had seen the papers that day.

Yes, he had.

It would, therefore, be useless to attempt to shut him into the study with them.

"Don't, I beg of you, think of entertaining me in any way," Mr. Mindy begged earnestly. "I am perfectly content walking about this delightful garden and talking to you."

Laura resigned herself.

Her faint, scarcely recognised, hope that a miracle might take place, and a cook appear at the desired moment, had failed to eventuate, and she was able to spend the evening in justifying to herself her determination that, cook or no cook, she would go to Great Quinn on Wednesday.

The Temples, by eleven o'clock that night, their heads buzzing with information, exchanged only one comment on their visitor.

"Does that fellow ever answer anything with plain yes or no?" demanded Alfred.

And Laura replied with conviction: "I should think never."

She woke next morning with the thought uppermost in her mind: "The servants are going to-day, and there'll be no cook."

Dejection possessed her.

On principle, Laura always pathetically strove to put worry away from her in the presence of her children. She resolutely produced a smile, and made her step elastic, as she walked into the nursery.

"I've left Edward in bed, madam, after the night he's had," said nurse lugubriously.

"Was he ill? Why didn't you fetch me?"

"He's been coughing, off and on, the whole of the night. Sometimes in his sleep, no doubt, but sometimes the fits were so violent that he woke himself up."

"I've thought he had a little cold, for a day or two— he's coughed once or twice—I'm afraid he must be in for a bronchial attack." Laura hastened to the night-nursery.

Edward, sitting up in bed, and sharing bread-and-milk with Fauntleroy, looked perfectly well.

"Nurse thinks you've got a cold, darling. Is your throat sore?"

"No, not a bit," said Edward brightly. "Can I get up after breakfast?"

"We'll see."

Reassuring discoveries followed. Edward had no temperature and no symptoms. He did not even cough.

"Nurse must be an alarmist," thought Laura. She made enquiries about Johnnie. Johnnie was quite well.

"Well, I really see no reason for keeping Edward in bed.

He can't be sickening for anything, or he wouldn't be so hungry and so eager to get up."

Nurse gave Laura a peculiar look.

"Well, madam, there's whooping-cough about, isn't there?"

"Whooping-cough!"

"They can have it without ever whooping at all, for that matter, or they can begin with an ordinary cough, and then go on to whoop, and, as often as not, they're perfectly well in between the fits."

"Do you suppose that Edward is beginning whooping-cough?"

"It sounded to me very like it," replied nurse with a deadly calm.

Laura felt as though she had never before so fully realised calamity.

"If there's the least doubt—certainly, there *is* whooping-cough in the village—we'd better send for the doctor. I suppose it's no use trying to separate the boys now?"

"Not the slightest use, madam. It may be days, or even weeks, before Johnnie begins it, but he's bound to have it."

Nurse's unconditional surrender to misfortune left Laura aghast. She herself had no experience of nursing infectious illness and she was fully prepared to believe that nurse knew what she was talking about.

"How long does it usually last?" she asked faintly.

"The actual catching stage would be about six to eight weeks, though I suppose they're never really safe to be with others until the cough is gone. And my word, doesn't it hang on! I've known a child to whoop the whole of the year round, when she'd started it in June."

"And this is August," said Laura.

"They say it goes in May."

"And that would be ten months."

Nurse shook her head.

"Whooping-cough is like that, madam. I ought to know. I lost a little brother and a little sister with it, besides nursing the little girl in my last place. Poor little mite, she'd turn black in the face, when she'd a whooping fit on. Many's the time I've thought she must choke to death."

"We must see what the doctor says," Laura unhappily repeated. "Don't let Edward or Johnnie know that we think it may be whooping-cough. Perhaps—perhaps after all it may turn out to be nothing."

But inwardly, Laura felt certain that it would turn out to be something.

She went to find Alfred, in obedience to the usual instinct for passing on bad news, but he had already gone downstairs, and from the dining-room she could faintly hear the steady booming of Mr. Mindy's voice.

The attention that she was able to give him, during breakfast, was even more perfunctory than that of the previous evening.

In response to a telephone message, the doctor came, assured Laura that Edward was probably beginning whooping-cough, and that Johnnie would in that case almost certainly catch it, and generally confirmed everything that nurse had said.

"It's like a nightmare," thought Laura. She had the exaggerated horror of childish ailments that belongs to the mother of only one or two children, and that is necessarily outgrown by a woman with a large family.

"He'll be all right," said the doctor cheerfully, referring to Edward. "Let me know if you hear a real whoop, or if he starts being sick after coughing. And watch the other little chap."

With this wholly superfluous injunction he went away.

Laura went straight to her husband.

"Edward has whooping-cough," she announced tragically.

"Who says so?"

"The doctor."

"Picked it up in the village, I suppose. Is Johnnie bound to get it too?"

"They think so."

"Well, I suppose it can't be helped," said Alfred—inadequately, his wife felt.

"They'll be infectious for about seven or eight weeks—perhaps longer, and it lasts ages and ages."

"I daresay. I remember being in the sanatorium with it myself at school, and I think I spent most of one term there. There's nothing particular to be done, I suppose?"

"Oh no, nothing. Edward doesn't seem in the least ill, although nurse says he coughed in the night, and Johnnie hasn't got it at all yet."

"The only thing to do is to go on just as usual then and keep them away from other kids."

"I shan't be able to go to Great Quinn," said Laura suddenly.

Alfred looked mildly surprised.

"I thought you weren't going anyway, because of the cook. I daresay I can run you in another time. In any case, Wednesday is early closing day."

Chapter XV

A NEW and painful line was inscribed in the domestic calendar of Applecourt forthwith.

"The summer when the boys had whooping-cough," was what it would ultimately become, but in these early stages, time, for Laura, was measured by "The day before Edward really began to whoop," or "Just after Johnnie was sick in the night for the first time."

The boys did not have to go to bed, as invalids. They pursued all their usual avocations, excepting their lessons, and every time that Edward ran across the lawn he had a severe fit of coughing, and every time that Johnnie thought his mother was not sufficiently harrowed by their plight he whooped until he was violently sick.

Sometimes they seemed to be getting better, and Laura said: "I daresay they'll have it quite lightly," and nurse replied: "Whooping-cough is like that. Coming and going. You'll see, they'll start again the first wet day."

And they always did start again, sometimes without even waiting for the first wet day.

Laura took Johnnie into her room at night, banishing Alfred to his dressing-room and forgetting to make even a pretence of compunction about it, and Johnnie's cough —which very often failed to wake him at all—destroyed her rest and seemed to tear at the muscles of her own throat and chest.

The telegram that Laura had sent Duke Ayland, explaining that she could not meet him in Great Quinn, seemed only one calamity amongst many, although on the day that she sent it, a phantasy, on stereotyped lines, had come unbidden to her mind. A mother and a dying child. Parents brought together again over a little cot. A passing infatuation driven away for ever in the stark light of tragic reality.

But Laura's love for Duke was not a passing infatuation. If there was one thing that she was certain about, it was that.

She had disgustedly dismissed her own morbid imaginations, and sought and found reality in the farewell speeches of Mr. Mindy, fetched away for his meeting.

The new cook came, and within twenty-four hours left, declaring that she hadn't known she was coming to a children's hospital.

The usual period of stress ensued.

Then, gradually, Laura found that she was becoming inured to the sounds of whooping-cough, to the smell of creosote, and even to the presence of a terrible little pink bowl carried about by nurse for emergency use, and callously spoken of by Edward and Johnnie as "the sickbowl." Once more there were two servants—faintly unsatisfactory—at Applecourt, once more Laura tried to write short stories in the evenings, once more she exchanged letters about books with Duke Ayland.

Then Christine wrote her.

Darling
　　It does seem a pity that I can't come to stay, and

that you, I suppose, can't leave the boys, because we could have rather fun just now. The fact is, that I am now formally and properly engaged to the richest commoner in England, and we shall be in "The Times" as soon as we've seen his parents. You'll like Jeremy when you know him more, although he's not in the least clever, but he has a sense of humour, and is quite-quite. I'm sorry for poor Lady K.B. but it's Baybay's own doing. He was honestly in love with her, and wanted to marry her and I am what Losh calls the "reaction."

I've met the parent Vulliamys—both very nice, in a Du Maurier style—and I think Jeremy has prepared them. He's writing to them to-day, and I daresay they'll ask you down there, when I go.

Anyway you simply must come up here for a day or two, when we begin to make plans. It'll have to be a Church wedding, of course, though not "obey"—and I really prefer it myself, because of a wedding-dress and so on. Is there any hope that the boys will be well in time to be pages? I am now—incredible to relate—in a position to say that I can give them their suits—and of course, I'd adore to. We shall probably be married in the last week of October, but I'll write again directly.

My engagement ring is one colossal emerald, square, set in platinum—absolutely heavenly.

Anything else we can talk over when we need. No, I won't be a pig! I know you're dying to ask if I'm in love with him. Darling Laura, I've never been in the least romantic, and I'm not now, but I'm quite enough in love not to feel that I'm taking a mean advantage of having

*been the first decent woman he met after the affaire Bé-
bée. I truly think we shall understand one another very
well, and ought to be very happy. For goodness' sake,
try and think of something I could call him instead of
that awful "Jeremy."*

Yours,

Christine.

Although Laura had exchanged speculations with her
husband on this very contingency, and had hoped, and
yet felt ashamed of hoping, that it would come to pass,
she felt something like a shock.

Christine and the richest commoner in England. . . .
Not that Laura wanted to dwell only on that aspect of
the case, but it persisted in obtruding itself. She strove
frantically to recall what Lady Kingsley-Browne had told
her. Norfolk and rhododendrons, and a general impression of great opulence, was all that she could recapture.
She could not, even, recall Vulliamy himself with very
great distinctness.

Certainly she would have to go to London. She thought
what fun it would be to help choose Christine's trousseau.

She sat down and wrote four excited pages to her sister.

"Alfred?"

"What?"

Alfred was doing something to a small plant that stood
in the bed just beneath the drawing-room window.

"Guess who's engaged to be married!"

"Bébée Kingsley-Browne."

"Good heavens no! She's still chasing A. B. Onslow

round America as far as I know. I don't suppose any decent man will ever look at her again."

"There are very few decent men about, nowadays."

"Well, one of the ones there is, is engaged to someone who's not her," said Laura, her sense of construction temporarily in abeyance.

"That friend of Christine's—the musical fellow—what's his name?"

"Do you mean Duke Ayland?"

"Yes."

Laura felt as if she had received an unexpected blow.

"No. Certainly not."

"Then it's Christine, I suppose?"

"Darling, you're quite right. How clever of you! Christine is going to marry that Mr. Vulliamy who played tennis here once. I saw him again in London. I think he seemed nice. I believe," said Laura as casually as she could, "that he is very rich indeed—or his parents are."

"If they're the Northfolkshire Vulliamys, they are very rich indeed," Alfred assented. "Well, well, I'm delighted to hear it. Congratulate her from me." And he went back to the little plant again.

Laura thought, not for the first time, that men were odd. Personally she felt that she could have gone on talking about Christine's engagement for at least another hour. Alfred, however, evidently considered that the last word on the subject had been said.

"Nurse will be excited, anyhow," thought Laura rather forlornly. "Servants always are."

After that, letters, and even telegrams, fell upon Applecourt in profusion. Dates were settled, and unsettled, congratulations were exchanged, and Laura and Alfred were invited by Jeremy's parents to spend a few days in Norfolk.

"It really is impossible," said Laura wistfully. "I'd love to go, and it's nice of them to ask us, and of course Christine wants us to—but I don't see how I can leave the boys."

"What d'you keep a nurse for?"

"Do you mean that you'd like to go, Alfred?"

"I think a change would be good for you."

She looked at him almost incredulously.

Theoretically, Laura was perfectly well aware that her husband loved her, and was solicitous for her welfare, but actually, he said so little about it, and that little so very seldom, that she was apt to receive any demonstration from him in touched astonishment.

"We needn't be away for more than three or four days, I suppose, and it seems to me only fair to Christine for us to accept. You're her nearest relation."

"The kindest thing might be to keep away," said Laura, humorously and quite insincerely, since the thought that the acquisition of the Temples as connections would be of advantage to the Vulliamys, who had made their fortune in trade only two generations earlier.

She accepted Mrs. Vulliamy's invitation, and passed in strict, and rather discouraging, review, Alfred's wardrobe and her own.

Nurse, who had been quite as much excited as Laura had hoped by the news of the engagement, and who had discovered for herself without having to be told, the wealth of the bridegroom, declared that the boys could be left without any hesitation. She even, reversing every former prediction, sought to persuade Laura that they could safely act as pages at the wedding.

"And walk up the church with the pink bowl between them," said Mrs. Temple sardonically. "No thank you, nurse. I'm sorry in a way, of course, but the excitement would certainly have upset Johnnie for days afterwards, and you know what he's like."

Nurse, who knew well what Johnnie was like, still refused to find either argument unanswerable.

The Temples decided to go to Norfolk in the car. Laura, who did not drive it herself, was persuaded of the economy of this method of travelling. "It saves two railway tickets," she declared, and ignored petrol, meals on the way, and the new tyre that Alfred was obliged to purchase before they could start.

It was long since Laura had stayed in a country house, longer still since she had stayed in one of the dimensions of Castle Gate.

Two centuries earlier, a coach-and-four was alleged to have passed round the hall, and up the staircase—although not driven by a Vulliamy, since at that date the Vulliamys, in so far as Castle Gate was concerned, had not existed.

But here they now were—very like a Du Maurier drawing, as Christine had said. Mrs. Vulliamy, tall, grey-haired, unjustifiably distinguished-looking, and wearing a string of very beautiful pearls under a carefully neutral-coloured woollen jumper, and Mr. Vulliamy, equally tall, grey-haired, and unjustifiably distinguished-looking, and with beautifully waxed tips to his white moustache.

They had produced Jeremy comparatively late in life and it was evident that they adored him. But they liked Christine. Mrs. Vulliamy called her "quite a dear," and Laura surmised that this was as enthusiastic a description as Mrs. Vulliamy's vocabulary would ever permit. She was as incapable of superlatives as though rank, instead of commercial ability, had characterised her ancestors.

Their plans for the well-being of Jeremy and Christine were astonishing.

They were giving them a house in Hill Street, a motor-car, and the services of their second chauffeur.

"When they want a little quiet in the country, they can always come here, and I daresay later on they'll find a tiny cottage at Hindhead, or somewhere, convenient for the summer," said Mrs. Vulliamy.

She was very nice to Laura, although it was a niceness that rather tended to make her into Christine's mother, instead of her sister.

Christine and Jeremy went for walks, and drove in Jeremy's car, and Mrs. Vulliamy and Laura strolled carefully up and down the immense terrace that was one of three terraces leading down to the lake, and went indoors as soon as the afternoon became a little chilly.

Nothing but the wedding, Jeremy, and Christine, was ever talked about.

"It's quite natural," Laura said to Alfred, dressing for dinner in a bedroom of great size and height, with thick and expensive rugs and curtains in profusion. "It's perfectly natural, of course. He's their only son, and of course his marriage is very important. I'm so glad they like Christine, and are so charming to her."

"But they're overdoing this wedding business," said Alfred.

Laura privately agreed with him.

"The housemaid means me to wear my blue to-night," she remarked pensively, looking at the mahogany bedstead and the lace coverlet, on the magnificence of which her blue looked very unimpressive indeed.

"Not that clothes matter very much here," she added.

"They have a good cellar," said Alfred.

"And a fire in one's room—especially *such* a fire—is pure bliss."

Thus did the Temples compensate themselves for the undoubted fact that, in the splendour of the Vulliamy establishment, they were slightly bored.

Laura did not actually count it a compensation, but it certainly crossed her mind frequently, that Lady Kingsley-Browne's daughter—so openly and so offensively thrust upon the notice of her parent's acquaintances—had, by her own unprecedented conduct, forfeited a very fair chance of occupying the position now awaiting Christine.

Mrs. Vulliamy only once referred in Laura's hearing to this episode in the past of her son.

"Of course, one has always wondered a little bit about Jeremy's wife," she temperately said. "I daresay you know that at one time he was very strongly attracted—

though it was never an engagement, or anything in the least like it ——"

"I know," said Laura.

"Poor Gertrude Kingsley-Browne! I was always fond of her, and one was quite prepared to welcome the girl. I thought her extremely pretty, too."

"She is certainly very pretty."

But Mrs. Vulliamy continued to speak of Bébée as of the dead.

"But she must have been quite, quite without any morals at all," she gently pursued. "Utterly depraved. One can only be thankful that it came out in time. Of course, I don't attempt to judge her. One should never judge others, I always feel."

"She is still in America."

"Ah, I daresay. America is like that, I believe," returned Mrs. Vulliamy.

What a woman, thought Laura, who might in theory agree that one should never judge others, but who frequently found herself doing so in no lenient spirit.

"Poor Gertrude's husband was a strange man. One heard tales. Not that I wish to dwell upon them. As of course you know, he is no longer with us. But I have often thought that heredity ——"

Mrs. Vulliamy sighed, and Laura said, "Yes! Of course! One does," and thought to herself, "How idiotic this conversation is!"

"Dear little Christine is very bright and sweet. A thoroughly natural, unaffected girl."

"Bébée was never unaffected, whatever else she was," declared Laura warmly.

"You felt that, did you? But I'm sure you must be a wonderful judge of character."

"I don't think it needed that ——"

"It was an infatuation," said Mrs. Vulliamy more gently and solemnly than ever. "A sort of madness. Jeremy saw nothing but her beauty. And of course, having always been devoted to Gertrude, I was as blind as he was. But when I heard that it was all over and that the unfortunate girl had completely gone to the dogs, I said to my husband: 'Mark my words, Anstruther, Jeremy is *thoroughly well out of it,*' I said."

Laura, unable to think of any adequate reply, could only bend her head assentingly.

"Is it perhaps growing a little bit chilly? *We,*" said Mrs. Vulliamy rallyingly, "are not in love. So I think we might perhaps seek the chimney corner."

Although the implications in this small and mild pleasantry were displeasing in the extreme to Laura, she felt obliged tacitly to accept them, and to follow her hostess to the magnificent warmth and splendour of the chimney corner.

On the whole, she preferred the conversation of Mr. Vulliamy to that of his wife. He was a grave man, with a passion for his rain-gauge, and another, lesser passion for travelling in the Europe of tourists.

Every night at dinner, Laura sat next to him, and they discussed the scenery and the hotels in those parts of France, Norway and Switzerland that constituted Laura's experience of foreign travel. She hoped, and believed, that he did not notice how very often they said the same things about these places over and over again.

Of her future brother-in-law Laura saw less than of his parents, but she perceived that Christine had been right in saying that he possessed a sense of humour.

"And does anything else really matter, after all?" was Mrs. Temple's not-very-happily worded enquiry, after imparting this opinion to her sister.

"Not much, certainly," Christine agreed dispassionately. "But as a matter of fact there are lots of other things I like about Jeremy. He is very generous, and easy going, and we both enjoy doing the same things in the same way, which is a great mercy. He can't bear gardening, and he likes going abroad, and we both like London, and we neither of us can endure playing Bridge."

"Have you ever thought what you'll talk about in the evenings after dinner, when you've been married some time, and there isn't anything new to say any more?" Laura solemnly enquired.

"I haven't written out a list of subjects suitable for keeping a husband entertained, if that's what you mean, but I have made up my mind that on evenings when we're by ourselves, if I can't be amusing, or amorous or interesting—then I shall go to bed with a headache and advise Jeremy to go to his Club," said Christine.

Laura left the Castle Gate fully convinced that Christine was about to embark upon the most successful phase of a thoroughly successful career.

The wedding was to take place in London. Edward and

Johnnie—subject to the approval of the doctor, and to the complete elimination, for some weeks previously, of the pink bowl—were to act as pages, and Alfred was to give away the bride.

"You and your husband, of course, will act in *loco parentis*," said Mrs. Vulliamy to Laura. "That will be so delightful."

"But I," said Christine privately to her sister, "am going to pay all the expenses. I've got quite a lot of money saved—truly I have—and I'm simply going to blue it on this."

"Christine, are you—I daresay you will think me very absurd and conventional—but are you happy?"

"Frightfully," said Christine placidly.

"I'm glad," said Laura, almost tearfully.

Christine shook her fair head disapprovingly, kissed Laura, and changed the subject. Laura never knew whether Christine placed to her discredit this brief dialogue as a merely sentimental impulse, or whether she suspected any of the stifled longing that possessed her sister for opportunities that it seemed to her she had never had. For Laura, confronted by Christine's security, Christine's contentment, and Christine's absolute conviction of present and future happiness, was obsessed by a positively frenzied sense of contrast.

She did not wish—except spasmodically and without real fervour—that Alfred had been rich, but she wished with a ceaseless, half-suppressed passion, that now coloured the whole of her days, that she could become possessed of Christine's freedom, Christine's detachment, and

Christine's powers of conducting her affairs with judgment and intelligence. Laura, in fact, shared with several hundred thousands of other people a vain desire to combine the opportunities of youth with the experience of maturity.

She was also in the grip of a variety of other desires, mostly incompatible with one another, such as a longing to be made love to by Duke again, and an exhausted feeling that it would certainly simplify matters never to see him any more, a conviction that she could never let Alfred know that she had fallen in love with another man, and a weak desire to tell him all about it in the hope that he would remain sufficiently unmoved to take away from her any sense of guilt.

"I suppose Freud would say that I had better set about murdering an infant in its cradle," reflected Laura, with stark and joyless humour, "in preference to nursing an unacted desire. What would Freud say to my present state of mind?"

Laura's question was purely rhetorical. If she had dwelt upon the subject, which she had no wish to do, she would have known too well that Freud, had he been in a position to pronounce a verdict, would have declined to look upon her case as being in any way peculiar, unique or interesting. For she could not deny that there is nothing either peculiar, unique or interesting, in wishing for more love, more admiration and more attention than one is ever likely to receive.

Edward and Johnnie received with varying degrees of enthusiasm the information that they were to be pages at their aunt's wedding. It had evidently been easy for nurse to inoculate Edward with some of her own excitement, but the un-suggestible Johnnie was inclined to parade his own originality by adopting an opposite point of view. The unfortunate Edward was torn between his natural tendency to enjoy whatever he was told was enjoyable, his unvarying instinct for imitating Johnnie, and his desire to propitiate nurse. It was left to Laura to make up his mind for him, and as usual she did so with a mild contempt for his vacillations, and a contrasting admiration for his characterful junior. In Edward she saw all the acquired characteristics that she least admired in herself, in Johnnie's those that she had not had the strength to develop, but that might once have been hers.

She wondered from time to time, remembering Mrs. Bakewell, whether it might not be possible to live in her children, as the phrase runs. It did not seem so.

Edward, physically independent and spiritually and mentally undeveloped, did not really interest his mother as an individual. She knew that more and more, as time went on, he would live in a world of games and machines and little, unrelated facts about things and animals— never about people—and that in that world he would, rightly, have very little place for her. The bond between them, such as it was, was unlikely to survive the needs of his childhood.

For Johnnie, her love was vivid, and even passionate. He possessed the power to hurt her. She was the secondary luminary in his ego-centric world. But his need of her, also, would diminish, as he came to realise more and more the importance—the, to him, supreme importance—of his own effect upon other people. Johnnie's very likeness to herself would defeat any attempt on Laura's part to monopolise him.

Nor did she seriously wish to do so—for she had read several very alarming works about the strange, and indeed scandalous, effects of what the authors rightly termed Vampire-Mothers, upon the subsequent careers of their children.

Laura, with a vague idea of sublimating her desires, thought of Alfred, of her own writing, and even—it must be admitted, as a last resource—of The Poor. But Alfred had already got everything that she had to give him, her writing was obliged to be subordinated to the claims of housekeeping, and The Poor, Laura honestly felt, were better catered for by existing organisations than by the manufactured activities of her own superfluous energy.

She arranged to go to London a week before Christine's wedding, and to let nurse, the boys, and Alfred follow at the last moment.

"I shall see Duke," she thought, her heart beating faster.

And, she added, tempering her own momentary exultation:

"This must be settled one way or the other. I can't go on like this—and it isn't fair on him, either."

A general sense of unfairness, in fact, possessed her. Things, she felt, were not fair on Duke, on Alfred, on the children, on herself.

Things must be redressed.

In this way did Laura, like a timid horse approaching an obstacle with sidelong steps, bring herself to the point of acknowledging that her love-affair was within sight of a crisis.

Chapter XVI

"I SHOULD like to hear about it. I am *interested*," said Lady Kingsley-Browne, with what Laura could not help feeling to be a creditable effort of generosity.

"I don't say that I was not surprised, but I was interested. I know you so well—I've met and liked your sister—the—the young man has stayed here. How did it all happen?" said Lady Kingsley-Browne, putting Laura into a difficulty.

For it was impossible to reply: "The engagement of my sister to the richest commoner in England was brought about by his astonishment and disgust at the atrocious conduct of your daughter, the original object of his affections." She decided upon a tempered truthfulness.

"Jeremy was very unhappy when he found that Bébée —that she cared for somebody else—and he happened to meet Christine just then. Of course, she knew the whole story and was dreadfully sorry for him, and he seems to have taken her into his confidence from the very start. And they made great friends."

"Ah, yes. So often—on the rebound."

"Oh yes," agreed Laura, perfectly understanding, and anxious to concede everything possible to anyone so profoundly humiliated as she felt her unfortunate hostess to have been.

"I think we shall find tea in the library," said Lady Kingsley-Browne, with her old, vague air of having no personal concern with the activities of her well-trained servants. "Come along, my dear. It's so nice to see you, and I have something to tell you."

Remembering the last announcement made by the same informant, Laura indulged in a brief variety of hair-raising conjectures as to the direction taken by latest activities of that informant's daughter, but she judged it prudent only to emit a wordless sound of interrogation.

"Come along," repeated her neighbour. "We can have an undisturbed chat over the fire. I hope your good man won't be in too great a hurry to pick you up on his way home."

"He is at a meeting. They always take a little while."

"It was nice of you to come," said Lady Kingsley-Browne rather wistfully. "And I always meant to thank you, dear, for writing to me yourself as you did, before the engagement was announced."

Laura felt touched.

"Christine and I didn't want you just to see it in *The Times*," she murmured.

"So very kind and thoughtful. But I must tell you that Bébée, poor darling child, has taken up quite a new line."

"Oh, what?" exclaimed Laura, her tone of dismay betraying her conviction that any new line followed by Bébée must necessarily be a disastrous one.

"She is leaving *him*—in fact, she already has left him. She has—it seems a most extraordinary thing, I know—but she has taken up religion. At least, I suppose you might call it a religion. Do come nearer the fire, Laura. I wonder if there are any scones, or anything hot? Oh yes—I see something in the fender. I do hope you like muffins?"

"Thank you. But do please go on ——"

"It seems as though Bébée has so much personality, poor darling, that she has to express herself in ways that might, in anybody else, seem almost odd."

"Yes."

"It seems that she has met a man—I'm sure things would have been just the same had it been another woman ——"

Lady Kingsley-Browne paused, but as Laura felt equally sure that whatever "it" might be, things would not have been the same had it been another woman, she made no reply.

"It just happens to have been a man—Ernest Blog is his name, but Americans so often have names that we think odd—well, he has discovered, or invented, a tremendous new creed, and he has quite converted Bébée to it. And the really bright spot is, that they are on their way to England, to—to try and spread it."

"They?"

"She has joined him," explained Laura's neighbour, with determined matter-of-factness, "as his secretary."

"Like she did with A. B.," said Laura reflectively.

"Mr. Blog is not married. You may say that simplifies things, in a way—but, of course, in another way, it makes them more complicated."

"Yes, I see it does."

"Bébée, I always feel, is a law unto herself," said Bébée's mother pleadingly.

"Indeed, yes."

"One really can hardly judge her by *our* middle-aged, matter-of-course standards. So much more idealistic and enthusiastic. I can't tell you how ardently she has taken up this new creed."

"What, exactly, is it?"

"Well, from the letter she wrote me—her handwriting is always a little difficult, but one could make out a good deal, here and there—Mr. Blog lays down just one or two broad principles. Nothing sectarian, you know—it rather reminded me of the Women's Institute movement, that I know you're so keen about, in that way. But sort of guiding lines, that make life simpler for all of us."

"One would be glad to hear of anything that would make life simpler," said Mrs. Temple, with some feeling.

"Yes, wouldn't one?"

"I should like to hear some of the—the Blog principles, if you can remember them. I am not laughing, really and truly. It's only the name that—just for the moment——"

"I know," said Lady Kingsley-Browne forbearingly. "It has a quaint sound, I am bound to admit. But the principles seem very simple and beautiful. She enclosed a sheet, with some Rules of Life written on it, put together by Mr. Blog. Nothing dogmatic, you know. Just: It is Better to Speak the Truth than to tell Lies, and Kindness is Right, but Cruelty is Wrong. Things of that sort. I liked all that part of it."

"Was there another part, as well?"

"Two other parts. One was about diet, which always

seems to enter so tremendously into any new kind of religion. I always rather wonder why. His—Ernest Blog's—idea is nothing *cooked*. Only things that have ripened in the sun—and, of course, in this country, that would limit one a good deal. But anything in the way of drink, and as much of it as one likes. Prohibition, you see."

"Not in England."

"I know. Perhaps he'll modify that part of it over here."

"And what else?" said Laura.

"Free Love," said Lady Kingsley-Browne, as one accepting the inevitable. "Oh yes, my dear, there's always a catch in these things, and though it's wrapped up in Universal Brotherhood and Spiritual Planes, I know exactly what it all amounts to. But I'm past caring. All the morals that you and I were taught in the nursery have been turned upside down, and if people don't do all the things they want to do, then they get complexes and repressions, and end by doing other, much worse things."

Laura remained dumbfounded, staring at the exponent of her own theories, that somehow seemed so strangely perverted when preached in conjunction with the evangel of Mr. Ernest Blog.

"It's all going to be terribly difficult to explain to people, I know, but Bébée has a wonderful way of carrying things off, and so few people see anything odd about anything nowadays. I thought I could go to her in London, but she is determined to come down here, and to bring

him too, of course. One will just have to make the best
of it, and after all, it isn't so bad as her infatuation for
A. B., who is so terribly well known. I hear he's had a
nervous breakdown, by the way, poor man, and his wife
has taken him to the south of France."

"Is he recovering?" asked Laura in a strangled voice.

"Quite, I believe."

The library door opened, and Laura and her hostess
stared at one another in a common dismay as "Major and
Mrs. Bakewell" were announced.

"Oh dear, I never thought ——" said Lady Kingsley-
Browne as she rose to her feet. "Well, this *is* nice of you!
How are you, Major Bakewell? I haven't seen you for
months."

A short contest in unselfishness followed, won, as usual,
by Mrs. Bakewell, and Laura sat down again in a chair
so placed that on one side she was scorched by the fire,
and on the other hampered by the tea-table.

She talked to Major Bakewell, about rope-making—a
subject that had presented itself she knew not how—and
heard with dismay fragments of the dialogue taking place
upon the other side of the tea-table.

"America . . . home almost directly . . . Blog, but
then American names *are* rather like that . . . It is a
Happier Thing to have Friends than to make Enemies
. . . But nothing cooked."

Mrs. Bakewell's voice perhaps from being employed in
a better cause, was more resonant a great deal than that
of Lady Kingsley-Browne.

"I always feel it so wrong to judge *anybody*," she said,

"even those who, to our poor finite perceptions, appear to have outraged every law of God and man."

Major Bakewell stirred uneasily, but still flogged gallantly at the now nearly moribund topic of rope-making.

"Universal Brotherhood . . ." came more faintly from Lady Kingsley-Browne. "So very glad to have her home again . . . unconventional, and even imprudent, perhaps, but then with magnetism like hers . . ."

"And to think that I knew Bébée when she was in the nursery!" exclaimed Mrs. Bakewell, suddenly and strongly, as who should say: "To think that Messaline was once an innocent child!"

At this Laura and Major Bakewell simultaneously abandoned all pretence, and gave themselves up to an attentive silence.

"Even in the nursery," said Lady Kingsley-Browne courageously, "Bébée was ridiculously attractive to men. I used to think it was her fairness. The man who came to wind the clocks, even, used to bring sweets for her."

"Cynthia has a bright smile for *everyone* who comes to the house. But I have never allowed my children to eat sweets. The first time I took Theodore to the dentist, he said to me, 'Mrs. Bakewell! This child has Perfect Teeth. I have never seen anything like it.' And Theodore—such a regular boy—spoke up before I could say a word: 'That's because we have never been allowed to suck sweets between meals,' he said. Dear little fellow, it was so like him. Always rational."

"How very nice," Laura murmured, already seeking

for an anecdote about Johnnie wherewith to counter the precocity of the insufferable Theodore.

She felt it unfortunate that, just as she was in the middle of it, Alfred should arrive, and that the politeness of her listeners should compel her to finish it in his presence.

She was not surprised that, on the way home, he should inquire:

"Don't women ever talk about anything but cooks and children, when they get together?"

"We hadn't mentioned either until the Bakewells arrived. I had been hearing about Baybay."

Even Alfred displayed comparative animation in begging to be furnished with a report of so sensational a conversation.

"But I'm glad I went," said Laura in conclusion. "We couldn't have let her see the announcement in *The Times,* just like everybody else. Though as a matter of fact, she didn't mind nearly as much as I should have expected. We hardly talked about the wedding at all, and I never even told her that we'd been to stay at Castle Gate."

"Why should you?" said Alfred, who—as Laura reminded herself—never did see any reason why anybody should ever be told anything.

She herself derived a certain amount of satisfaction from the interest aroused in the neighbourhood by the news of Christine's engagement—struck though she was by a tendency on the part of nearly everybody to speak as though Christine were her eldest daughter rather than her younger sister.

Christine, who had sold her flat to great advantage at exactly the moment when it best suited her to sell it, engaged rooms at the hotel from which she had decided to be married, and Laura joined her there a week before the wedding.

It was not until Duke Ayland actually met her at the terminus, that Laura suddenly realised afresh what this relationship meant to her. At Applecourt, it had lost poignancy from the sheer weight and force of other pre-occupations. Then, she saw him amongst the crowd making his way straight to her, his dark, eager face illuminated.

"Thank heaven you've come! I've been here two mortal hours, though I knew perfectly well what time your train was due. Here—give me your case ——"

He was masterful in the approved masculine way.

"I could go by Underground," suggested Laura, who did not, however, really intend to do such a thing.

"You're not going to," returned Duke.

It was the answer that her sense of the appropriate had already instinctively framed for him.

He opened the door of a taxi for her, tipped the porter who brought her luggage, and got in beside her.

"Right!"

The door banged.

"Laura!" said Duke Ayland, gazing earnestly at her.

He retained sufficient presence of mind to take off his hat immediately and throw it upon the floor, and Laura retained sufficient powers of observation to notice that

he did so, and to make her own deduction as to his mo-
tive for the action—nevertheless, both of them were nearly
suffocating with excitement.

The atmosphere was charged.

"Laura, I *must* kiss you!"

"No," said Laura.

Duke Ayland took her into his arms, tilted her face
gently up to his, and kissed her repeatedly. Then he
asked her to forgive him.

"I couldn't help it, sweetest. It's such an age since
I've seen you, and I've wanted you so dreadfully."

"So have I ——"

"Laura, we can't go on like this. We need one another . . . ."

Laura, equally convinced of the impossibility of what
was implied by "going on like this," had nevertheless no
solution to offer. She gave herself up to the extraordinary rapture of being made violent love to by a man with
whom she was violently in love.

In an incredibly short flash of time, the hotel was
reached, and the taxi stopped.

"Can I come in with you?"

"No, I don't think so. But ring me up to-night, at
seven o'clock."

When Christine met her sister she exclaimed:

"How well you look, Laura! That *is* a becoming hat.
How are the children?"

"Quite all right. Edward only coughs occasionally at
night, and Johnnie really had it very lightly. You

wouldn't know that there'd ever been anything the matter with them."

"How splendid! I hope they'll like the little girl brides-maids."

"The white Cromwell shoes for Johnnie are half a size too small. I've brought them up to get them changed at the shop."

Wedding preparations engulfed them both. Laura, whose shopping activities had for years been limited by a slender income to the resources of the shops in Quinnerton, and a very occasional order by post to the Army and Navy Stores, enjoyed herself very much.

She met numbers of Jeremy's relations, was assured by Christine that she had made a favourable impression upon them all, and saw again the pale and distinguished Mrs. Vulliamy and the serious Mr. Vulliamy. (It disconcerted her a little to find that she and Mr. Vulliamy instantly began to talk about hotels in Normandy, with words, phrases and sentiments identical with those employed at their last meeting—but then, as Mrs. Vulliamy might have said, some people are like that.)

She dined with Duke Ayland on the night after her arrival, and in the extraordinary relief and satisfaction of being with him again, and of finding him as much in love with her as ever—for Laura's inferiority complex had not allowed her to take this in any way for granted—she allowed the evening to pass without any very definite reference to the future.

"When can I see you again?" he asked her. "You come

to London so seldom. Can't we go somewhere to-morrow?"

"I'm here on purpose to help Christine—and Alfred and the boys are joining me in a day or two. We could do one thing more, perhaps, before they come. But meals are most difficult of all, because there are all sorts of Vulliamy relations, and if we're not lunching with them, then they seem to be dining with us."

"Keep your last free evening for me, won't you, Laura?"

"I'll try," she promised, and wondered why nobody had ever asked her so fervently for the privilege of an evening's tête-à-tête in the days when she could have acquiesced with no underlying sensation of guilt.

They made one other appointment, to look at a collection of pictures in a public gallery.

⁻The suggestion was Laura's.

"I don't in the least want to talk to you in a place like that," protested Ayland.

"If you don't want to talk, we can look at the pictures," Laura replied flippantly. She felt very happy.

But, as usual, after they had separated and after she had talked to Christine about the trousseau, and the bridesmaids' bouquets, and her own new frock and hat for the wedding, and after she had gone to her bedroom— as usual, Laura fell a victim to reaction.

It was a relief to her that the two or three remaining days before the wedding were crowded ones, and gave her no time for thought, and very little for conversation.

Christine was very nice to her, and so radiantly cheerful that it was impossible not to be infected, and she and Laura found themselves giggling like schoolgirls together in a fashion that neither ever achieved with anybody else.

"We ought to be more sentimental than this," Laura protested. "We never seem to do anything but laugh."

"A very good thing too. I think you ought to laugh a lot more than you do, Laura."

"Who with and who at?" inelegantly retorted Mrs. Temple. "Apart from Alfred and the children, nobody at Quinnerton is particularly likely to do or say anything very funny."

"Except Baybay. She is capable of almost unlimited funniness, isn't she? For heaven's sake, Laura, write and tell me at the first possible moment what she says and does when she gets home with her Yankee Tub-Thumper."

"They are going to spread the Blog creed in England."

"Beginning with unfortunate Lady Kingsley-Browne, I suppose," declared Christine. "And very likely ending with her, for that matter. Can you see Mrs. Bakewell, for instance, allowing herself to be converted by Bébée?"

"Neither Mrs. Bakewell nor anybody else in the neighbourhood, after the scandal she's caused. Everybody knows about A. B. Onslow."

"At least Blog hasn't got a wife, has he?"

"I believe not."

"Then whatever she does, can't be any worse than what she has done already."

"Do you think—seriously, I mean—that the A. B. Onslow business was—was very bad?" said Laura, looking with very great attentiveness at the fastening of a bracelet.

"Bad?" said Christine vigorously. "I don't so much mind the badness of playing the fool with somebody who is already married to another person, as the general futility, and senselessness, and utter vulgarity of it!"

Chapter XVII

"I'm not going on like this."

"But, Duke ——"

"Darling, you can see for yourself that it's impossible. I'm madly in love with you, and I can neither marry you, nor take you away with me. And to meet as we do at present is more than I can stand."

"You don't mean that you'd rather we didn't see one another any more?"

"Honestly, Laura dear, there are times when I feel that might almost be easier than—this sort of thing."

Ayland glanced round the semi-deserted picture-gallery, in the middle of which, on a long red plush seat, he sat with Laura.

"You've told me that there's no hope whatever of my having you altogether, because of your children."

"And because of my husband, too," Laura pointed out, with ill-judged honesty. "I'm fond of Alfred."

Duke winced slightly.

"I know. You've said so before. I cannot imagine why you tell me so often."

"Because," said Laura, with spirit, "you might very reasonably suppose, from the way I've behaved, that I didn't care two straws about him. And I *do*. I may not be in love with Alfred, but I'm very fond of him, and even if the children didn't exist at all I couldn't ever do anything that would hurt him."

"Then, my dear, you are not really in love with me."

"Duke!"

"How can you be! If you were, you'd want me as much as I want you."

"It isn't that ——"

The things that they were saying were not new. Almost identical words and phrases had already passed between them, and every fresh impetus given to the discussion made Laura rather more unhappy.

She sat now and looked, almost without seeing it, at a large painting of five wolves devouring three dogs in the snow.

She felt that Ayland was on the brink of saying something that she earnestly wished him not to say.

The next minute he had said it.

"Laura, darling—there's only one thing to do, if you can't come to me openly. Aren't you brave enough, or do you not love me enough?"

"You know I love you."

"Then be kind to me," he whispered.

"I can't. Deceiving Alfred . . . and after all I did make a promise when I married him."

"Which you've already broken, involuntarily, when you fell in love with another man."

"That was something I couldn't help. But what you're asking me to do would really be treachery. If I wasn't married, Duke, or if I was a widow, I shouldn't hesitate for one instant. Won't you believe me?"

"Believing you doesn't make things any better," he returned. "How do you intend this affair to end, my dear?

Am I to go on writing you letters once or twice a week in which I can't say a single one of the things I really want to say, and meeting you once or twice a year when you come to London, in restaurants, and public places, and getting perhaps five minutes alone with you in a taxi to kiss you good-night? I don't think you know what you're asking, if you expect any man to be content with that."

"At the very beginning, Duke, I told you that I was very fond of Al ——"

"Don't say it again, for heaven's sake!" He looked both angry and unhappy.

Laura also felt unhappy, but she was not angry. She was not angry with Ayland because she was still very much in love with him, and because she recognised that there was justification for his impatience, and she was not angry with herself because it seemed to her—as to so many—that acts and omissions that appear definitely wrong in theory, become, in practice, only unforeseen, almost unavoidable, results of the pressure of circumstances.

"Laura, will you give me one week? Come away with me somewhere?"

"How could I?"

"Of course you could. It's always possible to arrange things. You could go abroad, surely, to Paris or somewhere?"

"I've never done such a thing in my life. If I said I wanted to, I've no doubt that Alfred would let me, but

I should have to tell any number of lies, and I can't do it, Duke."

He gazed at her almost with despair.

"Don't answer now. Think it over. I shall see you again—besides seeing you at the wedding, I mean?"

"Yes."

Laura got up. For the first time she really saw the picture of the wolves and the dogs, bespattering the snow with their blood, and found it singularly revolting.

"How hideous that is!" she murmured. "We'll talk about it again. I must go now, but we'll talk later on."

But of what good was all this talking?

It was talking, indeed, that had brought them to their present pass.

Sometimes, reviewing the course of her acquaintance with Duke, Laura found it difficult to remember through what successive stages they had passed, in order to reach their present relationship, so unsatisfactory to at least one of them.

She had been herself far more happy than unhappy. The inward certainty that she stood to one man for the romantic ideal had comforted her in her matter-of-fact relations with another, and Ayland's love-making had brought to her the reassurance craved by her waning youth.

She felt that it would be impossible to let him go. But it would be impossible—and far more so—to break up her married life and leave her children.

A week—one week with Duke Ayland? "One week, out of all my life," thought Laura, as others, similarly circumstanced, have both thought and said before her. "After all, it wouldn't hurt anybody, as things are, and Duke and I would have something to remember."

In her mind was the vague conviction, still uncrystallised, that after that one week, she and Ayland would not again see one another very often. It seemed inevitable.

But it was quite illogical, as part of her consciousness well realised.

The frantic hooting of motor-horns and the yell of a passer-by roused Laura to a violent momentary activity, as she sprang back to the pavement that she had absently-mindedly endeavoured to leave.

"Dreamy-eyes!" said the taxi-driver who had nearly cut short Laura's perplexities for her summarily, jocosely satirical.

Laura blushed.

"*Fool!*" she thought.

She deferred the consideration of her problem until she had reached the Knightsbridge Hotel.

"There's a gentleman waiting in the lounge, madam," the porter told her.

Laura, in the hot, plush-and-cane chair discomfort of the lounge, saw Christine's friend, the medical student called Losh.

He looked, as before, unkempt, shabby, cheerful, enthusiastic.

"Mrs. Temple, do forgive me. I shan't be able to come and see Christine tied up, and I had to come and tell her so, and give her my final blessing. Any hope?"

"She said she'd meet me here for tea at five. It's nearly that now. Do sit down and wait till she comes."

"Thanks most fearfully, I think I will. Sure I'm not barging in?"

"Of course you're not. I'm sorry you can't come to the wedding."

"So'm I, but I'm taking Mids. Only just heard about it, as a matter of fact. Well, it's the beginning of the end for me, thank God! I shall have qualified by this time next year if I get through my Finals."

"What shall you do then?" Laura enquired, to humour him.

"Go to America, if I can wangle my passage money out of someone. They have the most topping Psychopathic Hospitals out there, and one can always get a job, once one's actually on the spot. I want to study their methods of dealing with juvenile offenders frightfully. They put them under psychological observation, I believe, for weeks and weeks."

"That's what you'd like?"

"Rath-er!"

"I suppose there must be a certain attraction about it. People are always interesting."

"Yes, aren't they, by Jove! You see, Mrs. Temple," earnestly said the young man, excitedly gesticulating with his bony hands, "everybody has a streak of abnormality in them somewhere. You're abnormal—I'm abnormal. Only we have it under control——"

Laura, gazing at him not without fascination, felt inclined to wonder whether we had.

"You'd be astonished if I told you of the impulses that perfectly decent, respectable middle-aged women sometimes experience."

"Should I?"

"You see, the Unconscious is so terribly Primordial. Of course, it's all hedged round and covered up with acquired things—civilisation and the fear of punishment, and so on and so on. But don't you yourself often find ——"

"Let's not talk personally, if you don't mind."

"I beg your pardon. Of course I won't if you don't want to."

He looked so much disappointed that Laura feared that she had hurt his feelings.

She said hastily:

"I daresay you could help me about the case of a— a woman I heard about. I don't know her at all well, but I—I hear about her quite a lot. I've often wondered ——"

Losh was gazing at her with even more than his usual intensity, and since it is always gratifying to feel that one is being interesting, Laura was encouraged to pursue the case of the hypothetical woman.

Perhaps Losh really might have some new and helpful light to throw on the question, she told herself, seeking an excuse for the relief of talking about her own complicated and distressing affairs.

"It's really this. She's married to a man ——" Laura paused, and then said with violence, "to a man she's really, thoroughly *fond* of—but with whom she isn't exactly in love. In fact, not at all in love. They've got children. And she—the woman—has fallen in love with another man."

Laura stopped again.

"Is the other man in love with her?"

"Oh yes. Yes, certainly."

"I only asked because it's quite usual for a middle-aged woman who's had no satisfaction out of her marriage to go off the deep end about pretty nearly any sort of fellow, good, bad, or indifferent, whether he's having any or not. It's a mild form of hysteria, very often."

"It's nothing in the least like that," Laura assured him, trying to keep a sense of profound indignation from quivering in her voice. "The man is quite as much in love as she is. More, if anything. In fact, he wants her to go away with him."

"The best thing she could do."

"But the children ——"

"Oh, I see. Did you mean go off for good, or just take a week-end together?"

"He has asked her to go away for good, I believe, but she won't. So it would be a—a—just a temporary experience."

Laura looked at Losh, and he looked intelligently back at her.

"She can't make up her mind."

"Is she religious? That sort of thing? I mean, would that stand in her way?"

"She isn't a conventionally religious woman."

"Not a Roman Catholic, or anything like that? We

have great difficulty with Roman Catholics, of course, because of their priests. They're dead against honest analysis every time."

"There isn't anything of that sort," Laura repeated.

"Then I don't see where the difficulty comes in."

"The husband. She hates the idea of deceiving him."

"Then she'll have to tell him."

"How can she?"

"Well," said the young man reasonably, "she must do one or the other, you know, mustn't she? What sort of fellow is he?"

Laura hesitated. In what terms could she make Alfred's personality apparent to Losh? At last she said:

"The kind of man who thinks that psycho-analysts are all humbugs, and that the people who go to them are always hysterical women."

Losh nodded.

"I get you. I know the type. Quite a lot of them about still. Believe in Church and State, and one law for the man and another for the woman, and to hell with all this new-fangled jargon of the day, if you tell them anything they didn't hear in Queen Victoria's reign. *I* see."

"But he's very nice," said Laura weakly.

"Oh, quite."

The niceness, or otherwise, of the subject under discussion, was evidently a matter of the utmost indifference in the psychological scale of values.

"Then I take it that there's no hope of your friend's being able to go to her husband quite simply and naturally, as you or I might do, and saying: 'Look here, old thing'—or whatever she calls him—'as you and I don't seem to click quite as well as we should like, what about giving the other lad a week at Weymouth'—or wherever they want to go—'and getting a little fun out of life, and then coming back a better and a brighter girl, so to speak?'"

"I don't think you understand," said Laura. "For her —it's most horribly serious."

"But, my dear, it can't be. Otherwise she'd do a bunk with the other fellow," said the medical student simply.

"The children. I told you she had children."

"I know. That's all right. If she puts the children first, well and good. Then obviously she must either chuck the blighter she's in love with, or start an intrigue —week-ends, and so on, like I said at the beginning. But you say, it's most horribly serious. And I say, it can't be. Because if it was, the kids simply wouldn't be in it. She'd leave 'em, and go to her man."

Laura stared at her adviser in the stricken silence of utter spiritual devastation.

"Would she?" she said at last.

"Obviously. But most Englishwomen have the maternal instinct much more strongly developed than the mating instinct."

"For the sake of the argument," said Laura in a slightly tremulous voice, "you can take it absolutely for granted that the woman I'm speaking of won't ever leave her children."

"Right," said Losh cheerfully. "Then it's not what the Russians call a Grawnde Passiong. Is the husband the kind of bloke who'd divorce her?"

"I don't know. I—somehow I don't believe he would."

"Good. What about the other johnnie? Is he married, too?"

"No."

"Well, honestly, the best thing she could do would be to go off with him for a bit. She must use her own judgment about putting the husband wise. From what you tell me, I shouldn't think it would be any use. No object in making the poor chap wretched."

"It's she who'll be wretched if she has to tell lies and deceive him."

Losh shrugged his shoulders.

"She sounds to me pretty spineless altogether. Not that I blame her. Women have a rotten time all along the line. But she's lucky, really, your pal is, to have a chance at all. Hundreds and thousands of women in this country would give the eyes out of their head for what you might call one illicit thrill, and there simply isn't anybody to provide it. I say, are you sure I'm not boring you?"

"Perfectly certain. I—I'm really interested in this particular question. I think my friend is rather—she isn't absolutely an average woman, in some ways."

"No? Well, of course you know more about it than I do. Only one gets a bit fed up with the woman who'll let a fellow go all out after her, and tell him that he's the love of her life and so on, and then, when he very naturally asks, 'Well, what about it?' throws a fit and says she couldn't ever wrong her husband and won't he just go on being friends?"

"When it's put like that, I agree—in a way."

"Well, of course. Any sensible person would. The fact is, of course, that such a lot of women live in their imaginations. They've no other outlet. A woman like yourself"—Laura hoped that she did not start—"can let herself go a bit in her writing. But these wretched, inarticulate souls, who can't do anything but yearn in silence—half of them are neurotic before they're forty. It's all rot, that about women not getting neurotic if they've plenty to do. Very often the more neurotic they are, the more they try and do, and then they get nervous breakdowns, and are worse than ever."

"And if they didn't do things?"

"They'd still be neurotic," said Losh.

"Oh!"

"It's a vicious circle, I know. But I don't believe in all this blinking optimism. Better face things as they are. I say d'you suppose Christine's got run over or anything? She's frightfully late, isn't she?"

"I expect she'll be here in a minute. Are you in a hurry?"

"No. So long as I'm not boring you."

Laura shook her head.

"You're interested in psychology, aren't you?"

"Anyone who writes fiction has to be."

"I suppose so. Well, do tell your pal that all this confession to the husband stuff is out of date. All she's got to do is to break away from her own repressions for a bit, and keep her own counsel about it."

"You don't think that lies and cheating matter?" said Laura bitterly.

"Of course they matter. But we live under such damned artificial conditions that we can't do without 'em. And anyway, other things matter more. Do you know what Freud says: 'It is better to murder an infant in its cradle than to nurse an unacted desire?'"

"Does he?" said Laura, considerably startled at this echo of her own recent self-communings.

"Not, mind you, that I'm prepared to go with Freud the whole way, for—— Hullo!"

Christine, composed and smart, unhurried in spite of her lateness, walked into the hall of the hotel.

She and Losh greeted one another with exclamations and tea was ordered.

They were noisy and merry, all three of them.

Laura perceived, without any very great surprise, that Losh assumed a considerable degree of intimacy to have been established between her and himself in their half-hour's tête-à-tête.

Presently she left him with Christine.

She went up to her bedroom—filled, after the manner of all hotel bedrooms, with crumpled tissue paper and chilly squares of white crochet-cotton—and sat down on the edge of the comfortless bed. She felt extraordinarily tired.

Losh had been interesting and sincere—if immoral. No, a-moral was the word that everybody used now.

Laura wanted to remember what he had said, and to think it over quite dispassionately, but she found that she was so very tired she could remember very little, and was quite incapable of any thinking over at all.

When Christine came upstairs and knocked at her sister's door, Laura was still sitting on the edge of the bed.

"You look tired, darling. Losh is so terribly in earnest, even when he's playing the fool, that he wears one out. You must have been a great success, by the way, while you were waiting for me to come in. He said you were a most frightfully interesting person."

Laura felt uneasy, rather than gratified, at this tribute.

"What sort of way did he mean?"

"You may well ask, knowing what his tastes are!" Christine returned, looking at herself in Laura's hand-glass. "(What shall I do, Laura, if I get a really plain fit on my wedding-day—such as I have now, for instance? I suppose I really ought to say, what will Jeremy do?) Losh didn't say, exactly, why you were so interesting, but I gathered that you'd been telling him the story of your life, rather. Losh is terribly discreet, really, although he does talk so much, and you're perfectly safe with him."

Laura felt that at the moment she did not care whether Losh had penetrated the feeble disguise of her fable or not.

"What are we doing to-night, Laura? I know Jeremy is taking us to another relation, but I've forgotten which

one. That's the only part of being married that's rather
a bore—all this digging up of relations that one's never
been to see for years, and will probably never go and see
again."

"You're lucky not to have old cousin Louisa and poor
Selina to go and see. At least, Jeremy's relations live
in get-at-able places, or if they don't, you can go to them
in a car comfortably."

"Well, who is it to-night?" Christine took out her engagement book from a brand-new crocodile bag, with her
monogram in gold. "Eaton Square. That's his aunt, I
think—Mrs. Arthur Hobbs. A widow with dogs, and
plays Bridge. It's a pity all his relations are such Phil-
istines, but it'll give the children a better chance.
The children of parents who are both brainy generally
turn out awful—either so precocious that they die young,
or so nervy that one can't do anything with them. Our
children ought to have decent physiques, *and* quite good
brains. Like your Johnnie, in fact."

"You do want to have children?"

"Oh yes. Not immediately, of course, and not more
than about three, at decent intervals. But we both want
a family, fortunately."

"You're quite right. Children," said Laura thoughtfully, "keep married people together."

"Darling, what absolute nonsense!" exclaimed Christine ruthlessly. "What can you be thinking about, to
say things like that? Married people who haven't anything else to keep them together except their children,
would surely be better apart. So terribly hard on the

wretched children, too, just to serve as links for chaining an unwilling couple together."

"I suppose I'm old-fashioned," gloomily said Laura, who would have repudiated such an accusation almost with frenzy at a more normal moment.

Christine did not hesitate to take advantage of her sister's mood of fatigue.

"Not old-fashioned, exactly, but conventional. Yes, darling, you are, in some ways. Your ideas of right and wrong, for instance, seem to me stereotyped. As though you didn't really feel that every single case in the world has got to be judged on its own merits, and not by some outside, arbitrary standard."

"If you lived at Quinnerton ——" began Laura.

"I know. I dare say I should. But I hope one of these days you'll make up your mind that you aren't actually rooted to the earth at Applecourt, and that ——"

The elder sister, long dormant in Mrs. Temple, had nevertheless existed in Laura Fairfield, and now woke again.

"I go away from home quite as much as I want to— we both do—and I'm quite satisfied with such standards as I *have* got, thank you, Christine."

"Well, well," said Christine thoughtfully. "I dare say my little head is rather turned by all this sort of thing," she waved her left hand, with its enormous glowing square of green fire. "I'm sorry if I was tiresome." She went away.

Laura felt all the annoyance of the person put in the wrong by the generosity of her opponent.

Christine could afford to be generous, and good-humoured, she reflected.

Apart from an inconspicuous—but after all, comparatively short—childhood, during which she had been entirely overshadowed by the Grecian nymph Laura, Christine had made a success of her life. By this Laura meant, as almost all women do mean, that Christine had attracted men, dressed well, and kept her head.

She was just about to be married to a man who was very rich, neither old, ugly, nor half-witted, and who appeared to be in love with her. Laura had not the slightest doubt that Christine would also make a success of her marriage, although she was entering upon it, so far as could be seen, without earnestness, without illusion, and without emotion.

Perhaps that was why.

"Only what," thought Laura—by this time on the verge of an uneasy doze—"what is to be done, if one is by nature earnest, and emotional, and desperately given to illusions?"

Probably there was nothing to be done.

Perhaps other people, even the successful ones, sometimes had doubts of their own competence, their ability to impress upon the rest of humanity exactly that aspect of themselves which they most wished to present. . . .

But did they take even such doubts seriously? Laura felt certain that they did not.

An hour later, she was surprised by the discovery that she had slept.

A symptom of middle-age, she decided pessimistically,

this dropping asleep in the daytime. But it might also be regarded as a symptom of justifiable physical fatigue, after strenuous shopping, and as a result of considerable nervous tension. By the time that Laura had looked in the glass, and seen that her eyes looked less tired, and her skin clearer, she had adopted the latter explanation of her unprecedented daytime sleep.

Chapter XVIII

ALFRED TEMPLE's procedure, when travelling with his children—a thing which seldom occurred—was entirely contrary to that of his wife, as she perceived when she went to meet them at Paddington station.

Nurse, Johnnie and Edward emerged from one third-class carriage, and Alfred, at the opposite end of the train, from another. He had deliberately separated himself from them. Laura's own journeyings with Edward and Johnnie, on such occasions as visits to the sea, or to relations, had been of a very different description, as she could not help remembering.

She had then read aloud, in a voice low enough not to disturb other people in the carriage, and yet loud enough to be heard above the noise of the train, she had told stories, had pointed out objects of interest to be seen from the window, and had provided—and prolonged as much as possible—a variety of meals.

"A railway journey is a nervous strain for little children," had been the explanation that she had given to both herself and Alfred.

It had also been a nervous strain for Laura, under such conditions.

Nurse, however, appeared calm, and the little boys cheerful and un-tired, although black with the unparalleled blackness only to be collected from the assiduous exploring of every part of a railway carriage.

Alfred—as well he might, thought Laura—said that they had had a very good journey.

Laura, clasping a little soft hand in each of hers, and looking from one small, beaming face to the other, was assailed by the quick rush of emotion that the sight of her children, after however brief a separation, would always rouse in her.

They looked so small, so pleased and innocent, in the noise and smoke of the big station. They were so manifestly confident of her power to protect them, and make them happy. . . .

"We're not waiting for anything, are we?" inquired Alfred. "There's no luggage."

"No, of course not. We'll get into a taxi at once. They must want their tea, poor darlings!"

In the taxi, Laura at once experienced the familiar difficulties of conversing satisfactorily with her husband and her children at one and the same time.

"Well, I suppose you've been busy, and Christine too?"

"Yes, but everything's ——"

"Mummie, have I ever been to London before?"

"Not to remember, Edward. You were once here when you were almost a baby."

"Why can't I remember it?"

"I suppose we go home the day after to-morrow? There'll be nothing to stay on for, will there?" said Alfred.

"Nothing. Mrs. Vulliamy is seeing about having the presents packed up and so on."

"Mummie, is ——"

"Wait a minute, darling. Don't interrupt Daddy."

But Alfred said nothing more, and Laura turned back to Johnnie.

"Is what, sweetheart?"

She was absorbed in the inquiries, that she found stimulating and intelligent, propounded by Johnnie.

Edward, in an endeavour to divert Laura's attention to himself, began to ask foolish questions in a high, unnatural voice.

"Is London as large as Quinnerton?"

"Shall we see the King?"

"Is it before tea, or after tea?"

"He's rather tired, I expect," said nurse, reproving Edward kindly by shaking her head at him.

"Now, what engagements have you made for to-night, Laura, and is anything on to-morrow morning?" her husband inquired.

"Christine and a few relations and people are dining with us to-night at the Criterion. It's really Christine's party, of course. And naturally, to-morrow morning there'll be plenty to do getting ready. We've got to be at the church at two o'clock."

"Well, when can I go to look at pumps in Victoria Street?"

"You could do that to-morrow morning, I suppose. It needn't interfere, so long as you're back for lunch at the hotel not one moment later than twelve o'clock."

"Shall we have all our meals downstairs with you and Daddy at the hotel?" Johnnie inquired, with round eyes

"Yes."

"Even breakfast?"

"Yes, even breakfast."

"Oh!" said Johnnie naïvely, "how lucky we are!"

Laura glanced surreptitiously at her husband, to see whether he was as much moved as she was herself by the trusting joyfulness in Johnnie's voice and face, but if he was, he gave no sign of it.

And the next moment Johnnie, with even more fervour, had exclaimed:

"What do you suppose there'll be to eat?"

The atmosphere of Quinnerton had, indeed, been transferred to London.

Nurse, in consideration of her unbroken three hours on duty in the train, was encouraged by Laura to remember the existence of relations who appeared to be humble prototypes of old cousin Laura and poor Selina, and to go out and see them.

Laura and Christine put the children to bed.

The bride-elect was as hilarious as they were, and seemed as much unconcerned at the prospect of the next day's ceremony.

"Isn't it incredible," she remarked to Laura, as they endeavoured to restore order in the bathroom, "that after this evening I shall have a lady's maid?"

And Laura, seriously and in all sincerity, replied: "Utterly incredible!"

"I need never darn another pair of stockings. It's unbelievable."

"Mum-mee . . ."

It was Johnnie's well-known note, and Laura hastened to the room where one double-bed with a bolster laid down the middle of it received both the boys.

"Mummie, couldn't you stop that noise?"

"What noise?"

"Outside," said Johnnie pathetically. "Motors and things."

"You'll get used to it, darling. Don't think about it."

Johnnie, justifiably enough, received his parent's counsel of perfection with contempt.

"I suppose nurse'll be back by the time we want to start for the Criterion?" said Christine aside to her sister.

"I hope so. I told her to be."

"Shall I sit with them while you dress?"

"They never do have anybody to sit with them," said Laura doubtfully.

"I haven't any room," said Edward loudly and suddenly, and pushed the dividing bolster with violence.

Johnnie pushed it back again.

"You go and dress, Laura. Keep still, boys, and I'll tell you a story."

Laura dressed herself frantically.

Her hair seemed lank and stiff, although she had washed it only two days earlier, the powder lay on her face in blotches, and on her nose not at all, and her neck and arms seemed suddenly to have become abnormally thin.

"I've looked perfectly nice all these days—why should I suddenly turn into a hag just when Alfred and I are dining out together in London for the first time in years?"

Laura silently inquired of her unsatisfactory reflection in the mirror.

Her black dress made her look sallow, and emphasised the shadows under her eyes.

Alfred knocked at the door, came in, and was appealed to by Laura.

"What am I to do? I've never looked such a sight in my life. It's this frock, I think. Black never suits me."

"Well, well," said Alfred kindly. "Don't worry, my dear. After all, it's Christine they're coming to see, more than us, isn't it? I dare say no one will look at your frock."

More dejected than ever, Laura went to the children while Christine went to dress.

She came back in apple-green and silver, her fair hair looking quite golden, her mouth artificially—and most becomingly—scarlet.

"Alfred is quite right," thought Laura. "Why on earth should anyone look at me, or my frock?"

She was very nearly relieved to know that Duke Ayland would not see her that evening. But the recollection that followed—that he would not see her on the following evening either, and that she was going home the day after that, made her miserable.

Nurse as nearly as possible made them all late for dinner, since Laura refused to leave the boys alone, and Alfred refused to receive his guests without her, but she arrived breathlessly just as Christine announced coldly that it was eight o'clock.

"I'm very sorry if I'm late, madam, it's such a way from Balham."

Laura remembered Queen's Park, where old cousin Louisa lived, and felt the parallel complete.

The Temple dinner party was too strictly a family affair to be wholly successful. The relations of Laura and Christine did, indeed, congratulate Christine warmly and kindly, but they also displayed a faint tendency to wonder whether she had ever done anything to deserve so much good fortune. And again Laura was sensible of a slight disposition on the part of everybody to treat her as though she were Christine's mother.

They were all very kind, and very cheerful, but there was none of the *abandon* that had characterised the gatherings of Christine's friends, as distinguished from her relations.

Family parties, Laura reflected, never display *abandon*. Impossible to present to one's relations any aspect of oneself beside the one to which they have always been accustomed, and which they expect. They labelled one, as it were, in one's nursery days: "Mary's Laura is so fond of reading," or "little Christine is the quiet one," and if, later on, one liked dancing as well as reading, or became animated, rather·than quiet, they did not seem to notice it.

Laura, in the view of her relations, had long been "Laura lives right in the country," and they adapted their conversation to her supposedly rural point of view.

It was comparatively early when the party came to

an end, and the Temples and Christine returned to the Knightsbridge Hotel.

"Good night," said Christine. "Thank you so much for the party. I thought it all went off splendidly."

They heard her singing in her bedroom:

> "The more we are together
> The merrier we shall be."

"I suppose," said Alfred, with some solemnity, to his wife, "that girls nowadays don't have to be *told* things the night before their wedding?"

"Certainly not," said Laura. "They didn't have to in my day, either."

Alfred knew to a week the difference in age between Laura and her sister, but even with him it seemed necessary to establish the fact that they really did belong to the same generation.

The wedding of Christine and Jeremy, next day, was to Laura a bewildering, exhausting medley of subjective and objective impressions.

She was, at one and the same time, the sister of the bride, the hostess, together with—strangely—the wealthy Mrs. Vulliamy, at a social occasion of some magnitude, the mother of two little pages, of whom everybody said, "Aren't they too sweet?" and the wife of Alfred Temple, who farmed his own land in the depths of the country.

And she was Laura Temple, loving, and loved by, Duke Ayland.

She wished that she could have been aware of herself in one of these aspects, and one only.

Her good looks, now for ever fallen between the two stools of Greek-nymph and woman of the world, were still under a cloud and she put on her coffee-coloured lace dress, and hat with a curving feather, very badly, because she was hovering helpfully between the respective toilets of Christine and the boys.

"Madam, they look a picture," said nurse, referring entirely to the boys.

"That blue suits them both," Laura answered with calm, for fear of making them vain, and gazing at them with untempered adoration in her face.   But she knew, and she knew that nurse knew, that Johnnie's curls—as usual—gave him a vast advantage over his brother.

She was, in her heart, glad to remember that both the little girl bridesmaids were taller, older, and plainer than Johnnie, and that the hair of both was perfectly straight.

Undoubtedly Johnnie—after the bride herself—would be the *clou* of the procession.

Christine's wedding-dress, her newly-acquired pearls, her lace veil with soft bunches of orange-blossoms on either side of her face, suited her admirably, and she had powdered her face artistically, and entirely omitted to rouge it.

She was so calm that Laura thought she must be inwardly a little agitated.

The sisters looked at one another, smiled, and then Laura kissed Christine, felt furiously indignant at the realisation that she wanted to cry, and said in a strangled voice:

"You look perfectly lovely. Alfred is downstairs, quite ready, and he's ordered the car to be at the door five minutes after we've started. I'm taking the boys now."

"All right," said Christine, in a perfectly natural voice. "Tell Alfred to walk up the aisle slowly. I never can bear a bride who *scuttles*."

"How modern one gets," thought Laura, absurdly, remembering the infectious agitation of all her own nearest relations on the occasion of her marriage to Alfred.

She had supposed that in the church she would see Duke Ayland, since he had taken pains to inform her of the spot at which he intended to place himself, but actually, she saw only the most unexpected people, such as Poor Selina, in a hat entirely composed of pink and mauve orchids, and a vaguely familiar smile, above white kid gloves and gold bracelets, that suddenly identified itself as belonging to Mrs. LaTrobe.

"Dear little people!" murmured Laura automatically.

There was a red carpet, and a striped awning, and the usual crowds of people outside the porch, and a group of clergymen with bald heads and fluttering white surplices, inside it.

Johnnie and Edward and the two little bridesmaids stared at one another with hostility, were reluctantly compelled into partnership, and left in charge of their nurses and of a competent and elegantly dressed person whom Laura never remembered to have seen before.

She turned into the church.

"Mummie! Are you going away?"

"It's all right, dear," said everybody, making reassuring signs to Edward.

Laura looked round frenziedly for nurse, who nodded.

"How does one wed?" she heard Johnnie inquire in loud, interested tones of the nearest clergyman, in accordance with his habitual instinct for focussing the general attention upon himself.

The church seemed wonderfully full.

A strange young man, with a face like a harlequin, murmured something that Laura did not hear, but to which she replied, "I am the bride's sister," and begged her to come with him.

She obediently followed him up the church, to a front row of chairs, of which two nearest the aisle were vacant. In the corresponding row on the other side, she saw the bending form and aquiline profile of Mrs. Vulliamy, and the tail-coated outline of Mr. Vulliamy beyond her. A Vulliamy aunt, with diamonds, and two expensively-clad, attenuated daughters, were immediately behind them.

They bowed gravely to Laura, who bowed back again.

The organ stopped and then began again. It played a well-known hymn that Laura recognised as the signal for the bride's entrance. In a sudden panic, she looked for Jeremy, about whom she had altogether forgotten.

But he was there, at the chancel steps, almost entirely indistinguishable, unless one knew him very well indeed, from his best man. But then, so are almost all bridegrooms.

Alfred was conducting Christine up the aisle . . . not scuttling . . . and her bouquet, that Laura had not seen before, and that must have been mysteriously waiting at the very door of the church, made her look even more exquisitely bridal. . . . Then the children . . .

But Laura really only looked at Johnnie, who was fortunately on the side nearest to her. He was the youngest, and the only one with a mop of curls, and he wore a serious, intent, innocent expression that made his mother want to burst into tears.

Then he caught sight of her, and at his sudden, joyful radiance, Laura, whilst smiling back again, felt two enormous tears roll from her eyes.

To cry at a wedding—could anything be more banal, sentimental and unmodern?

She bit her lip violently, and fixed her eyes upon the baldest and most prominent of the clergymen.

The service proceeded, and Christine Fairfield exchanged her name for the less euphonious one of Jeremy Vulliamy.

Laura was thinking of her sister, and of Alfred—who had said "I do" under pressure from the baldest clergyman, and had then looked rather appealingly at Laura, and come to occupy the seat next her—and of the boys, now fidgeting mildly, and of the words of the marriage service. But she was also thinking, retrospectively, of her own wedding.

Had she been more in love than Christine now was, or less?

Did it really matter whether one was in love or not?

She had been glad to be married, but not radiantly happy.

Not nearly as happy as on the evening when Duke Ayland had told her that he loved her.

Being glad to be married was not the same thing as being radiantly happy because one was marrying a man with whom one was in love.

Laura felt a pang of passionate self-pity, because she had not known that rapture, and would never know it.

In order to stifle it, she reminded herself indignantly how much less becoming her wedding dress had been than Christine's now was. There had been a veil over her face, too, and she remembered still how insufferably it had tickled the point of her nose.

A discourse was beginning.

Laura did not hear a word of it.

She allowed Johnnie to come and sit on her lap, and saw smiles of indulgence and admiration turned upon his infantile charms, and ignored Alfred's slightly disapproving shake of the head.

Then the procession re-formed, and the young man with the harlequin face beckoned violently to Laura and Alfred, and to Mr. and Mrs. Vulliamy, to come into the vestry.

Laura apprehended little or nothing of the brief interlude of document-signing that ensued, owing to her extreme astonishment at the fact that Jeremy, with courage and initiative, had kissed her.

Perhaps Christine had told him to do it?

Mendelssohn's "Wedding March" had resounded, Christine had taken Jeremy's arm and had, with great presence of mind, remained stock still when Edward stood firmly on her train, and Alfred had lifted Edward off again, and Laura had found herself entering a perfectly strange motor-car with Alfred, wondering anxiously if nurse had been at hand to receive the boys. She did not see them again until after she had shaken hands with an immense number of people, all of whom seemed to arrive at the hotel very much at the same moment that she did herself.

Then she found them at the buffet, eating composedly.

Johnnie gave his mother a severe shock by remarking uncannily:

"That Mr. Ayland is here."

"How do you know?"

"I saw him. He's looking for you."

"How do you know?"

"I just thought— Mummie, can I have one of those pink cakes?"

People surged in, and Laura, strangely disquieted by Johnnie's information, temporarily lost sight of him again.

But she saw Duke Ayland.

He came up to her.

"What about this evening, Laura?"

"The Vulliamys have asked us to dinner."

"And to-morrow?"

"To-morrow we go home."

"Couldn't you possibly stay on one extra day by yourself?"

"Not possibly. There are the children—and anyway, I couldn't. But I must see you again, Duke. Would to-morrow morning be at all possible for you?"

"I'll make it possible."

Laura saw Mrs. La Trobe coming nearer and nearer, inexorable as Fate.

"We shan't go till the one o'clock train. I am going to do some last shopping at the Army and Navy Stores. I'll be at the entrance—Victoria Street—at half-past ten. I shall have about ten minutes to spare. . . ."

"I've been looking for you, Mrs. Temple," said the contralto voice of Mrs. La Trobe. "What a coincidence, isn't it? Jeremy, whom I've known ever since he was a little chap, to be marrying your sister!"

"Champagne, madam?" said the waiter.

"I suppose I must, though really, I never do ——"

Under cover of Mrs. La Trobe's smiling apologies Duke said low and rapidly:

"All right. Only it's a perfectly certain spot for meeting everybody one's ever met in one's life. Wouldn't Westminster Cathedral be ——?"

Then he, too, was claimed by an acquaintance, and Laura was left in doubt as to where their *rendezvous* really was.

"How's Cousin Louisa?" she asked casually of Poor

Selina next moment, and then, as she waited for the voluble reply, wondered whether it would not have been kinder to let Poor Selina forget all about Queen's Park for the day.

But Selina replied with every appearance of enthusiasm, that Cousin Louisa was wonderful. Laura found herself glancing surreptitiously at her watch. It ought soon to be time for Christine to go and change her dress.

Laura felt extraordinarily tired, and knew that very soon her fatigue would show in her face and bearing.

Suddenly, with an incredulous astonishment that momentarily revived her, she saw a slim, well-known figure towering above its neighbours, topped by the painted, insolent, undeniably lovely face of Miss Kingsley-Browne.

"Bébée!"

"Hello," said Bébée unmoved. "How are you? Last time we met was at the A. B. Onslows'—dear people!"

Laura could think of nothing more brilliant than a bald affirmation in reply.

"Mummie is here somewhere, with Dr. Ernest Blog, a most wonderful man from America. You'll meet him at home, this winter ——"

"Shall I?"

"Christine looks topping," said Bébée affably. "Jeremy's frightfully lucky, as I've just told him. Of course, I'm rather *mal-vue* by his parents just at the moment, but as a matter of fact they ought to be grateful to me."

"Honestly, Bébée, I think that they are," said Mrs. Temple candidly, in an effort to take the wind out of

Miss Kingsley-Browne's unjustifiably inflated sails. But Bébée's eyes, according to their wont, were roving far away, above the head of her interlocutress.

"There's Ernest. I must go to him. Naturally, he doesn't know anyone here."

Laura made a desperate effort to see Ernest, but without success.

"We shall meet at home, I expect," Miss Kingsley-Browne said without enthusiasm. "I know mummie will be dying to talk to you about the bulbs."

Laura's first words to her newly-married sister, when she found herself upstairs in her room, were couched in the formula familiar to them both.

"*Did* you see Bébée Kingsley-Browne? Could you have believed it?"

"See her? Did I not!" ejaculated Christine. "Who could fail to see a giraffe like that? Though, I must say, she looked pretty. She must have a nerve of iron."

"She has. Poor Lady Kingsley-Browne!"

"Unfortunate woman! She was in charge of Hogg, or Blog, or whatever his name is. I saw him, following her about like a dog."

"What is he like? Here—I'll undo that."

"Laura, I think Jeremy's mother is coming up in a minute."

"Shall I go? I shan't mind if ——"

"No, no, truly. I want you. Here she is. I think ——"

Christine moved to the door, speaking rapidly over her shoulder.

"Blog, my dear, is exactly two foot high. No wonder Bébée doesn't want to walk about arm-in-arm with him, as she did with A. B." Then she opened the door.

Laura's sense of confusion and bewilderment deepened more and more. She noticed vaguely how maternal Mrs. Vulliamy, in her shadowy way, had become, and how ingeniously Christine combined responsiveness with a complete absence of sentimentality in her own manner.

Soon they were down stairs again, Christine transformed, in a frock that had been the subject of numberless conversations between herself and Laura, and an opulent nutria fur coat that Jeremy had given her as one of his wedding presents, and a little brimless blue hat with silver flowers that became her.

The best man—now completely distinguishable from Jeremy, who had changed into a grey suit for travelling —was to see them off at the station.

Laura, suddenly completely exhausted, felt that she desired nothing so much as to see all the guests depart instantly.

But when they had done so, instead of thereupon becoming a person who could look as tired as she felt, Laura found that she was merely the mother of two thoroughly over-excited little boys. It was too early to put them to bed, there was no garden into which they could be sent, and nurse displayed a strong disinclination to take them for a walk "in all that traffic" as she perversely designated Laura's suggestion of Kensington Gardens. Eventually, Laura sent her to pack and herself undertook the charge of Edward and Johnnie.

Alfred had vanished.

There was nothing to do except to answer the tireless questions of the boys, and to cudgel her brains until she could produce a story with which to amuse them.

"Mummie, may we have wedding cake again for supper?"

"No, darling, I'm afraid not."

Johnnie displayed unreasonable disappointment. At last they were both fetched away, to go to bed.

Alfred, as mysteriously as he had vanished, reappeared.

"Where *have* you been?"

"I had to have a pipe," said Alfred. "Did you say we were dining out?"

"With the Vulliamys. I cannot imagine how we could ever have been such fools as to say we'd go," sighed Laura.

"I expect you're tired. It's always the same thing, when you have the boys on your hands. . . ."

He spoke quite without rancour, but Laura, her nerves on edge, would have liked to scream.

Screaming, however, then as always, was impracticable, and a fresh item was added to the already long list of the repressions so much regretted by Losh on behalf of Mrs. Temple.

"I'd better go and dress," she said instead.

"Can we get off by the eleven o'clock train to-morrow?"

"We decided on the one o'clock. I want to go to the Army and Navy Stores in the morning. There'll just be time."

"All right."

Laura, without any shred of exultation left in her, contemplated the prospect of what must, in all probability, prove to be her last interview for an indefinite length of time, with Duke Ayland.

Chapter XIX

At the uninspiring hour of half-past ten next morning, Duke and Laura met in the prosaic atmosphere of Victoria Street, and with all the sense of limitation induced by the consciousness of Laura's imminent train.

"I *must* be back at the hotel at a quarter to twelve," were her first words.

"I can take you back in a taxi."

"Meanwhile—I'm very sorry, but I must go to the groceries' department. It won't take a minute."

It took several minutes, but presently it was done.

"Where do you want to go now? Isn't there a tea place, or somewhere we can sit and talk?"

"There's a tea-room upstairs, I believe. But we can't sit there unless we order something."

"Coffee. Will that do?"

Laura signed assent, and they went up in the lift.

Laura looked at herself in the glass with some dismay. She had not recovered from her fatigue, and her face showed it.

"We shall go home by the one o'clock train to-day."

"I know," said Ayland—as indeed he did.

The tea-room was comparatively untenanted, except by elegant waitresses, who displayed boredom at the sight of Laura, but revived when she was followed by Duke.

They tried to take a corner table, but the nearest one bore a discouraging card that said "Reserved," and that and the combined haughty gazings of the waitresses, caused Laura to sit down at a large table laid for four in the very middle of the room.

"Do you like this?" said Duke doubtfully.

"It'll do, and there isn't time to change," Laura replied feverishly.

"Darling, what's the matter?"

Laura knew that the true answer to this inquiry was expressed in the single word Reaction, but it reminded her too much of the medical student Losh, of the books of Havelock Ellis, and of several other things that she could not bear to recollect. So she answered instead, with an inanity that shocked herself as much as she felt that it disconcerted Ayland:

"Nothing is the matter. I'm just tired after the wedding."

"Laura, I thought we were always honest with one another."

Laura had thought so, too, until this morning, but she did not say so, because at that moment one of the languid waitresses came and looked unsmilingly down at them and said, "What can I get you, please?"

"What would you like?" Duke inquired.

"Coffee, I think," said Laura, feeling that it would probably choke her.

"Two coffees, please. And cakes."

"We ought not to leave here a moment later than half-past eleven."

"It's all right. I'll see you're not late."

A most unhappy silence ensued.

Duke handed Laura his cigarette-case.

She took a cigarette without looking at him, and lit it slowly and with great care.

"Well, my dear, have you thought what's going to happen?"

"About us?" Laura said, entirely to gain time—although with no idea as to how she would employ it when gained.

"Of course. You're going back to the country to-day and you say you've no idea when you'll come up again—and in any case, it's damned unsatisfactory only to meet like this. I can't stand it, Laura. I wish to God you'd come away with me altogether."

"If I was free I would."

"If you were free, we could be married."

"But I'm not. And apart from anything else, I'm very fond of Alfred. It would hurt him most frightfully to think that I cared for somebody else more. . . ."

Duke shrugged his shoulders, the first sign of impatience that he had given.

"But leave all that out of it. There are the children," Laura forlornly reminded him.

"Yes, I know. They settle it, of course. And as that's so, Laura, surely you can see that we shouldn't be doing any wrong to anybody if we took such happiness as we can get! Can't we take one week together, to remember, out of all our lives?"

"Bleck or whayte?" said the waitress abruptly, poising two vessels above the two cups on the table.

When she had finished with them, Laura looked at her watch.

"It's five minutes past eleven already. I mustn't be late. Nurse isn't quick, and I shall have to help her get the boys ready. Besides, there's so much traffic now that it may take ages to get to the station."

Laura had not, as might have been supposed from this speech, forgotten her own frantic desire to appear in a light other than one purely domestic, to Duke Ayland. But she had reached a stage of mental and physical fatigue in which she could no longer distinguish between the things she really wanted to say and the things she was in the habit of saying.

"Darling, please don't fuss. I promise I won't let you be late. I've never seen you like this before."

"Sometimes I think that we'd far better never see one another again," said Laura wildly and irrelevantly.

"Laura!"

"We shall spoil it if we go on like this. It's been the happiest and the most beautiful thing in my life, and I don't want, ever, to let it be anything less. If we were to do Alfred a wrong—I don't care what you say, it is a wrong—and besides, the children —— No, I couldn't bear it. Duke, I could say good-bye to you to-day. I could find the courage to, although, heaven knows, it's the hardest thing I've ever done in my life. We should always remember, even when later on you marry somebody else, as of course you will. I shouldn't have lost you altogether. And you'll know that you've had something from me that no one else has ever had, or ever will have."

Laura, at last, had spoken, with halting and belated eloquence, but with all the sincerity that was in her.

In the long, long look that she exchanged with Ayland, she felt suddenly that they had come spiritually close to one another again.

"Anything else I can bring you?" the waitress superciliously enquired.

"The bill, please."

"How many cakes?" suspiciously enquired the waitress.

"None."

The bill was made out and handed to Ayland.

"Ought we to go?"

"I'm afraid so. In case it takes a minute or two to get a taxi."

In unbroken silence they descended in the lift to the ground-floor, and in Victoria Street entered a taxi.

"We needn't hurry now," Duke said, and gave an order to the driver.

This time Laura surrendered herself to his embrace with no attempt at resistance. And the effect of it was to shatter the frail strength of her so recent determination.

When he had kissed her, and she lay breathless against his shoulder, her hands clasped in his, it was as though her words had meant nothing.

In real life, Laura dreamily reflected, a moment of crisis was always followed by days and nights and days of anti-climax. One had to go on. And the thing that had been real and sustaining melted imperceptibly into the thing that was expedient at the moment. . . .

"Don't answer me now, angel," whispered Duke.

"You're tired out. Think it over, and remember that I adore you, and then perhaps one day you'll feel that you can come to me, and give us both the most wonderful memory ——"

"Perhaps," murmured Laura, fired by his desire, and by the ardour of his love-making, and by the knowledge that she was going back to an existence in which love-making played no part at all. The emotional instant of renunciation had passed—defeated, as are all emotional instants, by sheer force of Time's continuousness. Impossible to renounce in a crowded lift and with a train to catch. Almost equally impossible to part as lovers should part in a taxi drawn up outside a London hotel. . . .

Duke and Laura achieved neither one thing nor the other.

She had renounced him, but she had also half-promised to give herself to him. It was an incredible, inconsistent, and nerve-racking state of affairs.

But things, Laura knew, are like that.

She crawled upstairs, the muscles of her throat aching from a sense of constriction.

The packing was finished, and the suit-cases stood in a pile in the middle of the floor. The beds had been stripped, and the slops had not been emptied—a peculiarly dreary combination of effects.

Laura looked into the next room.

Edward was alone, rather pale and heavy-eyed.

"Where are Johnnie and nurse?"

"He's having to be washed in the bathroom. He got

himself all black downstairs, while nurse was packing. Mummie, I think I've got a cold."

Laura's heart sank a little lower.

Edward's colds were tempestuous affairs, necessitating bed, and an immense number of pocket-handkerchiefs, a supply of cold cream, and frequently a subsequent cough-mixture.

It was Laura's belief that no other child in the world had such severe and prolonged colds as had Edward.

As she looked at him, the voice of Mrs. Bakewell seemed to ring in her mind's ears:

"We got through this winter without any colds at all. Just the simple, healthy life they lead, and the right sort of clothing. . . . Let me see, it must be nearly two years since Cynthia had a cold. The cold habit is really so unnecessary. . . ."

"Edward, are you sure?" said Laura.

But she knew from his face that he was right, and presently he began to sniff—a recurrent, irritating sniff, that would increase in frequency and violence until a second, worse stage was reached.

One could only hope that it would not be reached before the evening, and prophesy brightly:

"Well, I daresay it won't be very bad, and you can go to bed as soon as we get home."

"But I don't want to go to bed," said Edward, beginning to cry.

"Oh, darling, don't be silly!"

"I hate bed!"

Nurse and Johnnie came in.

"Why, what's the matter? Do I see a little boy crying? Who's this little boy?" said nurse, affecting not to recognise the tearful Edward. "Whoever's this? Our little boys don't cry. It must be some strange little boy."

"Johnnie dear, don't jump on the bed like that. Nurse, Edward tells me he has a cold."

"Yes. He has," nurse said decisively. And she added to Laura aside, "Overtired, both of them. But he was quite all right when I left him—quite bright."

Laura knew that it was she who had quenched her son's brightness, and she could see that nurse knew it, too.

She did not attempt to defend the position. "Would you like a cup of tea before we start, nurse?"

"Oh no, thank you, madam. I can never eat anything before a journey. I didn't touch any breakfast this morning," said nurse proudly. "But the boys have had some milk and biscuits."

"Here's daddy," said Johnnie.

"Are you ready? The man's here for the luggage."

"Quite ready," said Laura, taking a last mechanical, unsatisfactory look at herself in the glass.

The train was crowded.

Laura took Johnnie on her knee, and nurse took Edward, and Alfred stood in the corridor. Strange women, hatless, and in thick, hot, crumpled clothes, made advances to the boys and offered them food.

Johnnie became unendurably restless, and Edward sniffed, and occasionally sneezed.

"You ought to have his adenoids seen to," one woman

remarked to Laura, gazing expertly at Edward. "He *looks* like adenoids."

"What do adenoids look like?" said Edward in a pessimistic tone.

"They look like something perfectly *hidgeous*," Johnnie replied with the grave, perfectly unmalicious freedom of speech peculiar to the nursery.

Laura was unable to forget her own preoccupations in keeping her children amused, because there was practically nothing that could be done to amuse them, and she was equally unable to remain still and face her own thoughts, because of the constant, unrelated demands of Edward and Johnnie upon her attention. Alfred, in the corridor outside, imperturbably read the paper. From time to time he looked round at them, and once he came to the door of the carriage and spoke. (Laura's prestige went up when the hot and crumpled ladies opposite saw that she had a husband of so unmistakable a type as Alfred. They ceased to comment upon the probability of Edward's adenoids, and only smiled at him instead.)

Laura, in snatches of silence, wondered whether Alfred knew anything of the crisis through which their domestic life was passing. He behaved as though he knew nothing. And yet, even if he knew everything, she felt certain that he would behave in precisely the same way. Alfred was like that—imperturbable, unalterable, in many ways unobservant, and yet with peculiar qualities of solidity and kindness—qualities, as Laura well knew, eminently desirable in a husband.

She, however, wanted a lover.

Ayland's suggestion of a week to be spent together kept on recurring to her mind.

"Perhaps a long time hence," thought Laura, with a vague feeling that this procrastination made the project less immoral. But the real truth was that she was so much tired that the only kind of week she could bear to contemplate for the present would have been passed almost entirely in sleep.

At the Junction it was raining hard.

"We shall soon be home now," said Laura, with fictitious cheerfulness.

Eventually they were home—though not soon.

This time there were no flowers in the drawing-room, and the pile of unforwarded letters was formidable.

"Where is Fauntleroy?" said Edward, rushing out into the rain.

"Oh, stop him!" cried Laura.

Nurse and Johnnie also hurried out into the rain.

"Johnnie, not you! Come back!"

"Where on earth are the servants?" said Alfred, putting immoderate pressure upon the front door-bell.

"They only didn't hear us drive up. It's all right, Alfred. Here she is. Good afternoon, Mary."

"Good afternoon," said Mary, whose salient characteristic was that she never addressed either of her employers by any term of respect.

"Is everything all right, Mary?"

"Quite all right."

"We shall be glad of tea whenever it is ready," said Laura, rather intimidated.

"Take up those bags," said Alfred, kicking the lighter of the suit-cases.

Mary instantly obeyed, and was thus spared the sight of the boys' re-entrance into the hall, hilariously followed by Fauntleroy, and their subsequent progress up the stairs, leaving wet and mould behind them.

"Excited at getting home," said nurse benevolently to Laura.

"Edward had better go straight to bed after tea."

"I'll get their things unpacked the soonest possible minute."

Laura, expert in detecting the finer shades of meaning in domestic formulas, deduced that nurse thought she was being slightly inconsiderate.

"Send them down to me as soon as they're—as soon as you've all had tea," she said hurriedly, "and you can come for Edward when you're ready for him."

"Very well, madam."

"What about tea?" said Alfred.

"Dear, you've this moment sent Mary upstairs. She'll ring the gong directly the tea is in the dining-room."

Alfred walked into the drawing-room. He appeared to have no curiosity about his unopened correspondence.

Laura listlessly examined her own share. The letters all looked uninteresting, and yet as if every one of them would require an answer. Laura instantly felt that she never wanted to write another letter as long as she lived.

Her correspondence with Duke Ayland had been the most interesting one that she had ever known, until they had fallen in love with one another. After that, it was impossible to deny that it had become perfunctory.

She did not correspond regularly with anybody else, partly from lack of time, and partly because she had no very intimate friends. Although Laura could not be described as a man's woman, she rather unfortunately possessed the distinction of not being a woman's woman either, principally owing to her slender reputation as an author, which alarmed or alienated most of those who knew about it.

"If I could only talk to somebody about it all," she now thought unhappily. But there was nobody to whom she could state the bald facts of her predicament, without the certainty of finding herself coupled, ethically and intellectually, with the scandalous Bébée Kingsley-Browne.

Presently she stopped thinking about Duke, and about herself in relation to him. Dinner was rather an unsuccessful meal.

"She's not a good cook, is she?" Alfred observed truthfully, but, in this connection, tactlessly.

"I daresay not," Laura returned. "But all the same ——"

A bad cook, she meant, and Alfred undoubtedly would understand her to mean, was much better than a cook who had given notice. They fell into their usual silence, and Laura made her usual effort—excellent in intention, but poor in execution—to transform it into an interesting and intelligent conversation.

"I think the drawing-room covers ought to go to the cleaner's. Unless we can afford new ones this winter."

"We cannot afford new anything," Alfred said calmly. "This visit to London has just about dished our budget for the year."

"We couldn't not have gone!" exclaimed Laura. "And Christine paid every single thing for the boys."

"I know she did. And I know we had to go. I'm glad we did. But we shall have to be a bit economical, that's all."

"Shall we be able to have any painting done in the spring? The nursery passage is terrible—just where the little lamp always smokes."

"I'll see if I can give it a coat of whitewash myself one of these days. But the difficulty is to find the time. This is just the time when things want doing in the garden."

"I haven't planted my indoor hyacinths yet!" exclaimed Laura, in allusion to her solitary annual horticultural effort.

Alfred smiled kindly. There was little to be said about Laura's hyacinths save that she did not possess what is called *la main heureuse*.

Then Laura said *"What's that?"* with a start of apprehension.

"What is what?"

"It sounded exactly like ——"

She half rose out of her chair.

"If it's Johnnie, you can tell him that I shall come up and settle him if I hear another sound. I thought he'd given up that nonsense."

"But it wasn't. It sounded," said Laura in stricken tones, "exactly like the noise they made during the whooping-cough."

"I think it was your fancy. I didn't hear a sound. Sit down again, dear."

Without a word Laura rose and rushed from the room.

She had heard the sound again, and as she went upstairs and along the passage she recognised it beyond any possibility of doubt.

The cough that belonged to Edward's whooping-cough.

Outside the door of the night-nursery, beside the bracket on which the little lamp that smoked stood smoking, was nurse, listening attentively.

"It's Edward," she mouthed. "I don't think it's woken him—not from the sound, it hasn't. But I really thought he was going to be sick."

"But he can't have whooping-cough again!"

Nurse shook her head.

"It's like that, whooping-cough is. They get quite well, and then suddenly they catch a cold, and it's all to do again. Even after *weeks*."

"But it seems too bad to be true—the doctor never warned me. I wouldn't have taken him to London if I'd had the least idea. There, hark at him!"

Nurse shook her head.

"That's what it is."

Then she relented a little.

"It won't last, very likely. Just a sort of relapse, and then they pick up again. It's catching a cold that does it."

"What about Johnnie?"

"He may be quite all right. He had it very lightly, didn't he? And he doesn't get colds the way Edward does."

Laura, with a sensation that approached despair, told nurse to come and fetch her if Edward was worse in the night, and went down to her husband again.

Alfred did not reproach her for agitatedly dashing away from him, although she knew that he profoundly disliked and disapproved of both agitation, and of what he looked upon as undue anxiety about the children.

He read *The Field*, and presently he fell asleep.

Laura opened her letters, and found the usual proportion of bills, of advertisements, of business on behalf of the Nursing Association, the Women's Institute, and the Girl Guides, and a note from Mrs. Bakewell, who wanted to come and hear all about the wedding. To this last there was a postscript:

"Are your little ones attending the dancing-class this term? C. and Th. just longing to begin again."

Would Edward and Johnnie go to the dancing classes? There would be the same difficulty that there had been before about getting them to Quinnerton. It was too expensive to hire a car every week, and Alfred would not always have time to drive them.

Perhaps it was better for them to go occasionally, than never at all.

Laura looked at the clock.

It was half-past nine.

One of Laura's convictions was that people living in

the country, who went to bed regularly at ten o'clock every night, put themselves thereby in danger of turning —spiritually—into vegetables. Therefore some three-quarters of an hour must elapse before she could go upstairs. She thought of Duke Ayland, and of their passionate, and at the same time unsatisfactory, parting, and of the hope that she had not forbidden him.

"But what do I mean to do?" Laura asked herself, utterly bewildered. For whatever course of action she might contemplate, it always seemed to her that she was determined not to follow it.

"I hope to goodness the bath-water is hot," said Alfred, waking suddenly.

"You always have your bath in the morning."

"Not always. I want one to-night. But in any case, the water ought to be hot. I shall find out."

"Don't ring!" exclaimed Laura instinctively.

But he had already done so.

Moments elapsed.

"Oh, Alfred, don't ring again! They're probably gone to bed."

"Then they won't hear me."

But after an interval sufficiently long to suggest that Mary had been at least on her way to bed, at the end of a day's work, she came in.

"Is the water hot?"

"The bath-water?"

"Yes."

"The bath-water isn't hot. Not to say hot. We were going to ask you to have a look at the range, or something, in the morning. It's been giving Ethel and I the most awful trouble."

Mary went away again, looking more aggrieved than ever.

The fact that Alfred, also, was aggrieved because the water was not hot, evidently did not matter to her.

"Do you know," said Laura, a train of thought presented to her, "that Christine once said to me that she thought servants were rather like God—they live so close to one, and know so much about one. Only, unfortunately, they don't love one."

"Like God?" said Alfred gloomily. "Ours are a good deal more like the devil, if you ask me."

Laura could not but agree with him.

She took this exhilarating simile to bed with her, and although of the two subjects she would have preferred to think—however unsatisfactorily—about her unhappy and discreditable love-affair, she found that the atmosphere of the house was too strong for her.

She fell asleep to the accompaniment of a quiet, reasonable, conviction-carrying rebuke that should convey once and for all to Mary and Ethel Laura's standard of domestic requirements.

She woke to the realisation—one become just too habitual, in the course of years, to be called a pang—that there was nothing to look forward to, and that it would be necessary very shortly to go to the kitchen and to order dinner.

In the distance, the servants were moving—but it was a quarter-past seven, so they well might be—and farther away still, she thought she heard Edward cough—the raucous, open-mouthed, unrestrained coughing of a small, bored child wishful to attract notice.

A single shriek, only faint because it was so far off, told her accustomed ears that Johnnie, as usual, had interposed his own infallible methods of wresting nurse's attention from his brother to himself.

"I must see about another daily governess for them, if Miss Lamb isn't coming back this term," thought Laura.

Alfred had left her side long ago, without disturbing her.

If Duke had been her husband?

Laura neither pursued the question nor attempted to find any answer to it. Nothing was more certain than that to do so would be entirely futile.

She was in love with Duke, undoubtedly, but she could not, at a distance of two hundred miles, remain in love with him indefinitely—nor he with her.

Alas, for the brief-lived romanticism of an attachment between a man and a woman, unsupported by even occasional proximity! Laura at last admitted to herself that she and Duke Ayland, in common with the vast majority of their fellow-beings, were incapable of the ideal, imperishable, love for which the world was said to be well lost.

She would never give herself to Duke, but hers was not the Great Refusal that ennobles the refuser and remains a beautiful memory for ever.

The children, her marriage vows, the house, the ordering of the meals, the servants, the making of a laundry list every Monday—in a word, the things of respectability—kept one respectable. In a flash of unavoidable clear-sightedness, that Laura would never repeat if she could avoid it, she admitted to herself that the average attributes only, of the average woman, were hers.

Imagination, emotionalism, sentimentalism . . . what woman is not the victim of these insidious and fatally unpractical qualities?

But how difficult, Laura reflected, to see oneself as an average woman and not, rather, as one entirely unique, in unique circumstances. . . .

It dawned upon her dimly that only by envisaging and accepting her own limitations, could she endure the limitations of her surroundings.

THE END